CHRISTIE CLAYTON

BOND

THE BONDED VAMPIRE CHRONICLES

BITTEN

MYSTIC OWL

AN IMPRINT OF CITY OWL PRESS

BOND BITTEN
The Bonded Vampire Chronicles, Book 1

MYSTIC OWL
A City Owl Press Imprint
www.cityowlpress.com

Cover Design by MiblArt. All stock photos licensed appropriately.

Edited by Lisa Green.

For information on subsidiary rights, please contact the publisher at info@cityowlpress.com.

Print Edition ISBN: 978-1-64898-226-2

Digital Edition ISBN: 978-1-64898-225-5

Printed in the United States of America

For my husband,
the athlete who married the nerd and helped all her dreams come true.

PROLOGUE

ALL THE HUNTER'S DECADES IN THE FIELD, HIS YEARS OF RESEARCH and sleepless nights had led to this moment. He lit a cigarette and peered through the windshield.

His target approached.

The bait waited in a trap, blissfully unaware of the storm she'd unleash.

Lightning in a bottle.

His target opened the door to the coffee shop and sauntered inside with that arrogant grace the hunter despised.

Grinning so broadly it hurt, the hunter shook hair from his eyes, turned the key in the ignition, and listened to the relaxing hum of the engine. "Tick, tick, boom."

1

EMILY LEANED ACROSS THE COUNTER TO PEER INTO THE MAN'S FACE. His eyes had changed color. Not a trick of the light or subtle shift from blue to gray, but a one-blink golden brown to startling green transformation. She stared open-mouthed at the dazzling peridot that glittered beneath heavy lashes.

"How did you do that?"

A puzzled smile curved his lips. "Do what?"

"Your eyes. Do you wear contacts?" She squeezed the lip of the counter, surprised by her unconstrained curiosity.

"What makes you think that?" His flirtatious smile invited her to respond.

She shuffled her feet and tucked her hands into the pocket of her apron, ignoring the long line of customers waiting behind him. "They, uh, they sort of changed."

His smile retracted into a startled wince, and he stepped back from the counter. Those eyes held hers, and everything dropped away. They stared at each other. There was a significance to what happened, a significance to the weight and pull between them, a significance to the way her fingertips ached to touch his skin.

"Regular flat white!" Her middle-aged boss, Bob, cut in and placed a cardboard cup in front of the man.

The spell dissolved and fizzed into the harsh, bustling reality around them—the countertop, the noisy customers waiting in line, the sound of the cash register, chairs scraping across the floor.

She pushed the coffee toward him, unable to look away. "Can I get you anything else?"

"No, thank you."

He strode outside with stiff, measured steps and dropped into a chair at the table next to the shop's metal perimeter fence, where he sat on the edge of his seat, the afternoon light turning his ash-blond hair into an enticing gold beacon. The muscles in his back were taut, as if he regretted sitting down and might leave his coffee and bolt.

She took the next customer's order without shifting her gaze from his perfect outline and suppressed a sigh. He was tall and built like a Roman statue.

Emily continued to stare. He didn't move, not even to lift his coffee, which sat, forgotten, on the table. Three, four, five orders later, he hadn't so much as twitched.

"Hey, Bob," she called over her shoulder. "I'm going to clear the tables outside."

Bob grunted his approval, so she wove her way out from behind the counter, between the crowded tables, and through the glass front door, its tired wooden frame groaning shut behind her.

Catching the man's eye, she collected a couple of empty cups and swept a cloth over the tabletop. A blush heated her face.

She wiped cookie crumbs from another tabletop, hoping he'd say something before she ran out of surfaces to clean. She had two golden rules when it came to men, both learned as a child witnessing her parents' relationship unravel in a divorce that tore her mother to shreds while liberating her wayward father. Number one rule: ignore them until they paid attention. The thought of an unreciprocated attraction—or worse, unrequited love—made her shudder.

She didn't want to be *that* girl, the one making moon eyes and hanging off every word. If her mother had been less available from the start, maybe she wouldn't have married a man whose heart was never in it. Maybe she wouldn't have found herself alone without so much as a bank account in her name.

And that last part was why Emily had her second rule: never depend on a man for *anything.*

"Is there something wrong with your drink?" she asked with professional disinterest. She wasn't technically breaking her rule, she reasoned. Just doing her job.

He blinked up at her, his brows creased. She pointed to the untouched coffee.

"No, it's great, thank you." He leaned back in his chair, shifting from his rigid pose, and studied her face.

She pocketed the damp cloth and reached for his cup. "Let me get you a fresh one."

"No, it's fine, really." He stilled her hand, his fingers brushing hers with a misplaced tenderness that made her breath hitch.

He stood to leave, removing the wallet from his back pocket and then tossing several bills on the table.

She gaped at him. "Is that a tip?"

He shrugged.

"You're not from here, are you?" She eyed the money like a stray cat investigating a saucer of milk.

"I just moved here."

"Do you know anyone in town?"

He gave her a tight smile that made her heart flutter in a flurry of frantic beats that threatened to overwhelm her.

"No," he said, the smile fading.

She couldn't imagine moving to a place like Pine Lakes without family or friends nearby. It was a small town named after a nonexistent body of water—the closest thing they had to a lake was a reservoir out on the edge of the neighboring forest, and parochial didn't quite cover its limited opportunities for socializing.

"There's a party later. You should go." The words flew out of her mouth like missiles, blowing holes in her golden rule. She bit her lip, fiddled with the tie on her apron, and tried to sound casual. "I mean, there's not a lot to do on a Saturday night in Pine Lakes."

She retrieved a notebook and pen from her back pocket, aghast at the way she scrawled the address of the party, ripped out the paper, and offered it to him.

"This is where everyone our side of thirty will be," she said, trying to disguise her unsubtle interest in him.

He took it without looking away from her. "Will you be there?" His gaze fixed on her name tag. "Emily?"

"Maybe."

Resurrecting what was left of her rule—and dignity—she strolled inside without a backward glance. When she shut the door, her breath left her in a frustrated rush.

Emily *never* broke her rules.

At least she'd left his obscene tip on the table. She could've used the cash, but she had too much pride to grab it.

Bob stomped over and held out his hand. "Your shift ended five minutes ago. I'm not paying you for the extra."

She untied her apron and gave it to him, waiting until she was in the back to roll her eyes heavenward. She leaned her head against the bare brick wall of the industrial staff room, still reeling from her faux pas.

A familiar whoop broke the silence.

"The back door was open," Roxi said with a crafty smile.

Her friend's dark-brown hair was perfectly coiffed, her puppy-dog eyes laden with flawless makeup.

"So are you coming?" Roxi was bouncing with impatience, tapping her high-heeled shoes on the concrete floor.

Emily folded her arms. "I have an early shift tomorrow."

"Come on. It'll be fun, I promise."

Emily shook her head in a halfhearted protest. They both knew she would cave; she always did where Roxi was concerned. And broken rules aside, how could she resist the urge to see if her too-hot customer turned up?

Thanks to his distinctive eyes, the rest of his face was already a blur in her mind. She figured he was mid to late twenties, and she had a vague recollection of a sculpted, sultry upper lip, heavy brows, and dark-gold hair. Curiosity was shoving her toward the party with two hands.

Roxi rummaged in her large leather shoulder bag and held up a black sequin minidress with a flourish. "You'll look amazing in this. I just bought it. Isn't it worth coming so you can wear it?"

Emily trailed her fingers along a ridge of sequins and felt herself giving in. Years of friendship made her and Roxi oddly accommodating of one another, like two trees whose trunks had twisted around each other until they were indistinguishable.

It *was* a beautiful dress, a perfect contrast to Roxi's powder-blue miniskirt and cream top. She huffed and held out her hand. "You'd better have makeup and hairspray in that bag too. And I'm going home at midnight. No later. I have to be up at seven for my shift."

A triumphant dimple appeared in Roxi's cheek as she began Emily's five-minute makeover, dusting her face with translucent powder, sliding a gooey pink gloss over her lips, and scrunching her long hair into loose waves.

They crossed the parking lot, Emily linking arms with Roxi to keep from staggering in her half-size-too-big, borrowed shoes.

She snorted in disgust at a black sports car parked next to her ancient Honda. Then she saw the driver sitting in the shadows— Mr. Pretty with the chameleon eyes.

Perfect.

If she'd known he was another rich asshole passing through Pine Lakes on his way to Oak Ridge, she never would've invited him to the party. Big tip, flashy car, and no doubt an ego to match.

Just like Daddy.

Thanks to her father, she knew the type all too well.

Disappointment pinched at her gut as she slid behind the wheel and started the engine.

His car peeled out of the lot, the setting sun silhouetting it before it turned and disappeared down the street in a burst of speed.

Sebastian was barely half a mile down the road when he pulled over, stopping beneath a huddle of old pines. All he could see was long brown hair dancing in the breeze, judgmental gray eyes, and pretty pink lips twisted in scorn.

Most girls her age got starry-eyed and breathless when they passed a six-figure car, but she responded with a sneer.

Emily. Her name came to him, unbidden and unwelcome.

He scrutinized his face in the rearview mirror, picking up the repetitive train of thought he'd been riding in the parking lot: *It's started. It's happening. It's* her.

Brilliant green replaced the soft amber that'd looked back at him for the past 225 years. He'd spent decades willing it to happen, and after all that time, wishing and anticipating, he'd gone and won the shit-luck lottery and bonded to a *human*.

He didn't have anything against humans per se. He'd been one once, and even as a vampire, he'd dated countless human women, cloaking what he really was with careful habits and contrived weakness. Their warmth and guileless interest drew him to them time after time, just as their need for honesty and candor sent him spiraling back to the anonymity that was the cornerstone of his existence.

But bonding to a human was a whole different game. Bonding to a human was *beyond* dangerous.

A wave of nausea hit him, and he pressed the heels of his palms into his eyes. If he accepted it, if he succumbed to the bond's compulsion, to the powerful urges already pushing and tugging at his thoughts and limbs, they would be tied to one another forever. But that wouldn't mean the kind of uncomplicated "ever after" he coveted. That only happened when vampires bonded to vampires.

He knew the old stories well, and he'd read the reports on the recent atrocities. Bonding to a human used to be something so rare it was the stuff of legend, but now it was the stuff of official Circle investigations, the clandestine organization's findings circulated by secure email to the vampires they sought to protect. In the twenty recorded incidents of vampire-human bondings, five were no more than ancient oral folktales passed on from the oldest among his kind. Fifteen happened in the last twenty years, and not one of them had a happy ending. Instead, they all culminated in bloodshed and large-scale massacres the Circle struggled to conceal.

With a sigh, he fished his phone out of his pocket and dialed, huffing at his friend's voice mail. "Max, I'm coming over. Be there. It's important."

He hung up and put his head in his hands, resisting the urge to punch the steering wheel. Max was better connected and informed than any other vampire he knew. Maybe he could help him avoid a full bond. Because finishing what had started would be madness. *Literally.*

He glanced down at his watch, realizing he'd been at the side of the road for an hour, which was nothing short of pathetic. Revving the engine, he set off in the direction of Max's home. It would take over an hour to get there, but he needed to see him in person. This was going to be the kind of conversation that took all night and several bottles of vodka.

But the farther away from Pine Lakes he got, the more acutely he felt a persistent crawling sensation whisper over his skin. He slowed, letting the engine idle at the legal speed limit. Perhaps he should go to the party. Perhaps he should find out more about her before he spoke to Max. Perhaps he ought to make sure she was safe. That dress was short enough to tempt a saint.

He shook his head and groaned and then turned the car around. So this was what being bond-whipped felt like. Goodbye freewill, hello obsessive-compulsive stalking. Romantic.

With a curse, he smoothed out the crumpled scrap of paper she'd given him and hit the accelerator. He lifted a brow when he turned onto a street littered with beer bottles and cigarette butts. The air hummed with the beats of loud music coming from a lone house a few yards ahead.

He parked across the street from her, stepped into the road, and inhaled until he caught her syrupy scent among the throng of warm bodies, cigarettes, and alcohol. He'd hang back, make sure she was okay, and see her home safely, and then he'd slip away. There was no reason for her to even know he was there.

"You're really losing it," he told himself, shaking his head and making his way past the overspill of revelers in the open front door.

"Hey, cool contacts!" an intoxicated blonde said, her words slurred. She staggered into his path, squinting at his shiny new cat's-eyes.

Before he could push past, two friends joined her, hands on their hips as they leaned in to get a better look. So much for being inconspicuous. He lowered his gaze, hoping they would disperse, but they stayed there, all three pointing expectant smiles at him.

The blonde edged closer, the spearmint punch of her gum hitting his nostrils. "You look lost."

"I'm looking for someone."

She pressed closer still.

There were so many bodies in the dark hallway he couldn't back up any farther.

Standing on tiptoe, she brushed her lips against his ear. "Maybe you've found her."

"I don't think so. Excuse me." He pushed past, ignoring her reproachful stare.

Her two friends parted to let him through with reluctant, shuffling sidesteps that finally gave him a clear view of the hallway. It ended in a narrow staircase, each step occupied by groping couples and raucous drunks. He caught Emily's sweet scent again, and his nostrils flared, his senses sharper now that Gum Girl was out of his face.

Shit.

Emily was taking the stairs two at a time, vaulting over the couples and clusters of smokers. Had she seen him?

He'd come to make sure she was okay from a distance, but her squirrel-up-a-tree flight had him itching to pursue her. It was an unsettling urge, both predatory and protective. He wanted to find out what spooked her, but he also wanted to give chase.

Either way, her panicked ascent compelled him to follow, and he found himself weaving through the crowd in her wake. He had to get to her, to guard and claim and possess.

2

EMILY LEAPED UP THE LAST STEP, TEETERING IN HER HEELS BEFORE regaining her balance and charging along the landing.

Typical, typical, typical. Why had she broken her rule?

She'd decided she wasn't interested the minute she spotted his ridiculous car, but seeing him hesitate on the threshold tonight, his luminous eyes flitting over the sea of shadowy faces in an apprehensive search...

She thought he was looking for *her*. She thought maybe she'd been unfair and he wasn't an Oak Ridge playboy after all. But a split second later, he was chest-deep in a trio of rapt girls.

A hand grasped hers from behind, and she stumbled, the strong arm that slipped around her waist the only thing stopping her from slamming face first into the floor.

"Hey, Ems. Sorry, I didn't mean to knock you off-balance."

She sighed with pleased relief at the warm, masculine voice and leaned against the firm chest behind her. "I didn't know you were back in town."

Heath was her high school crush. His arrival during her senior year set pulses racing, but in accordance with her previously unbroken golden rule, Emily made herself stand back while her peers pouted and flounced around him, an unassuming friendship developing in place of the romance she craved.

She pivoted in his arms and turned to hug him. "You've been shitty at keeping in touch, you know that?"

He held her at arm's length and looked her up and down, his sugar-brown eyes sparking beneath the shock of blond hair he always let hang over his face. "You look good, Emily."

"Oh, really?" She intended her delivery to be sarcastic, but she couldn't quite suppress her smile—at least someone had noticed her tonight.

"Come on." He took her hand and led her into a bedroom off to the right. "We should catch up."

Emily flopped into a broken desk chair while he closed the door, shutting out the noise of the party. "Where have you been, Heath?"

"College, work, around..." He smiled and bit his lip, the dim light of a lamp on the dresser behind him casting shadows over his face. "You really *do* look good."

"Shame you didn't realize that five years ago."

He sidled toward her, pulling her out of the chair and into an awkward hug that sent a thrill up her spine. His hands circled her waist, and he lifted her off the floor, spinning her around until she found her back against the cool bedroom wall.

He planted a hand against the cracked plaster on either side of her shoulders, lowering his head until his eyes were level with hers. "I realized."

She parted her lips in anticipation. It might be unexpected, but after her earlier fiasco, Heath's flattery was more than welcome.

She lifted her hand to his hair, about to sweep the blond mop away from his beautiful face when the door burst open, hitting the wall behind with a loud smack that fragmented the tired plaster.

Emily blinked in mute surprise at the burning green eyes that held hers with such ferocity.

She wriggled in Heath's embrace, puzzled by the grin that softened his features as he eased away from her.

Understanding replaced aggression in the strange eyes watching from the doorway, judgment peppering the gaze that hadn't wavered since he'd barreled inside. "Everything okay here?"

Indignation stiffened her spine. Not only did he arrive just in time to blow up her moment, but he also had the nerve to look as if he found her doing something she shouldn't, when only minutes ago he'd been pressed up against a leggy blonde and two curvy brunettes.

She pushed herself away from the wall with her elbows and straightened. "Why wouldn't it be?"

He scowled.

Heath threw him a provocative smile. "We're cool, aren't we, Ems?"

"Absolutely."

Heath swaggered up to her stranger, locking eyes with him in a moment that threatened to erupt into violence if one of them didn't look away. They were evenly matched—both tall and stacked with lean muscle. Neither one of them backed down, and Mr. Pretty narrowed his eyes at Heath's cocky smirk.

Unexpected guilt made her clear her throat. Mr. Pretty was only here because of her, and playboy or not, she ought to stop him from getting his nose broken.

"Heath, this is, ah..." She paused, waiting for him to introduce himself.

"Sebastian," he said through gritted teeth.

After a couple of drawn-out seconds, Heath turned and nodded to her. "I'll see you around, Ems." His silhouette blocked the doorframe a little longer than necessary, and then he was gone.

She glared at Sebastian. "I didn't think you'd actually come." She infused her words with a pinch of hostility—just because she didn't want to see him get punched didn't mean she had to play nice. He had no right to come charging in like that, as if he had some kind of claim on her. She'd invited him to a party, not proposed he be her one and only, and it wasn't as if he hadn't been flirting himself just a few minutes earlier.

He studied her with impassive precision from across the room. "Neither did I."

"I'm guessing wine bars and fancy restaurants are probably more your scene." She scuffed the pointed toe of her shoe on the wooden floorboard peeping through the threadbare carpet.

"It's not that." He pushed his hands into the pockets of his jeans, the rose gold of a bulky watch standing out against the stiff charcoal denim.

"Oh?" She found herself taking a step toward him. "So you are staying...?"

He dropped his gaze, shuttering those eerie verdant eyes with dense, feathery lashes.

She took another step toward him and held her breath. She was only a foot away when his eyes met hers again, and she staggered, thrown off-balance by their impossible glow.

He gripped her wrist and steadied her. "For now."

With that, he released her arm and took a deliberate step back.

Emily caught herself surging forward again and frowned. What was wrong with her? She didn't chase boys, no matter how pretty they were. How many times did she have to remind herself of that in one day?

She took a breath and strolled toward the door. Whatever the attraction was—and she couldn't deny that even though he appeared to be every inch the rich pretty boy, there *was* an attraction—walking away was her best option.

"Enjoy the party," she said over her shoulder as she exited the room.

She made it less than three feet before a girl in a glittery gold tank top and skinny jeans wobbled into her path.

"Hey, uh, the girl you came with could use some help."

Emily sighed. Collapsing in a drunk heap had become something Roxi did with alarming regularity. "Where is she?"

"Second bedroom on the right."

"Thanks."

Emily marched down the hall and stopped outside the room. "Rox?"

She pushed open the door to reveal Roxi sitting by the bed, surrounded by the contents of her purse. Based on the way she slumped, she was really, really drunk. Roxi turned when she heard her close the door.

"Ems, you're here!" she said, a drink in one hand and a broken high heel in the other, holding her arms up like a child.

Emily crouched beside her on the worn blue carpet. "Come on, up we get." She took the sticky plastic cup from Roxi and held out her hand.

"No!" Roxi slammed the broken shoe against the floor. "I'm staying. I just need to fix my shoe."

Roxi was more drunk than Emily anticipated. She clenched her jaw, and with a heave, she managed to get her friend onto her feet.

"Come on, Roxi, let's just go. It's pretty late now."

"No." She squirmed out of Emily's grasp only to tumble back onto the grimy floor.

Emily sensed, rather than heard, Sebastian come into the room.

"Do you need a hand?"

"No, I got this."

Roxi was back on her feet, staring open-mouthed and swaying. "Who the hell are you?"

Roxi lurched toward him, and he caught her, supporting her with his left side as he turned his head to Emily. "Look, I'm sorry I interrupted you before. I shouldn't have come."

"Why? Too rough around the edges for you?"

"I already told you it's not that."

"Let me guess, you have a girlfriend waiting for you back at the country club."

He arched a brow. "Assume much? Let me guess, you think a generous tip plus a fast car equals an arrogant trust fund parasite looking for a good time."

Yes, but more importantly, she thought it equaled a man like her father, and what was the point in even having a conversation with someone like that?

She made herself look away from his quicksand eyes, feeling their pull even when she turned her back and squatted to gather Roxi's scattered belongings. "Am I wrong?"

"Why don't you let me take you to dinner so you can decide for yourself?"

She froze, her hand poised to pick up an open lipstick peeping out from beneath the bed.

"And let me take you both home?"

She grabbed the lipstick and pushed herself up, holding on to the edge of her dress so it wouldn't ride up any farther. "I'm good to drive. I average one beer to her twenty."

"Then at least let me help you downstairs." His tone made it obvious that he expected no further protest, and in one smooth sweep, he picked up Roxi while propping the door open for Emily.

Roxi squealed and then began to giggle.

He inclined his head toward the noisy stairs. "Lead the way."

With no other easy way of getting Roxi down the stairs and out of the house, Emily stormed past him.

He stopped a few feet away from her car, a distant streetlamp doing little to illuminate the dark road. "Give me your keys, and I'll drive you both home."

She laughed and folded her arms. "I already told you—I'm good to drive. And only an idiot would hand their car keys to a stranger."

His gaze traveled from her rusty Accord to his matte black sports car across the street and then back again. "You think I'm going to steal *that*?"

She bristled at the disdain in his voice. "Whatever. I don't know you, so thanks but no thanks. I'm sorry you wasted your time coming here, but I can drive, and my friend can walk to my car." She glared at Roxi, willing her to get out of his arms and prove her point.

He sighed. "You've been drinking, even if it is only one beer. I want to make sure you get home safely, but my car only has two seats."

Emily snorted. "Expensive and impractical. You have *great* taste."

He set Roxi on the asphalt but continued to support her weight with his arm. "I'm trying to help you out."

"I don't need your help."

He let go of Roxi, who took several unsteady steps and slumped against the car with a happy chuckle before sliding down to the tarmac.

"Ems?" Roxi burped and giggled again.

"What?"

"You can't drive with *those*."

The words were slurred, but the meaning became all too apparent as Emily followed the direction of Roxi's pointed finger.

"Shit!" She rushed to Roxi's side and kneeled to inspect the flat tire.

The rubber sagged around a jagged slash.

"S'all of them." Roxi leaned her head against the bumper. "Now you'll *have* to let him take you home."

Emily circled the car, kicking the fourth flat tire in frustration. Now she had two problems: getting home *and* paying for new tires. Why would anyone slash her tires and leave the look-at-me motor across the street untouched?

She wheeled round and jabbed a finger at Sebastian, who watched in silence. "Did you do this?"

He held his hands up, irritation igniting his eyes. "Yes, I went to a coffee shop this afternoon just hoping one of the staff would invite me to a party so I could walk in on her kissing some guy and slash her tires."

"One of the *staff*? Fuck you. And I wasn't kissing him. And you and your three friends looked pretty cozy earlier too."

He looked up at the opaque navy sky and shook his head. "What about an Uber?"

"They won't come out this far. Not to this address anyway."

His brow puckered, and his eyes focused on something in the distance, his tempting, full mouth settling into a hard line.

She turned to find Heath lounging on the front steps, the glowing end of his cigarette contracting and expanding as he inhaled and then blew out ash-white breath. She whistled to attract his attention, though it was clear he was already observing their little sideshow. He ground his cigarette out with the heel of his boot and crossed the dead grass of the front yard.

"Everything okay here?" Heath smirked at his imitation of Sebastian and slipped an arm around her waist.

Sebastian waited, arms crossed, jaw clenched, the hollows of his cheeks and the sultry swell of his lips standing out in menacing relief.

Emily looked up at Heath. "Did you see who did this?"

"Nope."

"Well, can you take us home?" There went rule number two.

He tilted his head to one side. "Roxi lives fifteen minutes east of here, and your place is another fifteen minutes in the opposite direction. Taking you both home would mean an hour round trip to get back to the party."

Determined to retain some semblance of independence, she reached into the little black bag she wore across her body and pulled out a twenty. "I can pay you."

"No need. Your boy over there's got you, right?"

Sebastian gave a tight nod, his expression wrathful.

She fixed Heath with a stern stare. "His car only has two seats."

"Then I'll take Roxi, and he can take you. I need to stop by the liquor store on the way to her house anyway."

"God, you can be an asshole, you know that?"

Heath grinned. "Yeah, but you love me."

"Look after her, okay?" Emily said.

"Of course." Heath took Roxi's hand and helped her to her feet.

Emily sighed. "Call me when you get in, Rox."

Roxi gave her a sheepish half smile, a sure sign she was sobering up. "Always do."

She watched them leave to make sure Heath helped Roxi into what she assumed was his car at the end of the street.

As the taillights disappeared, Sebastian cleared his throat. "Do you want a ride or not?"

"What I want is four new tires." Emily was aware she was showing all the gratitude of a mulish teen, but she also resented having to depend on anyone other than herself.

He leaned against his car, maddeningly calm in the face of her ire. "Is that a no?"

She looked back toward the house. The chances of finding another designated driver in that crowd were slim. Most of them would pass out as the sun rose, sleeping off their excesses before trickling home sometime in the afternoon. She sighed and crossed the street. He opened the door for her, his eyes capturing hers and sending her heart into a sprint.

He started the engine and pulled away from the curb in a smooth arc. She glowered out of the window.

"You're upset," he said.

"I'm pissed off."

"Because your friend wouldn't take you home?"

She huffed with impatience. "No, because I have to find a way to pay for new tires."

"Do you live alone?"

She shot him a suspicious look. "No, I live with my mom."

"Will she take you to work tomorrow?"

"What do you care?" She sighed, realizing how bratty she sounded. Taking a deep breath, she tried to contain the discomfort she felt in needing and accepting his help. "She works nights, so I'll take the bus. She's usually in bed by the time I leave."

Her shoulders slumped at the thought of the forty-minute walk to the bus stop. It was past midnight, so she'd be lucky if she managed five hours' sleep.

"What about your father?"

"What about him?"

"Can he help you out?"

She rolled her eyes in the darkness, unwilling to share that bitter bowl of lemons with him. The father she despised would be last person she'd ask for help, especially when it would present him with another opportunity to pitch his Faustian pact to her—an offer to make all her dreams come true as long as she took those dreams far, far away from him. "No."

They drove in silence after that, except for Emily's reluctant directions. He pulled up outside the small house and startled her by getting out and opening her door.

He extended a hand to her, and she took it with a grudging smile, allowing him to pull her onto the sidewalk. "Thank you."

"You're welcome." He looked about as happy as she was to have entered into their polite little dance.

She walked up the porch steps, retrieving her key from her bag. The metal clinked in the lock, but the silence beyond her movements told her he was still there, watching.

The door swung open, releasing a surge of warm, white light. Emily turned back to the dark figure. "Good night."

He backed away, staring as he opened his car door, jewel-green eyes shining from the shadows. "Get some rest, Emily."

3

SEBASTIAN'S THOUGHTS CHURNED AS HIS AUDI R8 ATE UP THE ROAD between Pine Lakes and Basingdale, the secluded hamlet Max chose to call home these days.

He ignored the miniature lightning strikes prickling his skin with each passing mile and the way his heart stormed and thundered in his chest.

Get used to it.

He couldn't succumb to the bond's pull. He could only imagine how Emily would respond to him lurking in her wake twenty-four hours a day—with a call to the police, no doubt. She'd already accused him of slashing her tires.

He found her defensive posturing and attitude fascinating.

The bond had its hooks in her too, though as a human she was spared its full force. He'd pitied her confusion when she edged toward him at the party, but the ease with which she shook off the compulsion terrified him, a precursor to show how effortless it would be for her to walk away.

He pulled onto a gravel drive that stretched to an angular glass property, the stones grinding out a muffled protest beneath the car's wheels. Pine Lakes's proximity to Max's home was one of the reasons he'd listened to his friend's insistence that property there was a good investment. He still wasn't convinced, but at least he was close enough to share his current predicament in person.

He knocked on Max's door as the first glimmer of dawn crept across the sky. The manicured grounds were silent and still, the vast house exuding the empty, unlived-in feeling of a second home. He turned to the broccoli-green hills beyond the perfect lawns and took a steadying breath. The hushed movement of the door alerted him to Max's presence.

"Sebastian, what took you so long? Life in the country slowing you down already?"

While Sebastian had erased his accent, Max chose to retain the gentle Southern French lilt, and it permeated his words.

Max's grin vanished at the sight of Sebastian's preternatural jade eyes. He exhaled and ushered him through to the modern interior.

Unlike some older vampires, who liked to hang on to old-fashioned clutter long after it outlived its original purpose and style, Max abhorred antiques. He preferred floor-to-ceiling windows, polished concrete floors, stark white walls, and minimalist furniture.

"Breakfast?" asked Max, who was dressed and groomed despite the early hour, his mousy-brown hair deliberately tousled.

Sebastian nodded. His friend poured a glass of blood from a pitcher on the coffee table and passed it to him.

Max dropped into an armchair and stretched his long legs out in front of him. "So it's happened."

Sebastian took the pristine white sofa, sitting on the edge and dangling the glass between his legs. "I guess so." He took a sip and winced. Stored blood was so unappealing, but Max disliked the logistics of the hunt, using his connections to buy blood reserves instead.

"So why do you look so grim?"

"She's human."

"Shit." Max was silent for a minute. "What are you going to do?"

Sebastian reached for the brandy decanter next to the pitcher of blood and poured a substantial slug into his glass in answer.

"Shit."

"You said that already."

"It's just... It's dangerous, Sebastian, for both of you."

"I'm aware."

"Have you had sex with her? Is the bond consummated?"

Sebastian raised a brow. "No, of course I haven't. I'm not an idiot."

"Good, that's good... I mean, if you end up like the others... That's a fate worse than death."

"Not making me feel any better." Sebastian sat back and leaned his head against the sofa, looking up at the featureless white ceiling in defeat. "Haven't there been any cases that played out differently? I thought maybe Marie might know of other incidents, ones that haven't been shared with the rest of us."

Marie, Max's on-off love interest, was a senior Circle official prone to bringing her work home with her. They'd both served under her command during their period of conscription to the organization, a twenty-five-year stint that all unbonded vampires had to serve every two hundred years. Marie often told Max more than she should, divulging information, research, and intel not intended for the wider vampire community.

Max didn't answer, and a subdued silence settled between them as they considered the dark future ahead for Sebastian.

No matter what he did, life from this point on was going to be a fight.

"I have an idea." Max set his glass on the coffee table with an agitated clink and paced over to the window. "The bond is only a risk because she's human."

"I hadn't realized that." Sebastian swallowed his sarcasm with another frustrated gulp of his drink.

"So what if you turn her *before* you consummate the bond?"

Sebastian stared at the contents of his glass and thought about it, swilling the maroon liquid around in a tight circle. In theory, it *could* work. The only problem was *her*—her naked hostility and wariness. He'd struggled to coax her into a car with him. What hope would he have of talking her into changing her entire world?

"I'm not exactly her type, Max. I'd have to persuade her to get to know me before I even attempt to convince her vampirism is a positive lifestyle choice, and even *if* we end up together and I give her my best sales pitch, she might still say no. Not everybody craves immortality and youth more than family and humanity."

"Do you really need to convince her though?"

"I won't force her."

"But once she's turned, nothing that happened before will matter. She'll feel exactly as you do. You'll have a true bond, one you can complete safely."

"It would have to be her choice, Max."

"But what alternative do you have? You know what's at stake for both of you. If you don't turn her, her days are numbered."

Sebastian stood and paced over to the window. "There's no telling how long it could take to actually turn her, Max. You know how much it varies. It could take years. I won't put her through that unless she's sure she wants it."

"Or it could take days, and then it would be done. Mind-shattering, life-threatening crisis averted."

"No. I won't start the process without her consent." He ran a hand through his hair. "I'll get to know her, try to figure out if she's emotionally equipped to cope with all this. If she is, I'll tell her the truth, and she can decide for herself."

"And if she says no? Putting all the other risks aside, would you break with Circle protocol? Have you even thought about what that could mean?"

"If it comes to that, I'll negotiate a deal in exchange for her freedom. Their offer is still on the table." The Circle had been trying to recruit Sebastian since his conscription ended. He was sure they could come to an agreement, if necessary.

"That's going to take time. What if the hunters find you first? They've been swarming vampire-human pairs for the last twenty years. If they hear…"

"Have you forgotten what I can do to hunters? The Circle hasn't."

"You weren't bonded then, and you had an entire regiment to command."

"I just need some time to figure her out. As long as the bond doesn't progress any further and I don't tell her what I am, we can both still walk away from this."

"Are you sure about that?"

"I'm not saying it will be easy."

Max sighed. "Have I ever told you that you're the most stubborn bastard I know?"

"Once or twice."

"You need to call it in, whatever you decide to do."

"I know."

"Tonight, Sebastian."

He looked away. Calling it in would make it real. It could take away her choices and his. He didn't know what strategy the Circle had in place for vampire-human bondings, but there was a reason they had made reporting them mandatory, and it wasn't so they could congratulate the happy couple.

Emily woke with a start, scrambled out of the bedcovers, and pushed a tangled curtain of hair from her eyes. With a clumsy tap of her sleep-stiffened fingers, she shut off the persistent drill of her phone's alarm and collapsed onto the pillows.

A Sebastian-shaped dream tried to pull her back to bed. His gold-green eyes taunting, the curve of a seductive smile reeling her in despite the domineering rich boy vibe even her subconscious version of him emanated. She groaned and rolled over, embarrassed by her own dream and unwilling to give her unwelcome crush any further thought.

She yawned and trudged the few steps to her little bathroom, turned on the shower in the dated apricot tub, and tried to ignore the memory of Sebastian's fingers brushing hers.

The spray hit her face as she tried not to think about the way he looked at her or his oddly protective behavior—its intensity both irritating and charming.

Instead, she thought about her father. That would pour plenty of acid on her misplaced attraction. She thought about her father's shiny, polished, perfect Oak Ridge family, living in their sought-after Oak Ridge mansion. The exclusive spa town in the hills was where the rich and famous went to rest, play, and rehabilitate in private, and where her father chose to live with his second wife and their two daughters. Off the beaten track, away from the prying eyes of the masses and accessible only to the wealthy few. Sebastian probably grew up somewhere like that.

She lathered her shampoo with unforgiving vigor, frustrated she hadn't put more distance between herself and *that place.* With a sigh, she reminded herself she was still in Pine Lakes, living with her mother and serving coffee, because she was saving up for something better. A move to a big city a thousand miles away from Oak Ridge, or a new life painting portraits by the sea. Except the truth was, she didn't want to abandon her mother—that would make her as bad as her father. And she struggled to paint her nails, let alone portraits.

She stepped out of the steam, the dull sound of her phone vibrating on the dresser hurrying her into a frayed towel that did little to absorb the water clinging to her skin. She tripped on the bathroom's torn linoleum, stumbled forward, and stubbed her toe on an abandoned book on the way to answer.

Hopping in pain, she hissed a quiet greeting into the phone so she wouldn't disturb her mom. "Roxi, why aren't you sleeping it off?"

"I'm doing a yoga cleanse thing."

"Sounds relaxing. Unfortunately, some of us have to go to work."

Roxi was starting grad school in a few weeks, so her summer had been a relaxing blur of parties, shopping trips, and lazy afternoons in the sun.

"Do you need a ride?"

"No, I'll take the bus."

"Are you going to tell me what was going on last night?"

"What do you mean?"

"I might have been drunk, but even I noticed the way you were looking at him."

"Who?"

"If you pretend you don't know who I'm talking about, I'm hanging up."

Emily rolled her eyes. "I guess he's kind of attractive."

"*Kind* of attractive?" Roxi scoffed. "Even my booze-addled brain remembers those eyes and that mouth. He was so pretty my eyes hurt."

"So?"

"So why did you give him such a hard time?"

Emily toweled off her hair with her free hand and slipped into clean underwear. "I wasn't that bad."

"You accused him of slashing your tires."

"Well, maybe he did." She reached for her deodorant, coughing at the sickly strawberry cloud that came out of the aerosol.

"You're being ridiculous."

"Am I?"

"Driving a nice car doesn't automatically mean he's a dick."

She wriggled into jeans and grabbed a clean T-shirt. "Hmmm."

"Are you going to go out for dinner with him?"

"You remember that too?" She dropped the phone and pulled

the shirt over her head, picking it up again as she ran a comb through her wet hair. "Were you really drunk last night, or was it all an act?"

"Are you?"

"I don't know. He seemed... Look, I invited him to the party, and the second he got there, he started flirting with a group of girls and..."

"*You* invited him?"

"Yes."

"You broke your rule?"

"Yes, so I can't have dinner with him."

Roxi was silent for a moment. "You must have felt something, Em. You *never* break your rules."

Emily grabbed her bag and keys off the floor. "Can you just drop it?"

"What are you going to do if he calls you?"

"He won't. He didn't ask for my number."

"You sound disappointed."

She didn't answer as she crept down the hall and inched the front door open to make sure it didn't creak. Outside, she squinted in the early-morning sunshine and froze.

"Ems, are you still there?"

"Can I call you back?"

She didn't wait for the reply, ending the call and shoving the phone in her back pocket as she bounded down the porch steps.

Her car was parked on the street, and it had four perfect new tires.

When Emily got to work, Bob was muttering and cursing because the chef he'd spent the last week training had handed in his notice. He was brusque with everyone, his stout legs doing angry laps of the space behind the counter. Emily and the other waitresses did their best to avoid aggravating him further by pasting on their warmest welcome smiles and ringing up orders with false enthusiasm.

By late afternoon, tiredness scratched at her eyes and weighed on her limbs. She cleared a table, the cups and saucers balanced in a haphazard heap on her tray, and wondered for the hundredth time that day who slashed her tires.

She knew who had the audacity to replace them and return her car, and though the throwaway patronage of the gesture made her stomach churn, it also meant she had to drop her suspicions about Sebastian.

She placed a half-empty cup on the top of her mound of china, straightened, and lifted the tray, her eyes focused on the unstable load.

"Hi."

She watched the crockery slide to the edge of her tray and cursed when that last cup pitched free of its companions. With the barest of movements and an exasperating grin, Sebastian caught it.

"You startled me."

He replaced the cup on the pile, his peridot eyes melting her agitation. "Long day?"

"Long night." She took the tray over to the counter where Bob hovered. He nodded at the clock on the far wall as she made her way to Sebastian, letting her know he was timing the conversation and docking her pay accordingly.

"How much do I owe you for the tires?" she asked, partly because she wanted to make it clear she intended to pay Sebastian back, and partly because she wanted to dampen Bob's undisguised interest in their exchange.

He answered with a playful half smile. "Can I take you out to dinner?"

She tried to suppress her own involuntary smile, twisting her lips in embarrassment as Bob's face took on the blank expression of someone who was listening very hard. "Why would you want to do that?"

He lifted a brow in reply, as if the answer was obvious.

"Couldn't you persuade those girls at the party to go out with you?" She pouted in mock sympathy. "They seemed so *interested* too."

"That wasn't what it looked like." He reached out and squeezed her shoulder, as if his touch would have more impact than his words.

"That's what all the boys say."

"I'll pick you up tonight."

"I haven't said yes, and you haven't told me how much I owe you."

"I'll be at your house at seven. And the tires were a gift."

She shook her head. "I don't need handouts. I'm paying you back."

Amusement lit his eyes as he backed away. "*You're welcome.*"

4

It was still hot, the sun melting a molten trail across the dusky blue sky, when Emily strode across her cracked driveway to greet Sebastian. She wore high-heeled sandals and her best dress, a short crepe shift with a pink, white, and blue pattern. She fiddled with her hem and hunched away from the lingering daylight and into his shadow.

He leaned against his car, its black metallic shell a contrast to those strange olivine eyes, which he fixed on her. He sported jeans and a fitted black shirt, as posed and flawless as a model on a billboard.

He smiled, and her breath quickened, her heart clattering in her chest like a bird trapped in a chimney. She hadn't even wanted to go out with him, and now she was nervous, pulse-falteringly nervous.

"Good evening, Emily." He opened the car door for her.

"Hi."

She forced her nerves back under the surface and raised her chin, determined not to look impressed as she slid into the plush leather seat. He set off, and the town sped by, heads turning at his flashy ride. Sebastian relaxed behind the wheel, anticipating what was ahead and maneuvering the stick without effort.

"Do you have a curfew?"

She flushed. "Living with my mom doesn't mean going to bed early and eating my vegetables."

"I meant do you have to be up early for work tomorrow? If you do, I'll make sure I get you back earlier than last night."

"Oh." Her flush got hotter, and she picked at a seam on her dress. "I don't work on Mondays, so it doesn't matter what time I get back."

She looked out of the window at the dying sun clinging to the pines of the forest road, dense dark green against a bloody sky. Her nails pricked her palm as she realized the route they were on climbed out of Pine Lakes's small suburban sprawl to Oak Ridge.

And it was Sunday.

She swallowed, her throat dry at the prospect of the probable encounter that lay ahead.

Thirty minutes later, her heart sank further as a French maître d' ushered them into the snooty little town's most exclusive restaurant. A light sweat moistened her palms, and she followed the immaculately dressed older man past the bar. She should have known this was where someone like Sebastian would take her.

She kept her head down as he whisked them past the sea of Botox-filled faces in the downstairs dining room and out onto the first-floor terrace. Her fingers bit into the soft leather of her clutch, Sebastian a few steps behind her. The open-air upper level, with its creeping grape vines and stone balustrade, was where all the "somebodies" ate during the summer months.

"Monsieur Blake," said the maître d', gesturing to a table in the middle of the terrace. The *only* table. He pulled out a chair for Emily with a flourish, poured two glasses of champagne from a bottle chilling in a silver ice bucket, and backed away discreetly.

Emily looked around at the empty space, relieved she hadn't

seen the one face she would do anything to avoid. "You reserved the entire terrace?"

"I like my privacy."

She suppressed the censure on her lips, instead asking, "What brought you to Pine Lakes?"

"It was time for a change."

"From?"

"I move around a lot."

"For work?"

"You could call it that."

He leaned back in his chair and ran his finger around the base of his champagne flute, his expression sphinxlike. "How long have you worked at the coffee shop?"

"Too long."

"Is there something else you'd rather do?"

She toyed with her napkin, reluctant to discuss her limited job prospects amid the showy opulence of Oak Ridge. "There are a million things I'd rather do."

"So why do you stay?"

"I don't have a short answer to that question."

"I'm listening." He leaned forward, as if he really wanted to hear her uneventful life story.

"Pine Lakes isn't exactly a hotbed of opportunity, but I won't leave my mom behind so I can chase rainbows and play at being a careerist. She's my only family, and she's more important to me than professional aspirations and money. I know that's not a fashionable way to think, but that's just the way it is for me."

"Couldn't you take her with you, if you left?"

"She won't leave. She has a life in Pine Lakes."

"As do you."

"Meaning?"

"Your stance is refreshing. It's laudable that you value family above all else, but are you living *your* life or shadowing your mother's?"

Emotion slammed into her with the weight and force of a speeding truck. Unnerved by his steady gaze and the threat of unexpected tears, she knocked back a large gulp of champagne, its bubbles fizzing on her tongue with an acrid bitterness.

Looking down at the table, she felt the warmth of his hand on top of hers, the thrill of his gentle touch killing her harsh retort before it left her lips.

The caress, both unsettling and soothing, trapped her wrist with calming, captivating circles, even as the maître d' reappeared and began lifting dishes from a silver tray carried by a stiff young waiter.

"Goat cheese curd and beetroot jelly with a minted pea froth," he announced with pride.

Sebastian released her hand and gestured to the tiny cube of cheese. "I hope you don't mind. I preordered the tasting menu."

She smiled and tried to look composed, pushing the threat of a lifetime serving coffee and living with her mother to the very back of her mind where it belonged.

Lifting the silver fork to her mouth, she bit into the tiny square, long buried memories of family dinners in this restaurant assailing her as the sharp, condensed flavors hit her palate.

Emily ate with practiced, delicate movements. Sebastian had wondered whether the fussy restaurant, with its celebrity patrons and elaborate menu, would be too pretentious for her, but he couldn't face the steaks, tacos, and pizzas the Pine Lakes Grill offered, and the only other places to eat had chicken wings and subs on the menu. He'd trained his body to accept exceptionally cooked cuisine, relearning how to appreciate the flavors and textures, but junk food made his stomach riot.

He saw now that she'd been here before, more than once. Course after course arrived, and she selected the correct cutlery each time without thought or hesitation. What he couldn't work out was who she'd been here with and how long ago. An ex-boyfriend, perhaps? Judging by her modest, well-worn home, he couldn't imagine it had been with her mother.

He steered the conversation away from the emotional black hole he inadvertently opened up earlier by flirting, joking, and letting her tell him about the area and her friends. The tension that bunched her shoulders began to ebb, and he realized a complex vulnerability lay beneath the fierce bravado.

She used hostility as a sticking plaster to mask the insecurity of an old wound.

He would have to find the cause of the injury because, though he wanted to steep himself in her mellifluous voice, to see nothing beyond her fluid gestures and enthralling smile, he needed to keep his focus. He was here to see if Max's plan could work, if she could deal with the mind-bending prospect of life with a vampire, if she could entertain the idea of becoming one herself.

He batted away her offer to split the check and paid for dinner while she waited on the edge of the terrace, looking toward Pine Lakes, its distant citrine lights bright against the velvety darkness of the forested hills. He couldn't read her expression, but the slight twist in her brow told him she wasn't admiring the view.

He joined her, resting a hand on the guardrail next to her. "Ready to go?"

"Sure."

The breeze blew her hair into her face, and he swept it away, resting his fingers on her cheek, eyes on hers. His body thrummed with energy, the urge to kiss her contained only by the discomfort and sadness that played across her features.

He placed a proprietary hand on her lower back as they made their way downstairs, the heat of her skin through the thin fabric of the dress making him think about putting his hands in other places. He waited for a whip of sarcasm from her at the contact, but she accepted his touch. He wanted to believe she was warming to him, but it was this place that had caused the change in her demeanor, erasing all her confident sass like chalk from a board.

"Emily."

They were almost at the door when her name rang out in a clipped, imposing tone from the bar by the foyer.

She stiffened, her expression sour, and turned to a suited middle-aged man with salt-and-pepper hair. "Graham."

His face darkened, his lips thinning to a white line. "What are you doing here?"

"Leaving."

Sebastian put together the two pairs of sharp gray eyes, the warm olive skin, and the shared sugary note of both their scents.

The man looked him over, surprise registering in the slight movement of his heavy brows before he concealed it with a sneer. "You're so like your mother, Emily."

She shook her head, her body rigid. "Enjoy your evening."

"Did you think about my offer?" His voice had a hard, persuasive edge to it now. "It's still on the table."

"And the answer's still no. Excuse me."

"You're being foolish," the man called after her.

Sebastian took a step toward him, gripped by an alien impulse to defend her.

"Careful." Steely-gray eyes glared back at him, arrogant and fearless. "She might have conned you into thinking she's worth pursuing by telling you she's a Heart, but I assure you, she's her mother's daughter."

"Should the name mean something to me?"

The proud face flushed at the deliberate slight, and Sebastian turned away, quashing the bond's violent demand to escalate the stand-off. He followed Emily's swift little steps and pushed the door open for her so she could steam out into the cool night. She stopped at the curb, the breath she held hissing out in an angry rush.

He stood beside her. "So you don't get along with your father."

She laughed, the hollow, mirthless sound as jarring as a sob. "I haven't had a father to get along with for a long time."

"That's why you've been so tense. You knew he'd be here."

"He likes to have family dinner here every Sunday evening."

"He remarried?"

"I think upgraded would be a better way to describe what he did. Version 1.0 didn't meet his standards."

A valet appeared with the car. She slipped inside without hesitation and pulled the door shut before the flustered teen could close it for her.

They sped away from Oak Ridge, the streetlights alternating with the pitch night to wash her face in moving black and orange stripes.

Hands clasped in her lap, she glanced across at him. "Where are we going?"

"You look like you need a drink, and I don't think the champagne bar back there would be a good place to get one."

She laughed, and this time it was lighter. "You're learning."

He flashed her his sexiest smile. "I'm happy for you to teach me."

He was pleased when she rolled her eyes and chortled, her vulnerability fading. "There's a bar ten minutes from here. Take the next right."

The bar was the kind of crowded, shadowy place he liked to hunt in. Nobody paid any attention to them as they ordered their drinks and found a small table at the back of the badly lit room.

He let her take a swig of her beer before he hit her with another question about her family. "How long has it been since your father left?"

She dug her thumbnail into the soft wood of the table and took another sip of beer before she answered, her gaze pulling away from his to rove the busy space behind him. "Twelve years."

He hated picking at the scab, but he needed to know if her broken relationship with her father was going to be a problem. If he couldn't get close to her, if she couldn't trust quickly and completely, Max's proposal would never work, and he'd have to get the hell away from her before the bond took over.

She looked down at the table. "After he left, we had nothing. My mom was young when she married him, and he wanted her to stay home and look after me, so she never really worked or had any money of her own." She picked at the dent she'd made in the table, running her finger back and forth over the spot. "His family always hated her. The Hearts are kind of a big deal in Oak Ridge, and seeing their eldest son marry a nobody from Pine Lakes was humiliating. They accused her of being a gold digger. Eventually, he felt the same way. She made a point of asking for nothing in the divorce, but it didn't change his opinion of her."

"So when he said you were like her…"

"I don't usually date guys like you, not that he would know that." She tapped the neck of her bottle and hesitated, her gaze still glued to the table. "He only saw your clothes, your watch, your poise, and he assumed that was all I saw too."

"And what do you see?"

She lifted her gaze back to him, her expression quizzical. "I'm not sure yet. You're kind of cryptic."

He laughed and reached into his pocket for his buzzing cell. "Do you mind?"

She nodded in approval, and he answered Max's call, speaking in French in case anything sensitive arose. Max was checking in, so he wrapped it up after a brief exchange.

She contemplated him with interest during the short call, tilting her head to the side, long mahogany waves falling over her shoulder. "You speak French."

He slid the phone into his jeans pocket. "I speak a lot of languages."

"How come?"

"I've had a lot of time to travel and study."

"On account of you being so filthy rich?" she quipped.

He took the gibe with a grin and paused, considering how much to reveal about himself. "I come from France originally."

"You don't have an accent."

"It was a long time ago."

"When you were a child?"

"No, I was in my twenties when I left."

"But you're still in your twenties."

"Am I?"

"That or you have a really good plastic surgeon."

"Maybe I do."

"Are your family still there?"

He took a breath. Two centuries later, it still hurt to think about them. "No, they're all dead."

Emily flinched at the flat statement, horrified that her glib questioning had exposed such a wrenching revelation. "God, Sebastian, I'm so sorry."

"Don't be. It was a long time ago."

"What happened?"

"There was a fire at our home. I was the only one to make it out."

Shit. She'd been ribbing him about his money since they met, and the only reason he had it was because he'd lost his entire family. Shame took a bite out of her confidence, and she sat back, unsure what to say.

He reached out and took her hand. "It's fine, Emily, really."

He interlaced his fingers with hers, and heat curved up her spine, the unusual intimacy of their entwined hands sending a tremor through her body.

"Did you have siblings?" she asked.

"Two younger sisters, an older brother, and God knows how many half brothers and sisters."

She took a sip of her beer and waited for him to explain.

"My father liked variety in the bedroom."

She traced the line of his index finger with her thumb. Maybe his daddy issues were as complicated as hers. He squeezed her hand and began mirroring the back-and-forth movement of her thumb with his own.

"Are you in touch with any of them?"

He shook his head. "I never met any of them, but I heard the rumors."

"That must have been hard."

"Like I said, it was all a long time ago." He knocked back the last of his beer and stood without letting go of her hand. "Home?"

She nodded and stood, allowing him to lead her out to the parking lot, though she didn't want the night to end. His candor had blown her cynicism and distrust to dust, and without her protective shell of sarcasm, she was left with a naked attraction she could no longer deny. His eyes, shimmering panther green in the darkness, had transfixed her all evening, and her hands itched to touch his thick burnt-gold hair.

As they stopped by his car, he brought their tangled fingers to his lips and kissed the top of her hand, the appreciative smile he gave her sending feather-soft whispers dancing across her skin.

On the drive home, she refrained from chattering to fill the loaded silence that expanded between them. He instructed her to put her number in his cell as he drove, and her hands shook as those cat's-eyes watched her from beneath thick lashes.

He walked her the few short steps to her door. "Good night, Emily."

"Thanks for dinner." She looked at her car. "And for the tires— I'll get you the money as soon as I can."

He smiled and shook his head, and then he leaned forward to kiss her on the cheek. Her body ignored the formality of the kiss, roaring to life at his nearness, the feel of his lips against her face.

He pulled away with an amused smile and waited while she fished around in her clutch for her keys.

She felt the cool edges of her phone, the foil wrapper of a packet of gum, the smooth plastic of her lip gloss, and the sharp corners of a square compact. She shook the small bag and peered inside. "I know they're in here somewhere."

He pushed his hands in his pockets and stood aside so she could edge beneath the porch light. "Take your time."

"You can take off. I'll find them eventually."

He didn't move, and with an exasperated humph, she kneeled and tipped the contents of her bag onto the floor. The keys weren't there.

"Do your neighbors have a spare set?"

Tossing everything back into the small, impractical clutch, she got to her feet. "No."

"Can I drop you off somewhere?"

"Let me call Roxi."

She dialed and listened to the ringtone. She considered her limited options. She didn't want to bother her mom at work, and she'd rather not spend the next eight hours on the porch waiting for her to get back.

How could she possibly have lost her keys? She hadn't opened her clutch all evening.

"No answer?"

She shook her head. "There's a twenty-four-hour diner on the other side of town. Would you mind dropping me there? I'll call my mom when she finishes work, and she can pick me up on her way home."

"What time does she get off?"

"Seven."

He arched a brow and folded his arms. "You can't sit in a diner all night, Emily."

"It's fine."

"You could come back with me."

She squirmed. "Honestly, I'm happy to wait at the diner."

"Still don't trust me?"

"I wouldn't trust anyone I'd known less than forty-eight hours, Sebastian."

"Is trust something that takes a finite period of time to acquire?"

"Not necessarily."

She watched as an emotion she couldn't identify flickered in his eyes. Disappointment? She wanted to smooth it away.

"I think I've inconvenienced you enough already."

The emotion in his eyes sank beneath the surface, like a carp disappearing into the depths of a pond. "Well, maybe I'd like you to inconvenience me some more."

His mouth curved with sultry promise, and her body liquefied at the thought of spending the night with him.

"Do you have a spare room?" Her voice came out as an embarrassing, husky croak.

"Of course."

She inhaled and held her breath as he extended his hand to her. Meeting his mesmerizing gaze, she finally exhaled and clasped his cool fingers with her own.

5

SEBASTIAN DROVE TO THE EDGE OF TOWN, PAST WHERE THE SUBURBS finished and the forest began. With relief and foreboding, he noted the torturous crawling sensation had abated in Emily's presence, which could only mean it would worsen if he had to leave. His whole life was riding on this race to win her trust and affection, and she might not know it yet, but hers was too.

Glancing across at her moonlit profile, he wondered what it would have been like to meet her as a human, without the pressure of his volatile vampire bond. He didn't doubt he'd have wanted to wind his fingers in all that thick chestnut hair as much as he did now, to kiss his way up her neck and claim her mouth with his own.

Forcing his gaze back to the road, he took the well-hidden turn that led to his house, dense firs obfuscating the proud stone building until they were in its long shadow. He circled the large fountain in the center of the driveway, its four stone cherubs spraying gurgling water out of their mouths in greeting, and came to a stop.

He looked from the vast moon-washed property to Emily and waited for a reaction, but her features were composed. There was no shock or disgust, no adulation or avarice.

"Do you live here alone?" She took his hand as she got out of the car.

He tipped his head in self-conscious acknowledgement. "I know it's excessive for one person."

"You said it, not me." She shot him a playful grin that told him he could expect further teasing.

Inside, she wandered around the cavernous living space while he got them drinks in the kitchen. He moved around so often he no longer bothered investing time in decorating. Instead, he commissioned interior designers to dress the properties he owned, which resulted in fashionably furnished and utterly impersonal homes.

He carried two glasses and a bottle of cabernet sauvignon to the living room and set them on the coffee table.

Emily examined the only things in the house connected to him. "Who took these?" She scrutinized the series of framed black-and-white wildlife stills that ran along the wall at the back of the room. Her gaze flitted between a lone stag on the crest of a stark hillside and a close-up of a wolf in a snowstorm, its eyes narrowed in warning.

"I did."

"You like photography?"

"I used to—I've had lots of different hobbies."

"How did you get so close?"

He laughed, coming to stand beside her and snaking a hand around her waist. "I'm reckless."

She turned into his arm and leaned back to look up at him. He tugged her lower body against his and stiffened at the warm press of her thighs, the pulsing energy of the bond becoming a tangible, overpowering surge of desire.

His considered advance, intended to establish closeness and fledgling trust with controlled physical intimacy, had doused them both in gasoline. His body responded to her with incendiary force, torching all thought of restraint and caution.

His gaze fell to her lips, and he brought his free hand to her face to trace their arcing outline with his thumb. She moistened them while he watched, her pink tongue following the path his thumb had taken.

He stifled a groan and crushed his mouth against hers, pressing his right hand at her nape to bring her closer. Her lips pushed back against his, the scent of her arousal threading through him as his tongue met hers. Lust gripped and spurred him to run his hands beneath the hem of her dress, his fingertips brushing the base of the perfectly rounded globes of her ass.

Her legs shook at his touch, and that heady scent grew thicker, dewing the air. She kissed him harder and spread her thighs ever so slightly. Despite her well-established social prejudices, *she wanted him.*

Thank fuck for that.

But as she returned each fervent kiss and caress in kind, as she clung to his chest with a proprietary grip, his control slipped.

Unable to stop, he took her full lower lip between his teeth and sucked, and then he slid his right hand over the sheer lace of her panties. Panic chilled his skin, and he fought the exquisite lure of the damp heat that moistened his fingers through the fabric. With each stroke, the tremors from his internal battle intensified, shaking the foundation of his thoughts until there was nothing left but heart-faltering fear and toxic desire.

Burying his face in her hair, he sensed the flutter of the pulse in her neck and remembered that she was human, that if they did this, there would be suffering and death and horror. Terror stopped him from tugging the thin material aside and dipping a finger into her slick folds, from ripping open her dress and exposing the soft, feminine flesh it concealed. He wanted to see and taste all of her—her breasts, her blood, her sex. He wanted to claim what was his, to consummate their bond with the thrusting flow of his seed inside her.

But everything hinged on his ability to abstain. If he sank any further into this pit of sensation, he wouldn't make it out, and neither would she.

Pulling back, he dragged his eyes away from the temptation of her parted lips and met her heated gaze.

"You never did tell me what happened to your eyes," she said.

Relaxing his grip on her waist, he stepped back so there was space between their bodies again. "It must have been the light."

She was breathless, the rapid rise and fall of her chest tempting him to close the gap again. "I thought they were brown, but they're the lightest green I've ever seen."

He shrugged the comment off and went to pour the wine, doing his best to ignore the simmering tension between them. "I hope red is okay."

"Red is great." She accepted the glass and perched on the edge of a leather armchair, her fingers playing over the brass studs along its edges. "I'm sorry if I'm keeping you up."

"I don't need a lot of sleep."

"Do you have to get up early for work?"

He flicked his eyes away from the smooth, tanned expanse of her slender legs. "I set my own hours."

"What do you do?"

"Property."

He could have admitted that currently he didn't *do* anything, but he didn't want to watch her walls go back up in the face of more evidence that he was the two-dimensional stereotype she despised.

In truth, he'd built and sold more businesses than he could count in his long life and amassed more money and land than he would ever need. He'd once embraced the push and pressure of working life. His quarter century of conscription as one of the Circle's elite Primaries was the most devastating period on record for the hunters they'd crushed in countless battles. But almost a year after he'd completed his service and rejected the unprecedented offer the Circle made him, he was still drifting, aimless and untethered, the soulless revenue streams he once commanded holding little appeal.

She ran her index finger along the stem of her wineglass. "What kind of property?"

"Restoration."

That part at least was almost true. He'd spent decades restoring the ruins of his family's former home.

She sipped her wine and sat back, waiting for him to continue, her pursed lips daring him to pounce and fuse his mouth to hers again.

He leaned forward, hoping she couldn't see the thick erection still straining against his waistband. "I recently finished a project in France. A chateau."

"Oh, wow. I'd love to see a real chateau."

"Maybe I could take you one day."

A small, reproachful smile shaped her lips. "You don't need to reel me in with false promises."

"That wasn't my intention. I just... It would be nice to show it to someone who's interested, that's all."

She quirked a skeptical brow, but she let it go. "You must know a lot about history, restoring old buildings."

"Yeah, I guess I do."

He took a sip of wine, holding the rich berry-burst liquid in his mouth for a second before swallowing. There was no point in feeding her charming half-truths about himself. He needed to coax out her character traits, to gather information about her life and all the things anchoring her to it. He knew she was attracted to him. Now he needed to find out if there were any obstacles to the sacrifice she would have to make for them to be together.

"So tell me about Roxi."

She teased him with a giggle. "You're interested in Roxi now?"

"Only because you two seem close."

"We've been friends forever. She's kind of a loose cannon at the moment, but she'll settle down when she goes back to college."

"She's leaving?"

"She's going to grad school." Emily winced, as if the prospect was a painful one.

"Did you ever think about college?"

"Maybe one day, if I can find a way to pay for it."

Her grimace spoke volumes, and he let the subject drop. "And your mother? You're close?"

"Closer than close. After my dad left, all we had was each other, and things kind of stayed that way. I always thought I'd have moved out by now, but so far there's been no reason to leave, and even if I did, I'd probably end up living close by anyway. She likes having me around and vice versa."

And there it was, the insurmountable obstacle he feared the most. He heard the tick of the clock out in the hall, the rub of her legs on leather as she shifted position, the horrible, slow boom of his heartbeat, and the deafening crackle and hiss of the flames that were the soundtrack to all his nightmares.

He tried to pull his lips into a smile before he tossed back the contents of his glass and rose. "I should let you get some rest."

Emily set the half-full wineglass down on the coffee table and hurried after him into the hall. Her footsteps trailed his up the stairs, stopping when he shoved open the guestroom door.

"There are fresh towels in the bathroom."

"Thank you." If his brusque demeanor surprised her, she hid it well.

"Good night, then."

"Good night."

The door closed without protest, the soft disappointed thud of the wood settling back into its frame making him pause before he slunk downstairs.

He pulled out his cell and dialed Max, then wrenched the top off a bottle of whiskey and filled a tumbler.

"How did it go?"

"It's not going to work, Max," he said, his fingers contracting around the glass.

"She's still not into you?"

"No, she's interested."

"Then what's the problem?"

"There's a tie."

"A boyfriend?"

"No, worse than that. Her mother."

Emily woke early, propelled by the urge to get home where she could take a breath and slump into sweats and a T-shirt. She'd slept badly, the nighttime chill penetrating her skin as she curled beneath the cold duvet in nothing but her flimsy underwear. With no outlet, the torrent of sensation Sebastian's kiss triggered had left her restless, and that coupled with his abrupt withdrawal from their conversation made her brain swirl in an indignant frenzy until she'd shivered into a brief doze.

She tiptoed to the bathroom so she could shower, dress, and walk to the road. She'd call Roxi on her way, see if she could pick her up. Failing that, she'd have to hitch. She wasn't about to wait around for Sebastian. He'd been obliged to help her out too many times for her liking, and her pride staged a mini mental protest at the thought of seeing him again after last night's unsubtle rejection.

Yet she felt the flutter of a thousand butterflies taking flight when she thought about his mouth on hers—coarse silk, hot and wet—and the masculine weight of his body.

She wriggled out of her underwear, reminded of how differently the night could have ended. She couldn't work out what prompted the seismic shift in his mood, what she'd said to warrant his indifferent, cold good-night. But it didn't matter. She always stuck to her rules for a reason, and breaking them only proved her point.

She showered, doing her best to keep her hair out of the spray, and then wrapped in a plush white towel, she found a tube of toothpaste, squeezed a dollop onto her fingertip, and rubbed it back and forth across her teeth. Combing her fingers through her hair, she crept into the bedroom where she slipped into her underwear and dress and grabbed her shoes from the floor.

With her clutch wedged under her arm, she pried the door open, its thunderous creak sending her ricocheting down the stairs in hurried flight. She was galloping across the hall, reaching for the door handle, when she spotted an envelope with her name on it in her peripheral vision. She snatched it off the side table and tore it open.

Emily,
   I had to leave earlier than anticipated. There's food and coffee in the kitchen. A friend of mine will be here at 8:30. He'll take you home when you're ready.
   Sebastian

That was in ten minutes. *Shit.* She wouldn't even make it to the end of his private road before his "friend" arrived.

Fucking coward.

As much as she wanted to avoid Sebastian, arranging for someone else to drive her home stung like a slap to the face.

Agitated, she paced into the kitchen to get a glass of water, contemplating hiding in the crowds of fir trees outside until his "friend" had left. But that was an even more undignified prospect than accepting a ride.

The breakfast table, laden with pastries and muffins, a jug of orange juice, and a silver pot of coffee that smelled a million times better than everything they served at the Perfect Cup, brought her to a standstill.

A lone place setting with a folded linen napkin beckoned.

Why would he go to all this effort when he'd made it so apparent he was no longer interested? When he'd done everything possible to avoid seeing her again?

She reached for a croissant and bit into the warm, buttery pastry. Had he bought it all this morning? The bakery in Oak Ridge opened at seven a.m., so it was possible, but again, why would he bother?

She took another bite and poured steaming hot coffee into the waiting cup, too tense to sit down. She'd swallowed her second mouthful when she heard the front door opening.

With a quick lick of her fingers, she abandoned breakfast and strode out into the hallway. A tall, rakish man waited by the door, dressed like a very stylish librarian in a tweed jacket, expensively cut jeans, and brown leather brogues.

Oh goody, another Oak Ridge sophisticate.

"Emily?" His accented pronunciation of her name made it sound like *Amelie* instead of Emily. "I'm Max, a friend of Sebastian's. He said you might need a ride?"

"Did he?" The scowl that lowered her brow began to shape her words, giving them hard edges and sharp points. "And where is Sebastian?"

"Uh..." He ran his fingers through the fop of brown hair that had fallen across his forehead. "He was called away."

"And he couldn't call to tell me that himself?"

An apologetic shrug. "He's in a meeting."

"*Right.*"

"Do you want to leave now or...?"

She strutted past him in answer, stopped to slip her shoes on by the door, and then marched out onto the gravel driveway, his stride outpacing hers. He climbed into the waiting Range Rover and flung open the passenger door with an expectant look. She bounced into the passenger seat after an awkward high-heeled hop from the footrail.

To his credit, Max didn't laugh at her inelegant movement, his expression stoic as he started the engine and turned the car around. He pulled out onto the forest road in a smooth arc and said, "You like Sebastian, yes?"

"I don't really know him." She blushed, realizing how that sounded after she spent the night in his home. "I only stayed over because I lost my keys."

Max stared at the road ahead. "He would be with you, if he could."

The statement was so strange and solemn that Emily looked across at him, but he didn't meet her eyes. "What's that supposed to mean?"

He shook his head, an odd sadness weighing on his features.

They didn't speak again except for a cursory goodbye when he pulled up outside her home.

The door opened before she had a chance to knock, and her mood lightened at the prospect of fresh clothes and a morning at home with her mom.

"Hi, sweetie. Did you have a good night?" Still in her nurse's uniform, her mother's light makeup fought to conceal the fatigue that always shadowed her features.

"It was okay." Emily stepped inside and kicked off her shoes, tossing her clutch on the floor.

Her mom followed her through to her bedroom, handing her a pair of sweat pants as she wiggled out of her dress. "Just okay?"

"He took me to Oak Ridge." She pouted for emphasis.

"Did you see your father?" Her mother stepped in front of the mirror and examined a strand of hair streaked with gray, as if he might appear at any moment and find her appearance lacking.

"I spoke to Graham, briefly."

"He might not be a very good one, Emily, but he is still your father." She let go of the hair, tossing it over her shoulder with resignation. "What did he say?"

"He made a few of his usual snide comments and then brought

up his 'offer' again." She mimed quotation marks around the word offer.

"What did you tell him?"

"The same as always, Mom. I'm not stupid. And then I lost my keys, so I ended up having to stay at Sebastian's place."

"You should have called."

Emily pulled a T-shirt over her head. "I don't like disturbing you at work. I tried Roxi and got no answer, so he offered to take me home with him."

"I bet he did." Her mother crossed her arms, her face stern.

"It wasn't like that. He put me in the guest bedroom."

"You sound disappointed."

She sighed. "He was kind of confusing. Friendly then aloof, interested then detached. Hot and cold, I guess."

"Was that his car outside?" Disapproval lowered her mother's voice because, like Emily, she'd become wary of the trappings of wealth when her father and his well-heeled family had cast the two of them aside like litter.

"No. He wasn't even there when I woke up. He had a friend drive me home."

Her mother winced in sympathy and squeezed her shoulder. "Plenty more fish in—"

"The lakes. I know. Although there actually aren't that many decent guys around here."

"And you think he was decent?"

"I don't know. Probably not. His car looks like the Bat Mobile."

Laughter frothed out of both of them, rich and warm. Emily shook her head and decided to let go of the memory of Sebastian's fingers brushing hers, of his eyes studying every detail of her face, of the intoxicating energy that had rushed and surged between them.

6

Sebastian ran his finger along the rim of Emily's coffee cup, rubbing her barely distinguishable lip print and breathing in the trace scent that remained.

"Are you sure it's going to be a problem?" Max leaned against the doorframe, concern knotting his brows.

"Yes."

"Maybe you should give it more time. It might not be as bad as you think."

"There's no other family. No siblings, her parents are separated. And they're close. There's no way she'd leave her mother behind. I have to make a clean break. If I don't stop now..." He took in a breath, and an angry tremor shook his hand, rattling the coffee cup as he returned it to its saucer. "I might not stop at all."

"I still think you should consider—"

"No."

"In the end, it would be better—"

"It's barbaric."

"It's *safer*."

"Come on, Max. Would you really turn someone without consent?"

"If their life depended on it."

"Well, her life doesn't depend on it. As long as I can stay away, she'll be fine."

"Do you really think you can do that? Look at you. You're shaking, for fuck's sake."

Sebastian gripped the back of the dining chair to steady himself. "It wasn't this bad at first. I think this is withdrawal... because I spent so much time with her last night. Because I was close to her."

"You need to see a Circle physician."

"Fuck that."

"They have drugs in trials to suppress the early bonding hormones, make things more manageable for new couples. It could help."

"No."

"Have you even called it in?"

Sebastian glowered, the porcelain of his knuckles visible through the skin of his bent fingers, their grip forcing creaks of complaint from the chair. He closed his eyes, counted silently to three, and then released his hold. "I'll be fine. I just need to avoid close contact with her."

Max studied him with raptor-sharp eyes. "You need to speak to Marguerite."

"Don't you think I have enough on my plate?"

"She'll find out."

He shrugged. "So be it."

"It ought to be from you."

Sebastian sighed. "When I get my shit together, I'll call her."

Max reached into his breast pocket and pulled out a silver flask. He unscrewed the top and held it out to Sebastian. "You need to feed, and you're in no fit state to hunt."

Sebastian rolled his eyes and took the flask, forcing down a mouthful of dead blood. Though it slithered down his throat, stale and thick, it calmed him. He chugged the rest of it with greedy gulps.

"You need to feed regularly. Don't stretch it."

The tremors and the scratchy, crawling sensation that peaked in Emily's absence began to lessen, leaving a manageable discomfort behind. "Was she pissed off?"

Max smiled. "Enormously."

Sebastian's gut plummeted. "Good. Then she won't pursue this." He handed the empty flask back to Max.

"No, I suppose she won't." The unhappy compassion lining Max's forehead made Sebastian turn away. "Do you want me to stay for a while? Until you feel…?"

"Better? Come on, Max, I know that day isn't coming."

"We'll work it out."

He nodded to make his friend feel less helpless, to free him from the pitying obligation that would keep him by Sebastian's side day and night otherwise. "You should go. I'll be fine as long as I keep feeding and I stay away from her."

"I'll have some blood bags delivered."

Sebastian walked Max to the door. "All right."

"You'll call if you need anything?"

"I'm not an invalid."

Max clapped him on the back as he stepped outside, grinning. "Ah, but your heart is wounded."

Sebastian flipped him the finger, his friend's mocking humor relieving some of the dark, oily fear that congealed inside him. But Max's derisive words rang horribly true because Sebastian felt the bond's wounding pulse in his heart and every part of him—his organs, his bones, *his mind.*

Emily opened a pack of plastic cups and set them on the kitchen counter next to a lineup of soft drinks and alcohol. "Are you sure your mom won't mind?"

"She won't even notice. She's going to be at my grandmother's all weekend."

Tonight was Roxi's last Pine Lakes party, and she'd sent out an open invitation via a series of online posts earlier that week. Her roomy house was on the nice side of Pine Lakes. Well, *nicer* than Emily's, so attendance was likely to be high.

Emily picked up a crystal vase from the table and stashed it in a cupboard. "Even so, we ought to be careful it doesn't get out of hand."

"Ems, would you relax? I promise this is going to be fun."

People arrived after sunset, and Emily played hostess, sashaying around in a red dress and tan kitten heels on loan from Roxi. The dress fluttered around her thighs in a breeze that blew through the open windows and doors, animating the loose hair that fell down her back in waves. The blood-orange hue of the dress set off her light summer tan, making her look like she'd spent a week at the beach instead of months indoors serving coffee.

Another gust of summer wind lifted the dress away from her legs, and she swatted it down. Heath's gaze caught hers from across the backyard, and he cut through the crowd like a shark parting a shoal of panicked fish, thick waves of blond hair hanging in his eyes as usual.

"Hey." He kissed her on the cheek, his hand on her lower back.

"Hi."

"You look beautiful." His hand remained on her back, stroking a small circle that sent shivers skittering up her spine.

"Save the compliments. I haven't forgiven you for ditching me last week."

"I took Roxi home, didn't I?" His fingers continued to dance around her backbone.

Emily took a step back, and he grabbed her hand. "Don't be mad."

"I'm not." And she wasn't, but the feel of his hands jarred her.

For the thousandth time that week, she found herself thinking about Sebastian, the way his lips had moved against hers in a heady rhythm, the way he'd looked at her with unwavering focus, with *hunger.*

She jerked her hand free, irritated that her mind had wandered to Sebastian again. "I need a drink."

Heath followed her into the kitchen, watching as she mixed vodka and soda with a slice of lime. "That's a seriously boring drink."

"Maybe I like boring."

"Since when?"

She ignored him and added a couple of cubes of ice from a melting tray by the refrigerator.

"I should have taken you both home. I'm sorry, okay?" He was behind her, slipping his arms around her waist in that tactile, over-friendly way of his.

"No, not okay, but it doesn't matter." She shook off his hold and turned to face him, the kitchen counter at her back. "I'm not mad, so let's just leave it at that."

He leaned closer, planting a hand on either side of her waist. "Yes, you are." He pouted, his gaze falling to her mouth as it had the last time they were alone together.

"Cut it out, would you?"

He straightened and looked out of the window beyond the counter, a small smile tugging at the corners of his lips.

"See someone you know?"

"Only you," he said, returning his gaze to her.

"Move." She pushed at his chest, and he stepped aside with a theatrical bow.

She laughed despite her agitation. "Same old clown. What did I ever see in you?"

"Same thing everyone else did."

She shook her head and pushed her way out into the sea of bodies in the trashed hallway. With a sigh, she set her drink on a side table by the stairs and began collecting the scattered cups and dropped chips that littered the floor.

"Are you actually tidying up?" Roxi blustered toward her, her expression one of fond irritation.

Emily straightened and put the empty cups she'd been stacking next to her drink.

"Seriously, Ems? Let go, would you? Have a drink, or three. Here, you can start with mine." Roxi handed her a margarita and danced away to fix herself another.

Emily smiled at her shimmying rear as she disappeared into the kitchen. Roxi was right. This would probably be their last Pine Lakes party together, so she might as well make it one to remember. She downed the remainder of her vodka and soda and then took a swig of the citrusy cocktail.

Halfway through her second margarita, her heart started to rattle in a raucous, rapid rhythm, like it had on her date with Sebastian. She giggled at the thought before a swirl of dizziness made her lurch over to the sofa. Its blurry-faced occupants shuffled away from her.

Shit. She was really drunk. She bit her lip as she tried to tally how many drinks she'd had. Not that many—one vodka, one and a half margaritas. She tasted blood, hot and brassy on her tongue, and realized she was still chewing her lip.

What was wrong with her?

She clambered to her feet, tripped over a cushion strewn on the floor and staggered over to Roxi, who was dancing with Heath, her hands on his chest. Roxi swayed her hips and rubbed herself against him, grinning like the Cheshire Cat, her perfect white teeth gleaming beneath the dimmed lights.

Unable to form words, Emily waved to get their attention. Roxi waved back and blew her a kiss, continuing to bump and slide her body against Heath's.

Friends and strangers alike pressed in around Emily, and beads of sweat began to dampen her face and neck. Desperate for air, she weaved her way to the stairs and clung to the banister as she dragged her way up to the top. She fell into the bathroom opposite the stairs and then collapsed against the door in a grateful heap, the cool floor tiles easing the scorching heat of her legs.

Desperate to cool down and quench the sudden thirst that made her mouth ache for the feel of water, she leaned over the bathtub and turned the cold tap. Lapping at the water as it rushed out, she sucked up as much as she could, though it ran down her chin and soaked her dress. It wasn't enough, so she climbed in, pushed the plug down with an uncoordinated series of shoves, and allowed the chill water to rise around her.

Panic pulled Sebastian out of the shadows beneath the trees opposite Roxi's home, thrusting him through the throngs of people circulating in the hallway.

He tried to stay away, he really did, but the distance proved unbearable. In the few days he spent holed up in his house, a dark, frustrated obsession crept out of him until he was coated in it, transformed into a thrashing, angry creature full of destruction and wild, unchecked emotion. Tears punctuated hours spent smashing furniture and punching walls.

Upon Max's furious return, he'd downed one blood bag after another until clarity illuminated his thoughts and his ruined home.

The sinking acceptance that he couldn't stay away brought him here, where he could watch her, breathe in her sweet, addictive scent, and pick out the thread of her voice from the dozens of others and let it all lull him back into a normal state of being. He hadn't thought beyond this small, rationed fix of voyeurism, had no intention of getting any closer than he had to in order to maintain equilibrium. This was the new plan, this terrible compromise that allowed him to look but not touch, that meant watching that blond-haired idiot paw at her and fighting every instinct he had for the victory of doing *nothing*.

And now even this self-sacrificing scheme was turning to shit.

He cursed under his breath, and anxiety quickened his steps. Something was wrong. He hadn't heard her speak for a half hour or so, and her scent, imbued with alcohol and some kind of narcotic, had vanished altogether. There were several things that could affect a vampire's ability to follow a scent. Too long between feeds could dull their senses, although not to the extent of sensing nothing at all. The elements could make it difficult to pick up a trail. An ocean breeze might diffuse scent, or some things could trap scent, like sealed containers or water.

He tore through the open back door and interrupted Roxi flirting with a group of boys on the lawn. "Where's Emily?"

Roxi blinked, dumb recognition slow to animate her heavily made-up features.

"Where is she?" he asked again, hostility creeping into his voice.

She answered in a rush. "Ah, I don't know. I saw her just a few minutes ago."

Something wasn't right. Her pupils were dilated, and she seemed both unconcerned about her friend and unfazed that Sebastian had turned up uninvited.

"What have you taken?" he asked with quiet menace.

"You want some? I can get you some." Her gaze darted around in a directionless search.

He took her arm, returning her focus to him. "Did she say anything to you?"

"You're all she's talked about all week!"

"About where she was going?" His fangs began to sharpen.

"I'll find her for you. She'll be so pleased to see you."

He deserted Roxi with a frustrated huff and flew into the house, scanning everywhere for Emily.

A faint stammering heartbeat upstairs caught his attention, distinct from all the others in the way it stuttered and stalled. He tracked the noise to a locked door.

"Emily?" He slapped his palm against the smooth wood.

When there was no response, he forced the door open with a brutal shove. She was in the bath, its contents spilling over the lip in a morose waterfall as the tap continued to run. Beneath the surface, her dark hair fanned around her wax-white face, the red fabric of her dress floating like blood.

He wrenched her out and laid her on the wet floor, listening to the barest of breaths and the slightest pulse.

"What did she take?" he asked with deadly calm when Roxi appeared in the doorway.

"Nothing. She's not into all that."

Tears welled in Roxi's eyes as she tried to move closer to her friend. Sebastian shot her a warning look.

He lifted Emily into his arms, her wet hair and sodden dress soaking his jeans and shirt. "I'm taking her to the hospital."

"No! No, please, you can't do that. Her mom works at the hospital. You can't take her there." Roxi blocked the doorway and shook her head, tears sluicing down her cheeks.

"She could die! God knows how long she's been underwater."

Roxi stepped aside with a stifled sob. "I'll come with you."

"No." His tone paralyzed her, so he rushed past.

He sprinted for his car, parked out of sight on a neighboring street, unconcerned by the prospect of humans seeing the blur of a vampire moving at top speed. It would have been quicker to run to the hospital with her in his arms, but he couldn't stand the way the movement jolted her slight body.

He eased her into the car and strapped her unconscious form into position with the seat belt. Though he raced along the quiet streets, ran every stop sign, and pushed the car to its limits, he knew he wouldn't make it to the hospital in time. Her pulse continued to weaken, her skin chill and clammy beneath his fingers. He reached across to sweep her hair from her face, revealing lifeless, inky-blue lips. Who knew what damage had already been done?

"Damn it!" He slammed his fist against the dash and took the turn to his house.

There was only one way to help her now, but it would coat his already strong connection to her in steel, make it a thousand times harder to fight.

He came to a hard stop by the front steps, extracting her from the car with movements too fast for the human eye to track. In a blink, they were in the living room, where he laid her in front of the huge open fire, igniting it with the flick of a switch.

Kneeling behind her, he bit into his wrist and lifted her head onto his lap. "Emily, it's Sebastian. I need you to drink. Drink this, and you'll feel better."

He ran his thumb over her mouth, gently parted her lips, held his wrist there, and waited. A few seconds later, she gagged. Her eyelids quivered when he removed his wrist from her mouth to stroke her damp hair.

Her eyes opened, and her gaze flew around the room in wild sweeps until she focused on him. "What are you?"

A moment later, those astute gray mirrors glazed over, heavy lashes sealing them shut.

He pulled her into his arms and began a fearful watch of the descent and lift of her chest. They were blood bound now, the ropes of his bond to her transformed into unbreakable chains. His mind blanked at the awful prospect, offering no solution or way around their dangerous predicament.

By the time dawn's baby blues and lemon golds lightened the room, the fire had dried their clothes and restored the rose blush of Emily's lips and cheeks. He brushed his mouth over her forehead and closed his eyes at the welcome kiss of sugar that hit his senses.

EMILY JERKED UPRIGHT IN THE SILENT CONFINES OF SEBASTIAN'S guest bedroom for the second time that week. The covers fell away, revealing wrinkled red cloth, a sad echo of the vibrant dress she wore to the party.

What happened?

She remembered shutting herself in the bathroom and could only assume she'd blacked out soon after. But why? She didn't have enough to drink to put her down like that. And what was she doing in Sebastian's house?

She jumped out of the bed, fear strobe-lighting her thoughts. Had someone spiked her drink? Perhaps the same someone who'd slashed her tires? Her mind flew back to her missing keys. What if they weren't lost but taken? Each incident led to time alone with *Sebastian*.

Her gaze roved around the room, passing over the too-neat shelving against the far wall and its impersonal contents—fat white candles arranged in aesthetic symmetry, a smooth wooden bowl filled with wicker globes, and a squat lamp. Nothing she could use as a weapon if the horrible suspicion that forced quick, frightened breaths from her proved true.

She decided to move while the house remained quiet and stole out of the room, hoping Sebastian was asleep or gone. As she padded down the hall on near-silent feet, male voices drifted up from downstairs. Panicking, she slipped through an open doorway and gasped.

Broken furniture lay scattered across the floor like bodies strewn on a battlefield. Shredded bedsheets spattered the surfaces, and massacred pillows left their goose-down innards in trails along the hardwood boards. She prodded her memory, tried to recall anything that might point to this kind of destruction. Had she struggled? Tried to fight him off?

Opposite the bed, a decorative mantel supported a shattered mirror and a pair of tall brass candlesticks. Dumping one of the white wax stems on the bed, she gripped the hard brass in one hand, ready to swing it at Sebastian's face if necessary.

The male voices quieted, the tense silence warning her to get out while she could.

She tiptoed down the stairs and made a beeline for the front door, hesitating by the row of hooks and hanging keys to the left-hand side. If she took his car, she wouldn't have to risk him catching up with her on the long stretch of private road. She could figure everything out once she was clear of the property.

"Looking for these?"

She jumped and spun around, raising the candlestick to strike.

"Catch." Sebastian tossed her a set of keys from across the hall, his faded black jeans and a simple gray T-shirt doing nothing to conceal the honed, threatening physique beneath.

Her hand shot up reflexively, her fingers closing around the cool metal and plastic. "What happened last night?"

A flicker of emotion lit his eyes for the briefest of seconds. "You got sick at the party. I brought you here because Roxi didn't want me to take you to the hospital."

She could believe that. Roxi wouldn't have wanted her mother to see her like that.

"Did you call a doctor?"

"No. I took care of you."

"Why?"

"I could hardly leave you like that."

He hadn't moved at all. He wasn't trying to inch closer or block her exit.

"But why were you at the party?"

"I was looking for you."

There was a flat honesty to his words, though she sensed he chose them with care and precision.

"What was wrong with me?"

He tilted his head to the side, otherworldly eyes narrowed and assessing. "You mix with some interesting people."

"What's that supposed to mean?" The candlestick's smooth weight was slick in the clutch of her sweaty palm.

"Perhaps you should ask your best friend how some of her party favors ended up in your drink."

Her cheeks heated. "She wouldn't do that."

"Well, someone did."

"How do I know it wasn't you?"

He cocked a brow and smirked as she angled the candlestick back. "Emily, if I wanted you in my bed, I'd have had you there last week."

She flung the car keys at him and dropped the candlestick, the verbal barb burrowing into her chest as she turned on her heel. "I'll walk."

"You don't have any shoes."

She opened the door, sucking in the cool morning air that met her. "Where are they?"

"I don't know. You weren't wearing any when I found you."

She tried not to hobble as she stepped down onto the gravel drive, the last of her pride pushing her chin up and her shoulders back.

"Aren't you going to be late for work?"

Shit. She closed her eyes in defeat. "Can I use your phone?"

"Take the car, Emily. It'll be quicker than waiting for one of your hungover friends to come get you. I'd offer to drive you, but I wouldn't want you to think I was planning to assault you en route."

When she turned to face him, he was leaning against the door-frame, a dangerous sensuality curving his lips, the keys dangling from a single hooked finger.

She took each uncomfortable step toward him without flinching and held out her hand when she was a few feet away, so he had to close the remaining distance.

"Get out of here." He dropped the keys into her palm and strode back up the steps.

"Wait."

He ignored her, disappearing inside without bothering to close the front door.

She knew she should leave, take the car and figure out what happened later. But curiosity ate away at her fear, a persistent need to know combined with a strange pull, a compulsion to get closer to him.

Hurrying up the stone steps and over the threshold, she swung the heavy wood door shut behind her.

"Sebastian?"

She crossed the hall and slipped through the door to the living room, which was in the same state as the upstairs bedroom—coffee table overturned, sofas upended, the photographs she'd admired trapped beneath shattered glass and splintered frames.

Sebastian and Max stood in the middle of the debris, speaking in hushed French.

"What happened here?"

Sebastian pushed his hands in his pockets and exchanged a look with Max. "There was a break-in."

"Last night?"

"No, earlier in the week."

"And you haven't cleaned up yet?"

He tilted his head. "Pointers on housekeeping from a girl who still lives with her mother?"

She flushed, his words biting deeper because she was disheveled and barefoot and at his mercy again. "Is that what last week was about? You shut me down because you don't like the idea of me being close to my mom?"

Max said something in French, and Sebastian turned his back on her.

Something didn't fit, and his reluctance to explain only made her more determined to find out what. "Was anything stolen?"

"Are you still here?" He turned back to her, his lips bowed in an arrogant smile. "No, nothing was stolen."

"Did you call the police?"

"No."

"Don't you think you should—"

"No. This is my business, not anybody else's." He gave her a pointed look.

"You're fucking weird, you know that?" She whirled around, determined to get out of there before the frustrated tears welling in her eyes broke free.

Two voices locked in angry debate reached her as she yanked open the front door, the pretty patter of the French now fast and fierce. She dropped the car keys on one of the brass wall hooks and hurried down the steps, embracing the graceless gait that would get her out of there the fastest. She didn't need his cruel pity or his stupid car.

Two hours later, she limped through the back door of the coffee shop. She retrieved the forgotten jeans and shirt she'd left in her locker the week before, pulled them on, and forced a pair of ballet flats onto her swollen, blistered feet. She quickly used the bathroom, pausing in front of the dull mirror to run her fingers through her hair. Considering the night she'd had, her skin was smooth and lustrous, her eyes fresh and alert.

Tying her apron in a vicious knot, she pushed open the swing door to the shop front and braced herself for the coming onslaught.

"What time do you call this?"

"I'm sorry I'm late, Bob." She squeezed in beside him at the counter and took an order. "I got sick last night."

"And you couldn't have called to say so?"

"I meant to come in on time."

He grunted and pointed his chin toward the far corner of the room. "Your friends have been looking for you."

Roxi and Heath sat at a table, nursing large mugs of coffee. Roxi wore last night's clothes, her eyes bloodshot and framed by smudged mascara, the ghost of coral lipstick haunting the edges of her mouth.

"Go." Bob waved her away from the counter. "They won't leave until they've seen you, and her face is scaring the customers."

"I'll make it quick."

Emily scraped out from behind the counter and dragged her feet to the table.

Roxi jumped up, unsettling the contents of her mug as she grabbed Emily by the arm.

"Are you okay? Where did he take you? I thought..." Her voice wavered, and she looked like she might cry.

Emily shook off her hand. "You look like hell."

"Did Sebastian look after you?"

"The real question is, why didn't you?"

"I...I would have, but he wouldn't let me near you."

"So you let some stranger cart me away unconscious and you don't lift a finger to stop him?"

"You spent the night with him last week. He's hardly a stranger."

Heath leaned forward in his chair, his eyes wide with interest.

"I only stayed over because I lost my keys. *And nothing happened.*"

"Well, he was über protective."

"Yeah? Well, he's also an über asshole. I just walked for two hours to get here."

Heath's brow arched. "He didn't offer you a ride?"

"You're hardly one to talk."

Heath responded with a sheepish half smile and an apologetic shrug.

"Ems..." Roxi squeezed her upper arm. "Do you know what happened? I mean, did you just drink too much?"

Emily narrowed her eyes. "What do *you* think happened, Roxi?"

"I...I don't know." Roxi's eyes began to fill with tears. "Somebody spiked my drink, and the last thing I remember is drinking a margarita *you* gave me."

"I would never... Do you really think I'd spike your drink?"

Emily pinched the bridge of her nose and sighed. Whatever risks Roxi chose to take with her own body, she would never trick Emily into doing the same. "No, I know you wouldn't. I have to get back to work, okay? We can talk later."

Roxi nodded, still teary, and retrieved Emily's bag from beneath her chair. "You left this."

"Thanks."

Heath stood and ushered Roxi toward the exit, tossing Emily a sorry smile before the door swung shut behind them.

"You can't keep pushing her away, Sebastian. It's too late for that now." Max paced in front of him.

"She thinks I wanted to assault her."

"Can you blame her? She wakes up in your home with no recollection of how she got here, and the place looks like a fucking war zone." He swept his hand in an arc over the splintered, shattered debris that lay all around.

"We're not right for each other. Her life, her friends, her mother, her daddy issues... They're problems we won't get past."

"That's all irrelevant now, and you know it."

"There has to be another way. *There has to be.* I'll feed more. I'll take the fucking Circle meds."

Max eyed the growing pile of empty blood bags that'd been discarded by the fireplace. "We should clean this mess up."

"What's the point?"

"So that you'll look like less of a psycho when she comes back."

"I don't want her to come back."

"But you know she will. You're blood bound, Sebastian. Accept it."

Sebastian kicked a ceramic vase that survived the destruction, sending it hurtling into the far wall where it shattered into two jagged halves.

"Feel better?"

"Not really."

Max scooped up the two halves and held them out to him. "Get a trash bag."

Sebastian skulked out of the room. There was no point locking horns with Max—it wouldn't change anything. He was fucked, and there was no way out.

The telltale crunch of gravel under tires reached him as he retrieved a roll of heavy-duty bags from the kitchen. Glowering, he dropped the bags and followed Max to the front door. The gaze of an official-looking vampire with a severe French twist and a gash of red lipstick nailed him to the spot.

"Pascaline." He'd crossed paths with France's senior Circle official many times as a Primary based in Europe.

"Sebastian. How are you doing?"

He ignored her question, thrusting the bags and brush into Max's hands. "You called it in?"

"I had to, Sebastian. They can help."

"Fuck you."

"Sebastian, there are new things we can try, new drugs..." Pascaline sidled forward and lifted a large leather briefcase into view. "You have options," she said, tapping the case.

"I don't want to be your fucking guinea pig."

"You're not thinking clearly right now. We can fix that."

"Go back to France, Pascaline."

"I can't do that until I know you're stable. You were turned in my locale, and I'm responsible for your conduct."

"This is bullshit. I can manage my own conduct."

She craned her neck, her gaze tracking across the broken mirror at the foot of the stairs, the snapped spindles from the banister. "Clearly."

She exchanged a look with Max and backed toward the door. "I can't force you to take the meds, but I can't leave you like this either. I'll be staying in town, and a team of Circle Primaries will watch the perimeter of your home. If you leave, they have orders to contain you."

"I'm under house arrest?"

"Until you're stable."

"You mean until I start the meds."

"Just think about it, Sebastian. Please." With that, she nodded a goodbye to Max and swept out of the front door.

Max approached him with upturned palms. "Sebastian..."

"Fuck off." He stalked up to his ruined bedroom and slammed the door.

8

EMILY CLUTCHED A THICK WAD OF CASH AND RAPPED ON THE IMPOSING wooden door with three angry little knocks. She'd agreed to work a series of double shifts in exchange for an advance on her wages, the entirety of which she planned to use to erase her debt to Sebastian. Once she gave him the money for the tires, she could forget him. No more niggling urge to seek him out, no more nauseating anxiety, no more draining dread nibbling at the sides of her stomach.

Max opened the door a few inches, his towering body blocking the opening.

"Is Sebastian here?" She held up the crumpled bills in explanation, assuming his BFF would know about her tires.

"You're wasting your time. He won't take your money."

"He doesn't have a choice." She stepped forward, expecting him to let her pass, but he stayed put. "Is he home or not?"

"It's not a good time. I'll let him know you stopped by." He started to close the door.

The slight propelled her past him in a rush of indignant determination. "I came to talk to Sebastian, not you." She marched through the hall, ignoring Max's protests. "Sebastian?"

There was no response, so she strode into the living room.

Max hurried to her side and tried to make eye contact. "Emily, I'm asking you to leave. Sebastian will call you later."

She ignored him, turning on the spot as she looked around the disordered room. The broken glass and shattered furniture that littered the floor twenty-four hours ago had been cleared away, but fresh destruction lay in its place. Craters of cracked plaster marked the walls, as if they'd been hit with something hard and unyielding. A jagged crack split the solid stone fireplace down the middle. Her gaze fell to the figure sitting on the floor in the corner by the window, his head resting between his bent knees, the evening sun igniting the burnt-gold hair sticking out between his interlocked fingers.

"What's wrong with you?"

He raised his head, defeated eyes meeting hers with wary exhaustion. "Nothing."

"What's going on, Sebastian? What happened here?"

He didn't respond.

"Answer me."

"Not...now." He took a shuddering breath, and Max flew past her, placing himself in front of his friend.

She moved to the side, keeping Sebastian in her sight line. "Yes, now. You're going to tell me what the fuck is going on here."

Max stepped toward her, extending a hand in warning. "Emily, you need to come back later."

She was about to bite out a retort when Sebastian growled at Max, his face contorted with predatory threat.

Max tensed. "*Go.*"

Emily folded her arms. "No."

She skirted around Max, who hissed his irritation but didn't attempt to stop her, and kneeled in front of Sebastian, dropping the cash on the floor. "Are you okay?"

He lifted his head, troubled moss-green eyes meeting hers, holding them for several slow heartbeats.

"Leave us." He didn't look away from her as he spoke to Max, his voice hoarse.

"Are you sure?"

He continued to hold her gaze. "It's better"—he took another labored breath—"with her here."

Max's heavy footfalls faded down the hall, the door inching shut behind him.

Emily cupped her hand to Sebastian's cool cheek, his sorrowful stare dissolving her anger. He turned his face into her hand and kissed it. A surge of energy rippled through her, thrilling every nerve and drawing her closer to him, until their lips were almost touching.

"Emily." It was a plea. A wretched, broken plea she couldn't deny.

Emboldened by the emotional charge between them, she pushed him against the wall and straddled him, watching his lids go heavy with undisguised lust as she brought her mouth up to his. He slid his lips against hers in welcome, and she slipped her tongue into his mouth, drinking in his taste in slow, shocking pulls. She knew she should stop, but she couldn't. She didn't care if Max walked in on them. She didn't care if Sebastian was dangerous. She didn't care if he broke her heart.

She wound her fingers through his hair and felt him shake beneath her as his exploratory touch snaked up the back of her sundress and followed the curve of her waist up to her breasts and back down to her hips, where he guided her in a heady gyration of gentle thrusts.

She moaned at the feel of his thick erection between her legs, kissing him harder, tugging at his tawny-gold hair as violent need whipped her to push closer, move faster, and take what they both wanted. She fumbled with the fly of his jeans, intent only on having him inside her as quickly as possible.

Pulling down the waistband of his shorts, she freed his hard length, gripping it in her hand, the feel of smooth, velvety skin spurring her on. She bit down on his lower lip as she pulled her panties aside, a groan escaping his parted lips as she guided him toward her, running her thumb over the silky moisture that beaded his crown.

She cried out as the very tip of his erection entered her, a powerful, unexpected orgasm gripping her at this barest of penetrations. Quivers quaked up and down her skin, lines of energy lighting up in a fiery web of sensation. Aching with need, she prepared to inch more of his broad, silky length inside her.

"Emily. Emily!"

She didn't know how many times he'd said her name. She was boneless and dazed, confused at the overwhelming arousal that steered her actions.

"Emily!"

She met his gaze, realizing he was lifting her away from him. Embarrassed, she got to her feet, noticing the acrid smoke curling beneath the ceiling and the high-pitched screams of a fire alarm.

He fastened his jeans, took her hand, and hurried her out through the smoke-filled hallway and down the front steps. "Are you okay?"

She nodded as Max spilled out of the front door carrying a pan of charcoaled bacon. "*Désolé!*" He wafted the pan in a cartoonish circle as it continued to smoke. "I forgot. I'll stop the alarm."

Sebastian gave a small, tight smile. As his friend dashed back into the house, he turned to her, squeezing the hand he was still holding.

She cast her eyes down to the ground. "I should go. I only came to return the money I owe you."

"Can we talk?" He hooked a finger under her chin, tilting her face up to his.

She shrugged, shame and curiosity warring for dominance. "If you want."

He sank down onto the bottom step, and she joined him,

releasing his hand to sit a few feet away, and then stared straight ahead at the line of firs circling the property.

"I'm sorry I've been acting like such a dick," he said. "You probably have a million questions, and I want to give you answers, but it's...complicated."

"It's fine."

"No, it's not fine. I want to make it up to you. I *need* to make it up to you."

She dug the toes of her shoes into the gravel of the drive. "You could start with an explanation. The way you were yesterday..."

"I was pissed off. I'd taken care of you all night, and you more or less accused me of attacking you. You had a candlestick, for God's sake." He sighed. "Did you really think I would hurt you?"

"Why wouldn't I have thought that? After everything that's happened since I met you, the state of your home—"

"Emily, I swear the tires and the spiked drink had *nothing* to do with me." He crouched in front of her. "And I promise I'll explain what happened here if you do one thing for me."

"I don't like games, Sebastian."

"It's not a game. It's my way of making it up to you." He took both her hands, his eyes full of glittering intent. "Come to France with me."

She snatched her hands away, but he reclaimed them with a cool, persuasive grip. "Come to France with me, and I'll tell you anything you want to know."

Angry realization heated her cheeks. Only one man wanted her to go to Europe. He'd battled her refusal, cajoled, bribed, and threatened her for almost four years.

She stood and then backed toward her car. "Did my father put you up to this?"

Sebastian got to his feet in confusion, baffled by her accusation. "Your father?"

"Did he pay you?" Eyes narrowed in suspicion, she pointed at the large house behind. "That's why the place was trashed. You tried to back out."

"Whoa, Emily, you are way off the mark. I've only met your father once, *with you.*"

"He likes to do business over the phone." She kicked at the gravel, sending a cluster of stones ricocheting toward him. "God, I am so stupid."

"Emily, you're not listening to me." He raised his voice in dismay. "This has nothing to do with your father. Why would it?"

"Like you don't know."

"Humor me."

"The offer he asked about at the restaurant. He wants me to leave Pine Lakes."

"Why?"

"Some of his friends saw me waitressing. He's embarrassed. He offered to pay for me to go to college." She tossed her hair back and straightened. "I said no."

"Isn't that like cutting off your nose to spite your face?"

Her nostrils flared. "His offers come with strings attached. He wanted me as far away as possible, so he picked a school in Europe."

He stilled, taking in the angry set of her shoulders, the slight tremor of her hands. "I'm not asking you to move to Europe, Emily. I'm asking you to come away with me." He approached her with cautious steps. "Three, four weeks tops. It doesn't have to be France or Europe—it could be anywhere. I just want to get to know you."

She bit her lip, uncertainty lightening her glower. "I can't leave my job for that long."

"Two weeks then."

"Why do we have to go anywhere? Can't we get to know each other here?"

"That's not working out so well, is it?"

"Maybe that's because we're not a good fit."

He arched a brow. He'd tried to tell himself the same thing, but he could no longer deny his need for her. "I don't think so, do you?"

She drew a breath and scuffed the toe of her shoe on the gravel. "If what's been going on with you has nothing to do with my father, then what is it about?"

He reached for her hand, interlocking his fingers with hers. "I promise I'll tell you everything if you give me some time."

Placing his other hand on her nape, he kissed her, his body weightless at the sweet, maddening contact.

She broke away, stretching their arms straight as he refused to let go of her hand. "I should go."

"Will you at least think about it?"

She slipped her fingers from his and opened her car door with a noncommittal shrug.

Max approached, quiet as a cat as she drove away, and placed a hand on Sebastian's shoulder. "Sorry, it was the only thing I could think of to stop you."

"You did the right thing."

Sebastian took his cell out of his back pocket as they watched Emily drive away. "Pascaline?" He exhaled, knowing what he had to say and knowing he had to say it before the clarity Emily's presence lent him began to fade again. "I'll do it. I'll take the meds."

An hour later, he sat in an armchair while a Circle medic checked him over. Vampires couldn't die, their bodies healing and restoring themselves with smooth efficiency, but medics played an essential role in monitoring their only vulnerability: their mental state. The longer a vampire remained unbonded, the more fragile their mental state became, and the mental equilibrium of the handful of vampires who, like him, had bonded to humans proved to be downright volatile.

The medic tucked her cropped black hair behind her ears and scrawled in a thick notebook, talking while she wrote. "Your heart rate is higher than it should be, even for a newly bonded male. Dilated pupils, sharpened incisors, acute blood lust..."

"It's not like I've attacked anybody. I'm just drinking more than usual."

She perched on the edge of the coffee table Max had repaired and peered at him with thorough, analytical eyes. "But you *could* attack somebody." She continued to study his face, tilting her head back and forth. "You're lucid now. My job is to make sure you stay that way."

"How do we do that?"

"This is the first time we've had the chance to intervene before the completion of a vampire-human bond. You need to understand that we're conducting a trial, that what we're proposing is based on theory."

He nodded.

"The meds should level you off, dampen the hunger, and soften your mood swings. In theory, they'll restrict your sexual appetite too."

He quirked a brow.

"You've shown remarkable restraint, and I would recommend that you continue to do so."

She looked across at Pascaline and Max. "Turning your mate before you have sex is a sensible approach to what is essentially an unprecedented situation."

She opened a black leather bag on the table next to her and took out a plastic bottle of pills. "Take one every twelve hours. I'll see you again in four weeks, but in the meantime, call me if the treatment isn't having an effect, and we can go over your options."

She handed him a stiff business card embossed with the name Dr. Shilla Khan in straight-edged letters.

She nodded her goodbyes and showed herself out as Pascaline and Max closed in on him.

"You need to focus on persuading her to become a vampire

now." Pascaline wagged her finger at him like a frustrated school-teacher. "No more trying to avoid the inevitable."

He stood and popped the lid off his meds. "I get that, but how do I begin to explain vampires are real without looking crazy?" He tossed a pill into his mouth and swallowed it. "How do I make sure she doesn't tell anyone else? There are laws against human exposure for a reason."

"And the law protects candor in all things between *bonded* pairs for a reason."

"Only because it doesn't account for human-vampire pairs," Sebastian retorted.

"She won't be human for long, so your situation is no different to that of any other vampire who wants to turn a human."

He paced over to the window. "And if she says no? Will you treat her as you would any other human who declines a vampire's offer?"

"You need to make sure she doesn't."

Murderous, protective rage made him bare his fangs.

Max stepped in front of him and gripped his shoulder. "Let's talk about this later, after the meds have kicked in."

"I'm on your side, Sebastian." Pascaline sighed. "Don't forget that."

9

EMILY STARED AT THE BOUQUET OF FAT PINK CABBAGE ROSES AND tapped the airline ticket that came with them on the tabletop, reading the simple card attached to the stems for the hundredth time: *I'll meet you there. Sebastian x*

Presumptuous, mysterious, irritating.

But at least he'd left her to make up her mind without pushing, though the neat wad of cash tucked inside the envelope infuriated her. Why couldn't he just let her pay for the goddamn tires? She hated being in his debt, and the trip to France would be one more thing on her tab.

She bit her lip as the stinging splinter of doubt, the one that kept her from leaving, continued to pierce and prick her heart. What if the dizzying high of their encounter at his home, that gripping physical charge, was passing entertainment to him? What if he was toying with her? What if he truly was working for her father? The time they'd spent together had been intense but fleeting, enough to produce an extraordinarily compelling attraction on her part, but not enough to learn about who he was, his beliefs and values.

The ticking of the plastic clock above the faded pink sofa

seemed to get louder with every passing second, the air stiller and more oppressive. Her cell vibrated on the table, startling her into motion. She picked it up and scanned the message that lit the screen with details of a party. Same place, same people, same drinks, same music.

Did she really want to spend her life in Pine Lakes? And for what? A vicious need to spite her father? Loyalty to her mother? Her mom insisted she take the trip—take a chance on the man Emily wrote off as a rich, arrogant player.

"Not all men are like your father," her mother said when the flowers arrived. "And at least there won't be any prospective in-laws in your way."

Emily reprimanded her with a disapproving groan that died with a dismissive wave of her mother's hand.

"Sometimes you have to take a leap, Em."

Emily looked at the clock, the second hand seeming to stick and tremble in each new position before hauling itself forward again. Her stomach cartwheeled. "Fuck it."

She dashed across the room, hefted her bags, and then dragged them through the front door.

Sebastian waited behind the metal barrier at the back of a melee of jostling families. The chattering blend of different languages soothed him as he sniffed the air, his nostrils twitching at the first subtle hit of sugar and citrus. He leaned against the wall, relieved at the small but significant victory.

Maybe his luck was changing.

So far, the meds proved effective, giving him the freedom to put physical distance between them without pain or discomfort for the first time since bonding. He was calm again, able to think and act normally, and it gave him hope—hope that there could be something real underpinning the whip of the bond. Perhaps there was a foundation based on more than pheromones and fate.

He traveled to France two days ahead of her to check over the chateau and discuss their requirements with the handful of staff who lived and worked there. He hadn't been back to his family home in over a year, but thanks to their hardworking professionalism, everything was as he left it—dust free, polished to perfection, and bursting with French style.

Up ahead, a woman holding a handful of bobbing helium cartoon characters moved aside, giving him a clear view of Emily strolling down the walkway, luggage in hand, eyes scanning the crowd for him. Their gazes met, and a reluctant smile crept across her face. He strode to kiss her in greeting.

"You came," he said.

"Curiosity got the better of me."

"Just curiosity?"

She rolled her eyes and laughed. "Stop fishing."

He took her bag and led her through the milling families and couples still waiting at the barrier, taking her hand for the short walk to the car he'd rented.

"No hideous sports car?" she quipped when they stopped by the modest silver SUV.

"Disappointed?"

"Pleasantly surprised."

He tossed her bags into the trunk and opened the passenger door for her. "I'm glad you like surprises."

"I didn't say that." She folded herself into the car in a series of tense movements.

He slid in next to her and started the engine. "Relax, Emily."

"That's easy for you to say. You know what's going on here."

He reached out and brushed the hair away from her face. Her intelligent gray eyes looked up at him, and despite the meds, he felt that familiar pull again. He sensed her body respond to his touch, singing with the same magnetic energy that always hummed in the air around them.

He took her hand and squeezed it. "You'll get your explanation."

And he would explain. He would tell her everything, but not until she started to suspect. He knew from his own enlightenment that he couldn't just come out and tell someone he was a vampire. Better to wait until a small niggling belief in the impossible began to unfurl and stretch and scratch beneath their consciousness.

He pulled out of the underground car park and stole a furtive glance at her, her expression closed and guarded as she stared out at the road ahead. He wondered how she would react when she knew the truth.

Would she be repulsed?

His pretty face and enviable muscle tone were one side of it, the mechanics of fangs and feeding quite another.

How long would it take to arouse her suspicions? He would drop all the careful habits he used to hide what he was: the slow reactions, feigned tiredness, and show of eating that helped to conceal his vampirism. She'd already witnessed his eyes' incredible color change. How long would it be before she noticed his reflexes, agility, and speed?

"So where are we going?" Her words cut through his ruminations.

"To the Loire to see the chateau I restored."

Her eyes flared. "How long will it take to get there?"

"A couple of hours. Aren't you tired? I thought you might want to check into a hotel and get some rest first."

"Hell no." The wary veil she always wore had lifted, and a genuine smile lit her face with excitement.

He found himself grinning in response.

"Is anyone living there?" she asked.

"Not exactly."

"Will the owners mind us looking around?"

"No, it's cool. Actually, we can stay there if we want."

"Seriously? For the whole two weeks?"

"Unless you'd rather stay somewhere else or travel to other parts of France instead?"

"*Hell no.*" Her eyes twinkled with girlish anticipation.

He caught her chin with his hand, claiming a swift kiss as they stopped at a red light.

Emily stared out of the car window, submerged in the tapestry of vineyards and orchards that rolled across the landscape. Sebastian asked her how her week had been, whether her boss had been happy for her to take time off with short notice, if there was anything particular she wanted to see during the trip. But the polite questioning did nothing to suppress the sharp, carnal tension between them.

She leaned her body toward the door, frustrated by the heat pooling in her abdomen despite all the unanswered questions buzzing about her brain. Silence stretched between them as her impatience for the truth began to curb her enthusiasm for her new surroundings.

Sebastian clasped her fingers in a cool, masculine grip. "You're wondering when I'm going to explain myself."

She glanced across to find him scrutinizing her features. "Eyes on the road, please."

He smirked. "Yes, ma'am."

As he turned away, she said, "I hope you'll tell me what's really been going on soon, because right now I'm excited to be here, but I'm also fucking terrified."

He squeezed her hand. "I would never hurt you. Contrary to recent events, I'm not a psychopath, and I don't work for your father."

"I want to trust you."

"I want you to trust me."

"So start talking."

"I will, I promise."

"When?" Her tone was sharper than intended, and heat swirled across her cheeks as she stared at the road ahead.

"Soon, Emily. *Soon.*"

He turned the car down a road to the left, and Emily's pointed retort died on her lips. In the distance was a breathtaking tangle of turrets and spires, arches and columns, and more windows blinking in the light of the descending sun than she could possibly count.

They passed through two huge stone gateposts, the grounds on either side of the road becoming more manicured and ordered, the grass a rich, lush green, the trees perfectly shaped and spaced.

She wound down her window, letting the clinical kiss of the air conditioning disperse into the warm breeze that blew her hair away from her face. "This is like something out of a history book."

He nodded with a modest smile that was almost shy.

Something about his expression suggested both humility and pride, a nervous anticipation of her reaction.

Her eyes widened. "Sebastian, is this *yours*?"

"It's where I grew up," he answered quietly. "My great-great-great-great-great-great-great-great-grandparents had it built, and later generations added to it." He extended eight fingers, one for every "great." "It was in ruins until recently."

She swallowed. "So are you like...royalty?"

He laughed. "Not anymore. My family were part of the aristocracy before the revolution. And afterward, we were..." He paused as though he couldn't say the word "Nothing." His face was serious, and there was an odd sadness in his feline eyes.

"It's incredible that you can trace your family so far back. I want to hear the whole story."

She reached out and touched his hand. He smiled at her briefly before turning his gaze back to the long drive that led to the chateau's impressive entrance. They passed over a large stone bridge, the water beneath imperfectly reflecting the sun's orange haze as currents eddied and flurried below its surface. Emily struggled to take it all in, her gaze flitting from one architectural feature to the next.

He parked right outside the ancient entrance, the shiny silver car anachronistic in the shadow of the ornate stone crest above the door, its weathered lines carving out "Baux-Blosset 1549."

"Come on," he said, effortlessly holding both her bags in one hand while extending his other hand to her.

She took it, smiling, and he guided her over the threshold. It was dark and cool inside, but despite the absence of the warm summer air, the heavy stone walls were welcoming, as if all they needed was some company to bring them to life. He put the bags down in the expansive hallway, still holding her hand as she took it all in. A huge staircase with white stone steps and banisters swept into the distance, and two ornate stone archways to her left and right framed entrances to corridors so long she couldn't see where they ended.

"This is the oldest part of the building," he said. "That's why it's so dark and somber."

"I think it's lovely."

She understood why he'd brought her to this sheltered, protected place—it was somewhere they could both let their guard down, cut off from the world outside.

"I'd ask for the tour, but something tells me it might take a while."

His eyes sparkled. "Yes, it might."

"Thank you for bringing me here."

He looked at her intently for a moment and then leaned down to kiss her. When he tipped her head back and kissed her neck instead, she responded with breathless fervor. When a polite cough sounded, she jumped away from Sebastian.

"Henri," Sebastian said, before he turned to the smartly dressed man hovering in the doorway.

"Monsieur Blake, how wonderful to see you." Henri stood poker straight, his black hair slicked back in an old-fashioned side parting, though he didn't appear much older than Sebastian.

"This is Miss Heart."

Henri nodded respectfully at Emily. "Mademoiselle."

She smiled, uncomfortable with the realization that Henri was some kind of butler. She hadn't anticipated the presence of staff, but of course, a home this size would require people to keep it in perfect condition.

"Dinner will be ready for you at eight o'clock, Monsieur."

"Thank you, we'll take aperitifs on the terrace around seven, please."

"Excellent, Monsieur." The man nodded again and left the room.

"You have a butler?" Emily knew she was smirking.

"He's more of a custodian. He takes care of the chateau when I'm not here."

"Why aren't you here? I mean, your house is beautiful, but why live in Pine Lakes when you have a castle?"

He answered with a cryptic curve of his lips.

"Right, you'll tell me later." She rolled her eyes, frustrated by the prolonged mystery.

His fingers circled the back of her neck, sending heady shivers down her spine. "I can't stay in one place too long. I keep my distance from people, community... Pine Lakes is temporary, just like everywhere else I've lived."

Surprise quashed her urge to pull away. "Why? Who are you running from?"

"So many questions."

"You promised me answers."

"You'll get them."

She took a step back, hesitated to ask the question that had sprung on to the tip of her tongue. "If Pine Lakes is temporary, then would I only be temporary too?"

He tilted his head to the side, tall and seductive against the smooth stone wall. "I hope not." He closed the distance she'd put between them, sealing his mouth to hers in a hot, searching kiss.

She held back, returning the kiss with forced restraint in case Henri appeared.

"What's the matter?" Sebastian murmured into her hair as he broke away, his hands wandering the valleys of her waist.

She laughed. "I just got here. Can't I take a minute?"

He straightened and dropped his arms to his sides. "Shit. I'm sorry."

"Don't be sorry." She took his hand again. "Be patient."

He pushed his hands into his pockets. "Not a problem."

He looked so serious that she giggled, an embarrassing, juvenile sound that made her clap a hand over her mouth.

His laughter met her own. "Let me show you to your room. You can rest before dinner."

"Lead the way." She padded along behind him, up stone stairways and along thickly carpeted corridors. "This place is amazing."

She paused, inspecting the imposing paintings that hung on the nearest wall before settling on a display case in an alcove. Drawn to the bright stone sparkling within a gold cross behind the glass, she took a step toward it while Sebastian waited. "Is that a *green* diamond?"

He came to stand next to her with a sad smile. "It was my mother's. She wore that brooch every day."

"It's beautiful."

"Too beautiful to be hidden away." He tilted his head toward her. "Would you like it?"

She choked out an incredulous laugh. "Very funny. The insurance would bankrupt me."

"I'm serious."

Shaking her head with an amused snort, she continued down the corridor.

"Aren't you hungry?" Emily asked two hours later. They sat together at one end of a long, dark wood dining table.

"I don't eat a lot." Sebastian shot a pointed look at her untouched *steak frites*. "But don't let that stop you."

She gathered a forkful of fries, her gaze straying to his well-defined torso. "I guess you must be really strict with diet and exercise."

"Oh, I have a fairly restricted diet most of the time," he said, that now-familiar smirk back on his face. "What do you usually like to eat, Emily?"

She chewed a piece of beef with self-conscious hurry. "Breakfast is my favorite meal. I love pancakes, waffles, French toast, pastries..." She speared another mound of fries. "When I was little, we had a chef," she admitted, surprised to find herself talking about the privileged life she had before her parents' divorce. "He used to make the most incredible eggs Benedict."

Sebastian watched her with quiet intensity from the seat to her left, at the head of the table. "Do you miss the life you had before?"

"It's pretty much forgotten now. I still saw my father and my grandparents once a week for a few years after the divorce, but once he had children with his second wife, they lost interest."

"When did you last get together with him?"

"I don't know, eight, nine years ago maybe."

"It must have been hard."

She shrugged, reluctant to discuss the festering wounds the Hearts' rejection left her with when she was a million miles away from it all. It hadn't been the loss of the trappings of wealth that had been hard. It'd been the sense of worthlessness and unimportance that'd coated her like an oil spill when they all turned their backs.

The toxic anger would always be there, waiting for a spark to ignite it, but that didn't mean she had to focus on it. "What about you? If vanity didn't mean counting carbs and calories, what would you gorge on?"

He hiked a brow at her gibe but didn't take the bait. "Venison always tasted pretty good before."

"Couldn't you have said doughnuts? Or peanut butter cups?" She slid her knife through the perfectly cooked steak again. "How long have you been on this crazy diet anyway?"

"Too long."

She set her cutlery down and took a long sip of the red wine on her right. "So tell me about this place. How long did it take to restore?"

"Decades."

"Did your parents start the work?"

He steepled his fingers. "They made some alterations and additions."

She looked around at the wood-paneled walls, the enormous Persian rug, the terrifyingly old art that hung on the walls, and the precisely centered crystal chandelier, and took a breath, ready to start asking some of the questions she wanted answered. "At least everything here is neat and ordered."

"Henri does a good job."

"I meant at least it's not been trashed like the house in Pine Lakes."

He leaned closer. "I know what you meant."

"Are you going to tell me what happened? Do you know who did it?"

He paused and sat back in his chair, pinning her in place with those unflinching peridot eyes. "I did."

She started to cough, the steak stuck in her throat, her eyes watering. Sebastian poured her a glass of water from a pitcher on the table and pushed it toward her.

"Why?" she squeaked when she was able to speak again.

"Something happened that...threw me off-balance." The

considered flick of his eyes to the ceiling told her he chose his words with care.

She gripped the edges of her chair. "Should I be worried?"

"Perhaps. But not for the reasons you think. I'm on meds now to help me adjust."

"What kind of meds?"

"The kind that will keep me level no matter what."

She pressed against the front legs of the chair until her fingertips numbed and fought to keep her voice steady. "Sebastian, I can't trust you when you're only telling me half the story."

"I'm not hiding anything. I'm giving you all the information you need to figure out the rest of the story on your own."

"I'm not Nancy Drew. Can't you just be straight with me?" She tossed her napkin on the table and scraped her chair back, tired of whatever game it was he played so artfully.

He kneeled in front of her before she could stand, resting his hands on either side of her legs, his eyes searing hers. He pushed his lips against hers without looking away, taking her lower lip between his teeth and nipping it in reproach.

"I don't like this game," she murmured as he parted her legs and wedged his solidly muscled upped body in between.

"Are you sure?" he whispered against her neck as he dropped a trail of featherlight kisses down to her collarbone.

She nodded a silent confirmation that went unheeded, her breath coming in quick little pants as he pushed up the hem of her shift dress.

"Sebastian." She seized the hand that skirted the edge of her panties. "I want answers."

He returned his mouth to hers in a hungry kiss that left her mind reeling, his hands wandering up her thighs.

She pulled back and shoved his chest lightly. "Sebastian."

His gaze flitted between her lips and her eyes as he read her body language with a wicked smile. "Your choice." He slipped two of his fingers under the side seams of her panties. "Do you want answers? Or do you want this?" With a blatantly sexual bite of his full lower lip, he slid his thumb across her clit.

Her breath caught. "Why does it have to be either or?"

He lowered his head and spoke against the lace that didn't quite cover her core. "This is why."

Hooking a finger in the black floral fabric, he pulled it aside and silenced her with a slow lave of his tongue.

Legs trembling, she wound her fingers in his hair, disbelieving pleasure racing through every nerve ending as he opened his mouth around her and sucked in an intimate kiss that erased all thought.

"Do you want me to stop so I can answer your questions?"

Shaking her head, she spread her legs wider and felt his tongue edge inside her, hot and firm. She leaned back against the chair, and he pressed her thighs even farther apart, raising her feet off the floor as he held her there and began to suck her clit with hard, greedy pulls that left her core pulsating in a silent orgasm that paralyzed her with lashes of acute sensation. Pulling away and propping her sandaled feet up on his bent legs, he pushed two fingers inside her, slowly thrusting back and forth as he watched the unstoppable little spasms that gripped and released them as her climax continued. When it began to subside, he returned his mouth to her swollen clit and took it between his teeth, giving it a gentle tug that shoved her under the brutal currents again, forcing a harsh cry from her throat.

He stopped with a lingering, tender kiss on that sensitive spot and then withdrew his fingers and let her panties snap back into place.

Resting his head in her lap for a long moment, he finally looked up at her with a playful grin. "What was it you wanted to ask me?"

10

SEBASTIAN POPPED A ROUND PINK PILL INTO HIS MOUTH, FLIPPED IT over with his tongue, and knocked it back with a swig of cognac. He studied his face in the antique mirror that hung above the low mahogany sideboard, his moss-green eyes lamps that lit the foxed glass.

Emily had gone up to bed a half hour ago, her limbs heavy with languid satisfaction while her lips remained pursed with impatience.

He'd laughed and kissed her good night. "Sleep well, Emily. Everything will look different in the morning."

"It better, or I'll be on the first flight out." She'd pressed a rigid finger against his lips as he went to kiss her again. "You can't seduce me into silence, Sebastian."

"Tomorrow, then."

She'd given a curt nod as she shut the door.

With a sigh, he shook a second pill into his palm. The drug, which worked so well in Emily's absence, did not deliver the stifled libido promised when in her company. Her scent, her movements and gestures, the cadence of her voice, and the intensity of her velvet gray gaze were a pleasure-pain knife-edge to his senses. He hoped doubling the dose would be enough to prevent him from succumbing to the lure.

Panther-quiet footsteps fell behind him.

"You're late, Max." Sebastian turned toward his friend, who gave a disgruntled huff. "Don't you ever get tired of trying to creep up on me? You haven't caught me off guard yet. Perhaps it's time to give up?"

"One of these days..."

Sebastian poured a second glass of cognac and held it out to him. "Julien and Jean are waiting on the terrace. We were about to begin."

"I just got off the phone with Marie." Max picked up one of the abandoned billiards cues propped against the table and returned it to its holster on the wall.

"Oh?"

Max swilled the cognac round his glass before tossing it back and grimacing. "Marguerite called her, started asking questions about you."

"Did Marie tell her anything?" Sebastian set his glass down on the dresser and strode to the open French doors, a night wind billowing the curtains in and out.

"No, but Marguerite's half a millennium old; she has plenty of other contacts in the Circle."

"How did she find out in the first place?"

Max came to stand beside him, looking out across the breezy moonlit lawn at the front of the chateau. "People always talk about new bonds, and they positively scream about bonds with humans." He raised a hand to wave to Jean and Julien, who lurked by the hedged border on the far side of the grass, sipping beers.

"Can you find out who leaked it? If the hunters get a lead—"

"Marie is looking into it, but like I said, people talk, and it's likely to be more than one individual spreading the news."

Sebastian cursed. "Does Marguerite know we're here?"

"Not yet, but it won't be long before she figures it out. She knows you inside out, Sebastian."

"I wonder if the Primaries could spare a guard unit."

Max blew out a contemplative breath. "Do you really think that's necessary?"

"Who knows what she might do? I'd rather not take chances; this situation is volatile enough as it is."

"Perhaps if you spoke to her?"

"No. It's too soon. My focus has to stay on Emily." Beckoning to Julien and Jean, he strolled across the lawn with Max in his wake. "Let's do this."

He gathered his friends together to present Emily with the final piece of the puzzle—a demonstration of their superhuman strength and indestructibility that she couldn't deny or explain away. He wanted her to see the truth, rather than try to persuade her to believe in the impossible.

A pair of luminous bonded eyes similar to his own glinted in the darkness, Jean's jet hair falling over his forehead as he crouched low. Julien mirrored the stance, his lips thinned with predatory intent. With a bellow, Jean surged forward, Julien springing across the lawn with the same feline timing and speed. Max and Sebastian stood back-to-back, braced for the impact as the fight began.

Jean's foot hit Sebastian's jaw a fraction of a second later. Gritting his teeth, Sebastian twisted Jean's ankle and shoved. "Don't hold back."

Jean leaped up and ran at him again. "I won't."

Sebastian ducked into a crouch at the last second, took hold of Jean's legs, and wrestled him to the ground. With a snarl, he landed a blow to Jean's face and bared his fangs.

Max played a sight-blurring game of chase with Julien, popping up in one corner of the expansive lawn only to dash away and reappear on an opposite side. The irritating but effective battle technique exhausted opponents until they became careless. Patient and somber in the face of Max's cocky provocation, Julien retreated into the middle of the lawn, where he crouched, head swiveling in an attempt to predict Max's pattern of movement.

Distracted by the others, Sebastian lost his advantage, and Jean threw him off with a grunt. They scrambled to their feet. Roaring his ire, Sebastian charged him, taking them both down to the ground again where they rolled, each trying to throttle the other. Managing to haul himself on top, Jean pulled back his fist and slammed it into Sebastian's right eye.

"Ouch." Sebastian sat up and headbutted Jean, getting to his feet and lifting him in an unforgiving choke hold.

"I'm letting you win." Jean tried to grin as he squeaked the words.

Sebastian snapped his neck with a clean, sharp twist and stood back, glancing up at the only room without fully drawn curtains. He extended a hand to Jean, pulling the sputtering vampire to his feet. "Best of three?"

Emily's fingers hovered over her cell, the fight outside continuing with unrelenting force. Breath held, gaze fixed on the space between the thick blackout drapes, she flinched with each punch.

Certain now that Sebastian was a bona fide psycho, she looked up the number for French emergency services. While she scrolled, the man whose neck he'd broken with a vicious snap got to his feet, slapped Sebastian on the back, and resumed fist-throwing.

"What the fuck?" She dropped the phone with a muffled thud and pressed her nose to the glass.

The cacophony of grunts, yells, and curses rolled on, the apparently invulnerable opponents knocking each other down time and time again only to dust themselves off and start over. They moved with unnatural fluidity and speed, disappearing only to reappear yards away from where they'd been a millisecond before.

Sebastian went down, his neck broken with a savage twist

similar to the one he'd used to incapacitate his assailant moments earlier. Her chest heaved, and despite the fear chilling her skin and the terrifying impossibilities pressing against her heart, she willed him to get back up again.

"Get up. Get up. Get up. Get up."

He coughed, rolled onto his knees, swayed onto his feet, and then returned to his deadly dance of spinning kicks, punches, and shoves, expertly avoiding Max and the fourth fighter, who were now engaged in blow-for-blow combat that swept across the lawn in a violent blur. With a feral growl, Sebastian fractured his opponent's neck again and then collapsed onto his back where he lay panting, his gaze searching her window. She recoiled just as the lids of the man next to him fluttered open to reveal a pair of orange orbs, incandescent in the rich, satin darkness.

Slumping to the floor beneath the window, her back to the wall, she raced through all the oddities, contradictions, and discrepancies that'd tormented her since she met Sebastian. She dug her toes into the thick pile cream carpet and hugged herself, her thin cotton short pajamas doing little to stem the cold sinking into her pores.

With a frown, she realized she was so awestruck by the chateau she didn't notice the slight slip in Sebastian's speech when he talked about his family, or rather his ancestors. Family seemed too intimate a noun for the long dead relatives who'd lived here. Yet it was the word he chose.

But the real anomaly was his use of "we."

"Great-great-great-great-great-great-great-great-grandparents." She counted the eight greats on her fingers, as Sebastian had done, mentally averaging life expectancies and childbearing years as she tried to make sense of the timeline. But however she manipulated the numbers, the end date was always at least a couple of centuries shy of the year the chateau was built. The crest outside said 1549. She worked through the dates again and extended her fingers one at a time. An irrational, desperate voice in her head clamored for attention, and her hands began to shake.

Fuck. She dropped her head into her palms, pushing her hair back as she squeezed her temples.

He moved too fast. He got up and walked away from a broken neck. He brought her back from what Roxi claimed was the brink of death, and she didn't have so much as a hangover. His eyes changed color—she'd watched the soft bewitching brown dissolve into the dramatic gold green of a stalking panther's. His eyes *glowed,* for God's sake. If she really looked at them, they actually fucking *glowed.*

She couldn't bring herself to label the thought taking shape in her mind, the impossible monster every irregularity she recalled carved out in sharp relief. Beyond beautiful, beyond fast, beyond deadly...

Could it be that Sebastian was something *beyond?* In the literal sense?

She staggered to her feet and began throwing toiletries and clothes into her case. She wriggled out of her pajamas, tugged on jeans and a loose cotton shirt, slipped into a pair of flats, and looked up travel information on her cell. *Shit*—no flights until tomorrow afternoon.

She scurried to the Queen Anne chair in the corner of the huge room and wedged it beneath the door handle with trembling hands. Mouthing a silent prayer, she dragged her case in front of the door and curled up on top of it, tears wetting her cheeks. She'd thought Sebastian was like her father, that he'd use her until he got bored and then spit her back out into cruel, lurid reality. But he was much, much worse than that. She wasn't in a fairy-tale romance like her mother had been, one that would make the world outside seem harsh and unforgiving for years to come afterward.

She was in a nightmare—a real-life, breathing nightmare.

Emily woke with a start in disorienting darkness and silence. She lifted her head and the side of her face throbbed, reminding her she'd hugged herself to sleep on top of her case. The hard edges of her cell dug into her arm. She pulled it out and blinked at the illuminated screen. 17:45 p.m. Bile swept up her throat in a sickening surge.

Fuck. She'd slept all day.

Cursing her stupidity in not setting an alarm when she was jet-lagged and sleep-deprived, she veered into the bathroom, sagged over the sink, and fought back nausea.

She'd missed the flight she wanted to catch, but that didn't mean she had to stay another night. She would organize a taxi to Paris, check into a hotel, and work out how to get home from there. But what then? Pine Lakes was his home too. With a shuddering convulsion, she threw up, the contents of her stomach splattering the perfect white marble.

She couldn't run. It was foolish to think she'd even make it out of the chateau grounds when Sebastian could move so fast he blurred. Gripping the edge of the vanity, she studied the pallid complexion, thinned lips, and dark circles before meeting the hard, mercurial gray of her reflection's damning gaze.

Running the cold tap to wash away the ugly stains of her fear, she took a breath. With forced calm, she shut off the tap, closed the bathroom door, turned on the shower, and undressed in the comforting tendrils of warm steam.

When she stepped back into the bedroom, wrapped in a thick bath towel, she was ready to face reality—to negotiate rather than run. She felt her way over to the nearest window in the darkness and pulled the heavy drapes apart to let the last of the evening light into the room and gasped. A feast lay in front of her on the coffee table: pancakes, waffles, French toast, pastries. A scrawled smiley face on thick cream paper grinned above a handwritten note:

For the girl who loves breakfast. Served twenty-four hours a day because I don't sleep. And it's all for you, because I don't eat. Meet me on the terrace when you're ready.

xoxo

P.S. I really liked that chair. Next time use the key.

A second smiley face winked at her from the bottom of the page.

Bewildered, she looked across at the door and saw the key in the lock above the broken remains of the Queen Ann chair, which had been pushed aside, along with her luggage. She flopped down onto the bed and read the note again.

Unexpected, charming, funny, and penned by a monster.

Who drew smiley faces.

She pushed herself off the bed and took a waffle from the neat pile of food. She bit into the warm, sugary batter, groaned, and then took a bigger mouthful. There was nothing sinister or threatening in what Sebastian had just done. It was sweet. But then so was the gingerbread house with the witch inside.

11

Sebastian smiled with false warmth to mask the tension that coiled in his gut the moment Emily stepped onto the terrace. She wore a midnight-blue dress that shimmied in the wind, the flickering light of a dozen candles and lanterns exaggerating the anxiety and anticipation in her expression. The crickets' continuous hum softened the fall of her hesitant footsteps as she approached him.

This was it. His entire never-ending future depended on tonight, on her reaction, on his ability to persuade her they could have something good together—a wishful half prospect he wasn't even able to fully convince himself of, however tempting it might be.

"You look beautiful." He reached for her hand and leaned down to kiss her forehead, inhaling the scent of her hair. He gestured to the little wrought-iron table where there was an open bottle of wine waiting. "Shall we?"

With the subtlest of movements, she slipped her hand out of his.

His heart began to pound. "Emily?"

"I have to go back to Pine Lakes."

He looked down, felt the bitter smile curving his lips as she backed away. If she refused to listen, then there was no hope, no way out for either of them.

"Thank you for flying me out here, but I really have to leave."

He blinked, his mind stuttering with a crippling panic. "I...I'll ask Henri to take you to the airport."

"That's okay. I have a taxi coming."

He took her hand again. "You're afraid of me."

She shivered and bit her lip. "No. Yes, I'm afraid of you."

"Will you let me explain?"

"You don't have to."

"Please, Emily. I let you see what you needed to, to work out the basics. Let me fill in the gaps so you understand."

She shook her head. "Sebastian, I...I can't."

"I was born in 1761. I was reborn twenty-eight years later as a vampire. I can't die. I can't be permanently injured."

She recoiled at the rough torrent of words, but he gripped her hand tighter.

"You think I'm a monster. Would a monster make you breakfast? Or replace your tires? Or save your life?"

Emily's hand went limp in his. "I don't know."

"I would never hurt you, Emily. You're free to go. I only wanted you to have the truth I promised you. If you want to hear the rest of it, to find out why you're here, then please stay."

He let go of her hand and took a step back so she wouldn't feel threatened. If she freaked out, if she left, he would be all that stood between her and the Circle's assassins. Human life was dispensable, and their laws were merciless when it came to protecting the secrecy of their existence.

"Thank you, again." She shuffled backward, keeping him in her line of sight. "Maybe we could meet up in Pine Lakes some time." The words were flat and numb—an empty statement without intent.

He forced himself to freeze, though every limb, every muscle, every nerve, screamed to hold her close. "Emily, I'm bonded to you. That's why you're here. You're my mate."

Sebastian stood still as stone, his features etched in an uncharacteristic disquiet at odds with the genteel rose garden behind him. A lavender border threw a heavy perfume onto the warm evening breeze, the rich nighttime scents wrapping the scene in a kind of magical nonreality. He wore a tailored black suit with a white shirt, open at the neck, and against the backdrop of the chateau, he looked like a model on a fashion shoot, but beneath the peacock packaging, there lay a hint of power, of danger—a whispering ruthlessness, seductive and terrifying in its potency.

Emily's chest ached with the breath she couldn't release. She needed to leave, to run fast and far, but he enthralled her, and her own hopeless curiosity paralyzed her.

"What does that mean?" Her whispered words, mad and intrigued, kept her there, waiting for an answer.

"Do you remember the way my eyes changed when we met?"

She nodded. She would never forget the spectacular transformation from liquid amber to burning yellow green, the way they almost glowed. "When I asked you about it, you looked shocked."

"It's something that happens to vampires when they meet the person they're destined to be with." That serious gold-green gaze seared her.

She sucked in a breath. "But you didn't know me."

"I didn't know *about* you. But something in me recognized you, the strands and light and bones of who you are, and it bonded me to you."

Wonder was eroding her fear now, emboldening her, reviving her ability to question and challenge and dissect the information he was sharing. "Bonded you to me how?"

"Besides an overwhelming attraction, it's an instinct to stay close, to protect, to nurture and share. It overrides everything else —rational thought, restraint, free will, independence—the bond incinerates them all."

"And if I don't want you to do those things?"

A long pause. "Then we have a problem."

She stiffened, ready to start retreating again.

"*I* have a problem." He held up a hand to calm her, tapping it against his chest when she remained still. "It's my problem, not yours."

"Explain."

"Bonded pairs are drawn to each other, like magnets. The bond is a physical compulsion that neither party can fight."

She exhaled a startled breath. "Is that why I invited you to that party? Why I felt I needed to return your money in person?"

"You're human so the effect the bond has on you is weaker, more variable, but yes, it's likely to have compelled you to some small degree. The last time we were together in Pine Lakes..." He trailed off, pushing his hands into his pockets. "I'd say it was influencing us both."

Emily flushed at the memory of her shameless need for him, the way she'd thrust herself against him, greedy for more. She didn't chase boys, no matter how pretty they were, yet she'd pursued Sebastian from the start, unable to stop even though her actions violated all her self-imposed standards.

He looked skyward as he continued, studying the smattering of stars above. "When two vampires bond, it's just happily ever after, but when a vampire and a human bond, it can be disastrous." He strode over to the table and pulled out a chair. "This might take a while."

She floated across the terrace to the chair, submerged in what felt like that intangible place between sleeping and waking, where the most enticing reveries slip out of reach. Except this was too sharp, too complex to be a dream.

She dropped down onto the hard iron seat. "Tell me."

He took the seat opposite and leaned in to fiddle with the candle burning between them, his fingers tracing the flame.

"Vampires are physically invulnerable, but our longevity leaves us with mental weaknesses. Bonds help anchor vampires to the world, balance them. Older vampires who have not bonded struggle—some are full-on crazy."

"What's a crazy vampire like?"

"A horror movie." He ran his finger through a channel of hot wax. "The Circle usually locks them up pretty quickly."

"The Circle?"

"It's an organization that protects vampires' interests. Its primary role is keeping our existence secret."

"Why bother? If you're infallible supercharged immortals, why hide it?"

He flicked the solidified wax off the tip of his finger. "Hunting is easier if your quarry doesn't know you're there."

Emily pushed her chair back, ready to make a futile dash for the doors.

"Sorry." He sighed. "That didn't come out right. What I meant is that we're pacifists. If we were exposed, we'd be locked in continuous conflict with humans."

"Do you drink blood?"

He studied her with a defiant green gaze. "I'm not the kind-hearted vegetarian vampire you've read about in teen fiction, Emily. Human blood is an unfortunate necessity."

She swallowed, her throat dry and tight. "If you can't die, what happens when you go without it?"

He twirled his finger at his temple. "Like I said, our vulnerabilities are mental, not physical."

"Do you kill people?"

"I try to avoid it."

Her already racing pulse kicked up another notch. "But you have killed?"

"The Circle conscripts vampires for a quarter century every two hundred years to fight a small human hunting movement that's been targeting us since the beginning. I just finished my first stint, so yes, I've killed."

She forced herself not to react, to remain motionless and impassive.

His mouth creased in a soft, reassuring smile. "I'm not a dog, Emily. I won't give chase if you show fear." He reached for the bottle of wine and filled an empty glass with rich, red fluid.

"So bonding stops you from going crazy."

He pushed the glass toward her and began filling the second one with the same relaxed grace, as if they were enjoying nothing more than an aperitif before dinner. "In the long run, yes. But a newly bonded vampire is emotionally volatile. Unstable."

"That's why you trashed your house."

He nodded, acknowledging her astute insight with a half smile. "After our date, I realized that pursuing you wasn't the right thing to do. You're young, and you have your own life. You don't want to be shackled to me for the rest of your days. I tried to stay away, and it was hard, but I was managing." He set the bottle down and pulled his glass toward him. "Then you got sick at the party, and I had to give you my blood."

"Your blood healed me? That's how I got better?"

"I'm sorry I did it without your consent, but you wouldn't have made it to the hospital."

"It wasn't you who spiked my drink?"

He arched a brow. "Would you have come here if you honestly suspected me?"

She shrugged, frustrated that every answer spawned more questions. "Why were you there? How did you know I was in trouble?"

A sheepish grimace. "I was following you. It was the only way I could stop myself unraveling."

Unexpected pity framed her next question. "That was how you

were managing? You were planning to watch me live my life while you skulked in the shadows?"

He scowled, an indignant pout shaping his perfect lips. "I wasn't skulking. I was trying to protect you."

"From what?"

"Let's see, there's your drug-taking best friend, that blond creep who didn't even have the decency to drive you home, whoever it was who slashed your tires and spiked your drink..."

She gritted her teeth. "Carry on."

"Giving you my blood strengthened the bond. It's part of a three-stage process we call *the fall*. The first stage was the eye contact that triggered the bond."

"And the last stage?"

He looked at her with a naked desire so intense her skin heated in response, arousal blossoming despite her fear. "Oh."

He shuttered his eyes with heavy lashes, giving her a moment's respite from their powerful pull. "After that night, it became much harder for me to keep my distance and manage my emotions."

"Am I..." She swallowed, her throat dry. "Am I safe around you?"

"The Circle has developed meds to subdue early bonding hormones. I started taking them before I left Pine Lakes. As long as I keep taking them, I think we're okay."

"You *think*?" Her nails bit into her knees beneath the table.

"Bonding to humans is really rare, Emily. There's no handbook to say how we should approach it."

"What do vampires in this situation usually do?"

A muscle in his jaw ticked, indecision pursing his lips.

"Sebastian?"

"We're in a better position than most. As long as we don't have sex, the meds will keep me in check."

"And if we do have sex?" She blushed as she forced the question out.

"Then there's no turning back, for either of us."

"What aren't you telling me?"

He exhaled a slow breath. "Humans always leave, sooner or later. And the abandoned vampires are distraught, uncontrollable...dangerous."

She could taste the horrible conclusion in the acrid bile that coated her tongue, felt it squeeze her already thumping heart.

"They kill their mates."

Emily paled, but to her credit, she stayed put, her fierce silver eyes hard and determined.

He took a breath. "In the ninth century, a Norse vampire called Astrid bonded to a human man, Leif. Theirs is the earliest recorded vampire-human bonding that I know about. The details differ depending on the narrator, but all those old enough to remember agree they had a fiery relationship because of Astrid's possessive, jealous behavior—behavior that is typical of a newly bonded vampire. Leif's feelings for her were more sedate, more human. In the end, she drove him into the arms of a human woman. Astrid lost her mind and killed them both."

Disdain curled Emily's lip, her judgment of Astrid as a ruthless killer apparent in the hard glint of her steely gaze. "What happened to her? If vampires can't die, is she locked up somewhere?"

"She took Leif's body to a clearing in the forest near their home, and she lay down with him. According to her friends, she never left. They couldn't help her. In those days, there were no meds or containment cells strong enough to hold a vampire. So they protected the land from wandering humans, walled it off, and never left it unguarded. And Astrid lay there with Leif's body until the moss and the grass grew over them both." He spread his hands on the table and leaned toward her. "This isn't a fairy tale, Emily. She's still there."

She clasped her hands together, knuckles white. "So what

you're saying is I have to stay with you, or you'll go crazy and kill me."

"No, Emily. I would never hurt you."

"I bet that's what Astrid said."

He leaned forward. "I'm only trying to be straight with you, to make you aware of the gravity of our situation so we can find a safe way through this together, or apart, if that's what you want."

When she continued to stare at him in stony silence, he placed his hands over hers. "We have options. In the past, abandoned bonded vampires haven't just posed a risk to their human mates— they've mindlessly slaughtered any humans in their path. Containing the maddened vampires and covering up what they've done has become so challenging that the Circle has been working on various preventative strategies to make sure it doesn't happen again. Like I said, I'm taking their meds now, and they're monitoring my response. They'll contain me if I pose a risk to you or anyone else."

He refrained from telling her that they would also seek to turn or kill her to protect their secrets. And if she ran, they wouldn't stop hunting her until she was a vampire or dead.

This needed to be her choice, one that was freely made, and if she rejected him, he would find a way to guard her humanity.

Feeling her clenched fingers begin to relax beneath his own, he traced the outline of her crossed knuckles. "Say something."

She opened her hands, allowed him to lace his fingers through hers. "If Leif didn't love her enough because he was human, could she have made him a vampire? Is that how it works?"

"A handful of vampires have been born to bonded vampire parents. Most of us start out human, but the process of becoming a vampire is complicated. It can take years or days depending on the individual. Astrid may well have been trying to turn him."

"And the process itself? What does that entail?"

"Daily blood exchanges for as long as it takes. Each exchange has to happen within minutes for it to have an effect."

Revulsion dulled her eyes, forced her to swallow.

"I know it sounds disgusting."

"How long did it take for you to turn?"

"I was quick," he said, relieved at her interest. "One exchange and twenty-four hours later...vampire."

A deep breath followed a slight tremor in her hand as she lifted her wineglass. "Show me."

"Are you sure?"

She took a sip of wine and nodded, her somber mercury gaze focused and unblinking.

He strolled to the edge of the lavender border, taking a minute to allow his fangs to sharpen, his eyes to burn their brightest. Turning toward her, he cast his gaze down to the floor and waited.

He heard the scrape of her chair, her intake of breath, her heart striking a frantic, dangerous beat. Then he heard her footsteps and the hushed rustle of her dress in the breeze as she approached him.

Emily stopped with no more than a sliver of starlight between her and Sebastian, pulled to him by an invisible cord made of irrational, fearless threads of feeling.

He waited in the shadows, beyond the reach of the wavering candlelight, but even in the darkness, she could see his features were more beautiful, more striking—frighteningly so.

Protruding over his perfectly sculpted bottom lip were two sharp white fangs. At last he looked up, his surreal green gaze caressing her and stifling the gasp gathered in her throat.

Fear forgotten, she reached up and traced a finger along his upper lip, hesitating before she touched a pearl-white canine. "Is that real?"

He nipped her fingertip in answer, the sharp sweet sting shooting adrenaline through her in a tingling rush.

"Guess so." She held her finger up, spellbound by the tiny bead of blood on the tip.

Without looking away, he guided her finger to his mouth, releasing it after a single gentle flick of his tongue. To her surprise, a fierce, bold arousal started to bloom in her belly, unfolding like the bright petals of a dahlia.

A slow, pleased smile softened his terrible beauty as he recognized her body's raw, physical reaction. Winding his hands in her hair, he leaned down and kissed her, unleashing a hunger and intensity she hadn't felt before. As he slid his lips over hers in an intoxicating, dizzying rhythm, she quivered at the unmistakable graze of a fang. They stayed like that for a long time, kissing in the sweetly perfumed darkness. The way he held her, with tender, sensual reverence, was the reassurance she needed, and her response to his embrace was unguarded, honest abandon—a passionate promise not to run.

Eventually the night air began to cool, and he pulled back, taking her hands in his. "You're getting cold."

"I'm fine."

"And you should eat something."

"I'm not hungry."

He ignored her protest, leading her back through the open French doors and into the wood-paneled dining room.

Henri appeared as if summoned, and Sebastian rattled off rapid instructions in French. With a nod in Emily's direction, Henri strode out of the room.

Sebastian pulled out a chair for her and she sat, grateful for the hard, steadying wood at her back. "You said you don't eat."

He took the seat to her left, at the head of the table, waiting for her to continue.

"But you *can* eat."

"If I have to."

"And Henri, doesn't he think it's weird that you don't eat?"

"I'm not the only vampire you've met, Emily."

"Oh." She considered the possibilities. "Max too?"

He nodded, amusement flickering in his eyes. "Go ahead. You have questions."

Curiosity pushed her closer to the table. "If you can't die, what would happen if you lost your head, or if your body was burned to ash, or cut up into little pieces?"

An arrogant uplift of his brow. "Planning something?"

"Not today."

"Eventually we regenerate. A head might take a few hours to replace, a whole body, days." An amused half smile. "Burning me to ash might buy you a little more time than that."

"Good to know."

Henri swept into the room with a tray, setting down a second bottle of wine, fresh glasses, and a bowl of steaming tomato soup. He poured the wine and left on silent feet.

"Next question," Sebastian said as he raised his glass to his lips.

The soup smelled so good, the tang of freshly cooked tomatoes and sweet basil stirring her appetite. She lifted the silver soup spoon and dragged it through the rich liquid. "Who do you feed from? Do...Do people consent to it?" She couldn't quite keep the incredulity from her voice.

"Feeding is a gentle, hypnotic process. The humans we feed from aren't aware of anything more than a lingering kiss."

Emily's hand froze, leaving the soup spoon suspended above her bowl. "So you feed from women?"

An apologetic shrug. "Most of the time. Feeding requires physical nearness. It's just easier if the other party is attracted to you."

"And if you're attracted to them too." Unexpected jealously sharpened her words.

"If it's a problem for you, I can source blood bags. Stored blood tastes like shit, but it's easy to get hold of."

"You'd do that for me?"

He tilted his head to the side, unblinking eyes trained on her. "I would, yes."

Something inside her fluttered in acknowledgement of the unspoken promise that lay beneath his statement, that he would do anything she asked of him. She cast her eyes down, trying to process the overwhelming, plunging reality she was in.

"Eat." He nudged the forgotten bowl closer to her. "Henri will be offended if you don't. He used to run a Michelin star restaurant."

She took a spoonful of soup, savoring the burst of flavor for a second before she swallowed and took another. Sebastian watched her eat, silent and intense and every inch the patient predator.

A slight tremor ran through her arm, and the spoon rattled the side of the bowl loudly.

"I would never hurt you, Emily." He reached out and took her free hand.

She tensed and immediately saw the hurt in his eyes.

"I can't help what I am," he said, moving his hand away. "But I understand if it's too much for you to deal with."

"It's a lot to take in."

"I can give you some space."

He pushed his chair back, and she grabbed his hand. "No. You can't leave me alone with all these questions."

He squeezed her fingers, the soft, sweet pressure making her breath hitch, forcing her to articulate the fear that'd been taking shape all evening. "If we find our way through this and finish bonding, one day I'll be too old for you, won't I?"

12

Henri appeared and lifted Emily's bowl and spoon onto a tray with small, efficient movements. Sebastian nodded his thanks and waited for the other vampire to back away before he spoke.

"Not if I turn you. We could start the process any time you wanted." He hesitated, reluctant to share the alternative that could mean her rejecting vampirism altogether, an alternative that would ultimately mean a lifetime on the run. An alternative that brought with it the risk of execution for her and imprisonment for him.

Frightened, wary eyes met his, cracking his resolve.

"But there is another way for you to stop aging and stay healthy without becoming a vampire."

She straightened. "Your blood?"

He nodded, deciding to keep the terrible consequences of rejecting his offer to turn her to himself. He wanted to reassure rather than terrify her. "A drop a day is enough to halt the aging process. You can stop and age normally at any point, pick it up again whenever you want."

Content, she settled back into her chair. "If that was an option, then why did you choose this? Who turned you? And what about your family? What happened to them?"

"The revolution happened to them. We were aristocrats, Emily —our excesses made people hate us. The chateau was torched, and my mother and sisters died in the fire. My father got out, but the people seized him and took him to Paris where he was hanged."

Emily paled. Witnessing the veil of sympathy that fell over her features, he realized the scars of his family's demise still smarted and that his voice sounded bitter and heavy with impotent rage. His father was a selfish, reckless bastard, but even he hadn't deserved the violent humiliation the mob meted out to him.

"How did you get out?"

"I was already a vampire. A friend had the foresight to anticipate what was coming. She saw the hunger and desperation, the anger—all things she'd seen before in other times and places."

"She was a vampire?" Emily ran her finger around the base of the wineglass in back-and-forth semicircles.

"An old one. Her name is Marguerite. She told me what she was, warned me about what she thought was coming, and offered to make me like her—invulnerable, deadly, ageless. She turned me less than a month before the chateau burned."

"What about your family? Did you tell them what you'd become?"

"It's forbidden." He fixed her with a stern gaze, knowing he had to make sure she understood. "That goes for you too, Emily. Everything I've told you, you can't repeat it. I'm only able to share this with you because you're my mate."

He stifled a sigh because he knew the true cost of telling even a mate.

"Okay." Her voice was a tight whisper. "Couldn't you have turned them too?"

"There are limits. It wouldn't do to have millions of vampires roaming the planet. Even hundreds of thousands would be too many. The Circle allows each vampire to choose one protégé per century of life. I had another hundred years to go before I could even think about turning anyone. We can't turn older humans either—their bodies reject the change. Thirty, thirty-five, that's about the limit."

The color drained from her cheeks.

"What is it?" he asked.

"If my mom can't become a vampire too, then I can't ever tell her any of this?"

"No, Emily, you can't."

"But if I use your blood to stop the aging process, at some point she'll notice. Everyone will notice."

"Yes, but not for a long time. You can put it down to good genes, Botox, skin care. It won't be an issue for years."

She raised her eyes to the ceiling for a moment, as if she needed to mentally store the information to pull it apart later.

"Carry on," she said, returning her gaze to his.

He continued without breaking eye contact. "I hoped that in accepting Marguerite's offer I could protect my mother and sisters. If they survived the bloody times ahead, I would distance myself before they realized I wasn't aging."

"You weren't worried about protecting your father too?"

"I despised my father, but that's another story."

She gave a wry smile. "You don't need to explain that to me."

"Yes, we have that in common," he said.

"And the woman who turned you, Marguerite, were you close to her?"

He saw the slight narrowing of her eyes, the delicate flare of her nostrils, and realized she had a good idea of the kind of relationship they'd had.

"Yes, we were close."

"You loved her."

"For a time, yes, I did. But without a bond, all vampires tend to go their separate ways eventually."

"How long were you together?"

"Fifty years, give or take."

A disbelieving, uncomfortable smile. "Fifty years? That's forever."

"Not when you're a vampire, and I owed her everything."

The sentence and all it implied hung heavily between them, Emily's silence telling him that the idea of him in a half-century-long relationship brought home the stinging insignificance of their own short affair.

He leaned into her, looping his free hand around her waist and crushing her lips to his in a harsh, demanding kiss. "This is more than that."

An uncertain smile wavered and died on her lips. His stomach lurched as she pulled back.

"Maybe not for you, but it is for me," he said.

She released a small sigh. "I just need some time."

He could see she was getting tired, struggling to make sense of him and the long history that stretched behind him, but he needed to give her one final piece of information to sleep on. "There's something else I need to tell you."

She laughed, the soft swirling sound dispelling the tension that had gathered in his shoulders. "Are werewolves real too?"

"If they are, they're even more secretive than vampires." Grin fading, he continued. "The hunters I mentioned, they target bonded couples."

Her breathing quickened. "Are you saying we're being hunted?"

"Not yet, but sooner or later we will be, and you're human, so that makes things easier for them." He locked his jaw, withholding the fact that should she choose to remain human, there would be a second party hunting them too.

A frown shadowed her features. "Why hunt couples in particular?"

He studied her face for a moment, concerned by her renewed anxiety. "It's a strategy that's worked for them for the last couple of centuries. Bonded vampires are easier to identify and track." He pointed to his eyes to indicate the way the unusual color and slight glow made them stand out. "And the bond itself is a kind of Achilles' heel. It makes us easier to manipulate, our behavior easier to predict. Bonded vampires will do anything to protect their mates, and the hunters take full advantage of that."

"But why do they hunt vampires if you don't kill unnecessarily?"

"Officially, they say we're a scourge on humankind, dangerous parasites that must be contained. But blood that can cure all ills, heal wounds, halt aging—that makes us pretty valuable livestock."

"God, Sebastian, that's awful."

"The vampires they've captured in the past have never been seen again."

"How do they capture you? I saw what you can do last night. No human could match that."

"They train relentlessly, and they're amped up on vampire blood when they strike. We're not talking about lone wolves; they operate as an army would, entire regiments of fighters deployed to take down one or two vampires at a time."

"And you and I, if we don't...bond completely...if we go our separate ways, like you said, would we still be targeted?"

"Not by the hunters," he answered, trying to hide the fear that slithered over his skin at the possibility that she might reject his offer, making her the target of an even deadlier group of assassins.

He withdrew his hand and went to stand by the open doors, looking out at the moon-silvered garden.

Emily came to stand beside him. "I'm not saying that's what I want."

She reached up and brushed her fingers against his cheek.

He turned his face into her hand and kissed her palm. "Get some rest. We can talk more in the morning."

A shy lowering of her lashes. "Will you come with me?"

"Emily..."

"Just to sleep, or at least stay with me while I sleep."

He took a deep breath. "Go get changed. I'll be up in a minute."

She stood on tiptoe and kissed him, a brief sweet kiss that ignited hope and fear, burning desire and chilling dread.

Emily sat on the edge of the modern, king-size bed and brushed her hair. A chandelier lit the cavernous bedroom and threw into relief the intricate plasterwork on the ceiling, its gilded swirls and flicks coming together in a visual feast that distracted her buzzing mind enough to quiet its clamoring thoughts.

A soft knock on the door sounded.

She tossed her hairbrush onto the dressing table, stood, and straightened her oversize shirt. "Come in."

Sebastian smiled and shut the door behind him. He'd changed into sweats, his bare upper body all smooth honed muscle and flawless golden skin. An awkward shyness gripped her, and she bit her lip, holding it between her teeth, as he looked her up and down.

"Nightcap?" He slid his gaze across to the decanter sitting in the center of the coffee table.

"Sure." She followed him to the little sitting area, dropping down onto the small sofa on the far side of the table, careful to check her T-shirt covered her panties, though her modesty had gone up in smoke the night before.

He filled a crystal tumbler with amber liquid and handed it to her before pouring one for himself. "*Santé.*" He clinked his glass against hers and sat down beside her, his arm brushing hers.

"*Santé.*" She took a sip, savoring the way it burned the back of her throat.

"You look shell-shocked."

"I feel shell-shocked."

"But at least you have your answers now." A playful grin. "And you don't need to worry that I'm working for your father or slipping narcotics into girls' drinks."

"I wish I knew who did that."

"Perhaps you picked up someone else's drink?"

"No, I made all my own drinks, didn't leave them unattended. Apart from the one Roxi gave me."

He arched an accusing brow.

Emily waved a dismissive hand. "Obviously she's not made a good impression on you, but she wouldn't do that. Trust me. And it's not just the drink—it's the tires too. It feels off, deliberate."

The multitude of little mysteries that came with Sebastian had shunted the two strange incidents from her mind, but now the puzzling fog around him had lifted, she began to wonder about them once more. Swirling her drink around the glass, she watched the way it clung to the sides as she considered.

"Would anyone have a reason to target you?"

She shook her head. "My father's an awful man and he'd do anything to get me out of Pine Lakes, but bribery is more his style than low level crime."

"You should speak to Roxi, find out who she buys from. A town the size of Pine Lakes probably only has one supplier. Maybe they sold to whoever spiked your drink too."

"Perhaps, but even if they did, they're not going to offer up a list of names and addresses."

"I can be persuasive." Sebastian's face darkened, the predator beneath the surface stirring as if summoned.

She suppressed a shiver. "I bet you can. The stuff in my drink was different though. I mean, Roxi was fine."

"That doesn't mean it didn't come from the same source." He rubbed the back of her neck in small, soothing circles. "We'll figure it out."

Goose bumps broke out across her bare skin at the silent threat behind his words. "And then what?"

"We stop them."

"Sebastian..." She leaned away, twisting to look at him. "It's probably someone I know, and even if it isn't, violence isn't the answer."

He rolled his eyes. "Let's just find out who it is first and what their motives were." A long pause. "My money's on Blondie."

Now she rolled her eyes. "What is it with you and him?"

"He wants you." Obsidian ringed the pale gold green of his eyes.

She swallowed. "Well, *you* have me."

"Even after everything you've learned?"

Nodding, she placed a hand on his chest and flexed her fingers against firm muscle. "I don't know if it's the bond or not, but you're impossible to walk away from."

Heavy-lidded eyes met hers, and he pulled her onto his lap, spreading her legs to straddle him. "Good."

She kissed him hard and fast. She wasn't ready to talk about the fact that, impossible to walk away from or not, she'd never agree to become a vampire for him.

Sebastian's brain scrambled at the ferocity of Emily's kiss. All he registered was tongue, teeth, lips, and the aching grind of Emily's sex against his straining cock.

Pulling back, he watched her intently as he slid both hands beneath her shirt, squeezing her perfect breasts. She hissed and arched as he rolled a stiff nipple between his thumb and forefinger. With a wicked smile, she tugged the shirt over her head and tossed it to the floor, revealing a flat stomach, narrow waist, and beautiful, small breasts that made his mouth water.

Hands on her lower back, he pulled her toward him, guiding a nipple and its surrounding flesh into his open mouth. He ran a fang along the plump little mound, and she fisted the hair at the base of his head, guiding his mouth from one breast to the other.

With a groan, he tugged aside her panties, eager to free her scent, and thrust a finger into her slick core.

She cried out and lowered herself farther onto his finger.

"Emily..." Shutting his eyes, he blew out a hot breath.

She wriggled her hand beneath his sweats and curled her wicked fingers around his erection. "Fuck."

A sinful smile. "Yes, please."

His eyes shot open, and he was out from under her faster than her human gaze could track. He set her back on the couch and then streaked to the other side of the room.

"Is this a game to you?" The words were harder than he intended, thundered rather than said.

"N-No."

"Didn't you listen to anything I told you tonight?"

She pursed her lips in obvious pique as she stood. "Of course I did."

"Then should I assume your invitation is confirmation that you're in this for good? Because there's no way out once *the fall* is finished, and eternity is a long fucking time."

"No, don't assume anything. I need time to think this through."

"Then don't tempt me into doing something that can't be undone."

Angry red spots appeared on her cheeks. "What am I supposed to do? Hold your hand and wear a chastity belt while I make up my mind? I can't decide what I want without getting close to you."

Squeezing his eyes shut, he backed toward the door. "I'm sorry. I... It's the bond, it makes me..."

"Moody? Rude? An *asshole*?" she finished.

"You should rest." He opened his eyes, ready to disappear, but stopped.

Emily's laughter shook her body with silent gales, the sound muted by the hand she held over her mouth.

A confused smile creased his lips in response. "What?"

She dropped her hand, freeing the bubbling giggles to float around the room. "Are you sure you're 250 and not fifteen?" Her words were punctuated with hysterical giggles.

He scowled. "I'm 225."

She wiped a tear from her eye as her chuckles slowed. "All that time earlier explaining how new bonds affect vampires, you could've just warned me it'd be like dating a hormonal teenager."

She crossed the room to stand in front of him, laughter still dancing in her eyes. He tensed when she pressed her body against his, her head on his chest and her arms up around his neck.

"Relax, I'm giving you a hug." She sighed. "Come on, I'm tired."

When he didn't move, she tugged his hand, and he let her lead him to the bed. She pulled back the duvet and kneeled on the mattress, waiting for him to join her. "I don't want to wake up afraid of you. If you stay, I think the morning will be easier."

He remained at the side of the bed, undecided. "I don't want you to be afraid of me either."

She held out a hand, and he took it, stretching out on the mattress beside her. She draped herself across him, her head nestled on his chest, shoulder beneath his arm. She was warmth and comfort and heartbreaking, terrifying vulnerability.

Counting her breaths, he listened as they became slower and more even. He pulled the cord on the bedside lamp when he was sure she was asleep.

Praying that she accepted his offer of vampirism sooner rather than later, he settled back onto the pillow. Even with the meds, he didn't think he could trust himself around her. Her scent, her movements, and her candid willingness all made abstaining a much harder battle.

But he sensed an unspoken reluctance in her already, a resistance that told him his instincts were right when he identified her problematic tie to her mother. Circumstances had made them too close, made Emily excessively protective.

And she would not give that relationship up easily, if at all.

13

EMILY SANK INTO THE CAR SEAT, AND A HAPPY SIGH ESCAPED HER LIPS. "Where to now?"

Sebastian had played tour guide all morning, shepherding her from one breathtaking part of the chateau to another. He showed her ballrooms, dining rooms, galleries, libraries, vast suites, and a green maze of courtyards and gardens.

His eyes shimmered in the scorching afternoon sun that hit the windshield. "Swimming."

"Is there a pool I don't know about?" She beamed at the thought of cool water on her hot skin.

"In a river."

"Seriously?" Her desire to cool off shrank at the prospect of fast-flowing water. "I don't know if I'm that good a swimmer."

"I'll look after you," he said, clearly relishing the prospect.

She bristled. "No thanks, I can look after myself. If I'm not comfortable with the risk, I won't get in."

A nonchalant shrug. "It'll be your loss."

The river marked the edge of the chateau's grounds, winding along its borders in languid arcs, the water clear enough to see large fish meandering in its depths.

Sebastian parked by a sandy bank and retrieved an ice bucket, champagne, and two flutes from the back of the car while Emily wandered down to the inlet and studied the smooth stones strewn across its bed.

"What do you want to do first?" Sebastian came up behind her, wrapping his arms around her waist as he nuzzled her neck. "Drink or swim?"

"I don't have a swimsuit."

"Feeling shy?" He spun her round, his eyes full of boyish challenge.

She shook her head. "You first."

He appeared in the water in less time than it would have taken her to blink, his white shirt and denim shorts in a messy pile at her feet.

"That's not fair." Crossing her arms, she watched him tread water without effort, rivulets of moisture running down his body from his wet hair.

He splashed a shower of drops in her direction. "What are you waiting for?"

She couldn't resist his dare or the chill water that spotted her shorts and halter-neck top. Defiant, she held his hungry gaze as she kicked off her flip-flops and slid off her shorts. When she flung her halter-neck aside, leaving her in nothing but simple white panties, Sebastian's eyes became hooded. She removed the white cotton slowly in a purposeful tease, a tremor thrilling through her at his intake of breath.

She strolled to the water's edge and assessed the river's flow before taking a few cautious steps, Sebastian observing her closely.

Once the water lapped at her ribs, she began to swim, but found herself pulled downstream, the invisible current racing beneath the calm surface overpowering her within seconds. Sebastian was there before she had time to panic, sheltering her in his solid arms and holding her steady despite the river's force.

"You could have warned me!" She flicked water at him, but he dodged the spray with a chuckle.

"Vampire, remember?"

He dived under the water and popped up behind her as she began to drift. He put his arms around her and pulled her against his body.

Heart clattering, she turned in his arms and kissed him, pushing her wet body against his. He moved his hands down her back and circled her waist, his long fingers resting on her hips.

Feeling the now familiar point of a fang, she broke the kiss. "Are you hungry?"

He shrugged. "I'm always hungry."

Pulse quickening, she chewed her bottom lip. "Do you want to feed off me?"

"I'd be lying if I said I didn't. Hunger and arousal go hand in hand for vampires. But you're my mate, Emily, not my dinner."

An image of him fang deep in her neck flashed through her mind, igniting an unexpected trail of desire. "Can't I be both?"

"Don't tempt me."

"Maybe I want you to be tempted." She ran her hand down his chest before reaching beneath the water.

He caught her arm. "Did you absorb what I said last night?"

"Yes. We both know there's a line. Just because we can't cross it doesn't mean we can't play next to it."

Concern clouded his features. "It's safer not to go too far with me, Emily. If you take me to the edge, I'll pull us both over." He shifted away from her. "I won't be able to hold back, and when *the fall* is done, I won't care about your choice anymore. My focus will be on forcing a secure bond."

Swallowing, she held his gaze. "I don't believe you'd do that."

"I won't be myself."

Lost in thought, they swam in silence until Emily started to shiver. Once back on the sandbank, she wriggled into her panties and shorts.

"You really think you'd force me to turn?"

"I know I would."

"But you said it could take years." A breeze raised the fine hairs on her arms. "So you'd imprison me until it was done."

By the time she grabbed her top, Sebastian was fully dressed and waiting by the car, but she stayed put.

Hard, sad eyes met hers. "You would thank me in the end."

"It's not what I want." Tears stung her eyes.

"I know." A cold, courteous smile. "And that's why we can't take things any further than we already have. It's why we're here and not tangled in my bedsheets right now."

She turned away, sat back down on the sand, and hugged her knees to her chest. The last place she wanted to be right now was cooped-up in a car with him.

Ignoring the fact that he was still standing there, waiting for her, she fished the champagne bottle out of the pool of melted ice and began untwisting its wire cage.

She sensed him move closer.

"Emily—"

"This is fucked up. You realize that, right?"

Pulling rather than popping the cork, she poured herself a glass of the pale, hissing liquid, eyeing the label with disgust. "Dom Perignon. You really are like my father." She took a sip and continued. "Controlling, authoritarian, moody, *excessive...*"

He didn't say anything, didn't defend himself, didn't lash out at her, all of which her father would have done.

"Say something!"

"I'm not fighting with you, Emily."

"Won't fight with me. Won't feed off me. Won't fuck me. Do you just want to be friends?" She said the latter with a saccharin spite, now fully consumed by the temper that'd had clawed its way to the surface.

"Stop baiting me." He delivered the words slowly through gritted teeth. The low, rumbling warning rankled her.

"Or what, Sebastian?"

A few seconds later, the metallic clunk of the car door, the whirr of the engine, and the grind of the wheels over dry grass stuffed her heart into her smart mouth.

Sebastian shifted up another gear and sped away from the chateau —he didn't trust himself to spend another second with Emily. The more vociferous her demands for closeness became, the harder it became for him to hold back. He saw only passion in her drawn features and scrunched lips, a frustrated need for more that made him desperate to give her what she wanted. But she wanted it all with none of the strings attached.

It was for her sake that he held back, that he wasn't taking what he wanted without any regard for her future or her freewill. But she refused to see it that way.

He pressed the accelerator to the floor, pushing the speedometer to its upper limit. Racing past a group of college-age tourists gathered outside a local church, he wondered again if Emily was just too young to manage the challenge of his bond to her. If she found his moods difficult to handle now, how would she cope if he succumbed to his urges and finished *the fall*? Bile rose up his throat in answer because he knew that if things went that far while she was human, sooner or later, she'd run.

He drove until his agitation began to subside, stopping at a busy town popular with tourists shortly after the sun set. He ordered a bottled beer at a trendy little bar, took a seat at the back, and waited for its fashionable, young patrons to start arriving.

A group of women raucously celebrating a birthday spilled into the artfully lit interior, which had the feel of midnight though it was only just dusk. They noticed him immediately, their gazes flitting across to him every few seconds, assessing and excited.

As more people arrived, one of the women seized her chance,

taking a few hesitant steps over to introduce herself. Pretty and petite, her tousled copper hair framed a heart-shaped face and blue eyes. That was good. An attractive man picking up an attractive woman drew little attention.

She said it was out of character for her to talk to a stranger, even one as good-looking as him. She didn't really know why she was there except that for some reason, she couldn't not talk to him. He offered her a guilty half smile, knowing it was the irresistible magnetism of a hungry vampire that drew her to him, overriding her inhibitions. He smiled charmingly and flirted a little. Her eyes glazed over as he moved closer. He fed discreetly, his mouth cleaving to her neck as his fangs delicately pierced her skin. To her friends, it looked as if he whispered in her ear.

After a minute, he pulled away, his hunger dulled, leaving nothing but two pinprick puncture wounds behind. He touched her arm and looked her in the eye, taking her out of his thrall. It was strange the way humans succumbed as vampires fed—glassy-eyed and passive, with no recollection of it afterward.

Scribbling down a fake phone number, he suggested she enjoy the rest of the evening with her friends. She nodded, accepted the scrap of paper, and backed away. He finished his beer and slipped out before he attracted any further attention.

The chateau was in complete darkness when he got back a little before twelve, though his heightened sight discerned bats swooping for moths beneath the black sky and mice running for cover among the shadowy hedgerows. He let himself in and climbed the stairs without making a sound, pausing outside Emily's room to listen to her breathing.

He opened the door a crack.

"Sebastian?" The tension and anxiety in her voice pricked at his heart.

"You should be asleep."

She was lying on her side on top of the sheets, her shirt

bunched around her hips and waist. "I couldn't sleep. I didn't know where you'd gone. I thought... I'm sorry, about earlier."

"You don't need to apologize."

"I kind of have a short fuse sometimes."

He smiled. "I see that."

"I didn't mean to push you."

"Yes, you did, Emily, but perhaps your intentions are not your own."

She lowered her eyes, fisted the sheets in her hand. "Is it the bond?"

"I think that's a possibility."

A sigh. "What are we going to do?"

Kneeling at the edge of the bed, he cupped her cheek with a hand. "That's up to you."

Silence, ominous and telling, as he waited for her to respond.

She reached for his free hand, interlocking her fingers with his. "Where did you go?"

"I had to hunt."

"Oh."

"And it seemed like you needed some space."

She looked sheepish. "I thought you'd come back. It took me an hour to walk here."

"And did you feel calmer at the end of it?"

She sat up, releasing his hand and pulling her legs up to her chest. "I thought you didn't care."

"One day, Emily, you'll realize that for the rest of my immortal life, all I get to do is care about you."

She looked down at her knees, failing to hide her smile. "I'm still kind of mad at you."

He laughed. "Get some rest. You can tell me how much you hate me in the morning."

"I don't hate you. Can you stay? Or is it too difficult for you to lie with me in the bed while I sleep?"

"Of course not, Emily. That's not what I meant earlier."

She blushed.

"Do you want me to stay?"

She gave a little nod.

He undressed and lay down beside her, his body sighing at the way she nestled into him.

"Is it boring for you?"

"No." His voice was hoarse, almost a whisper. "It's perfect."

"I want to be with you," she murmured.

"I want to be with you too."

"So we'll figure this out?"

"I hope so."

14

Sebastian found Pascaline waiting in the morning room, her chic black pantsuit out of place amid the old-fashioned opulence, though she herself was very much at ease with the antique dark wood furniture, rich lemon velvet drapes, and priceless paintings. It was one of the few rooms in the chateau decorated and furnished entirely in keeping with its age, an age that Pascaline, like Sebastian, had lived through.

He'd left Emily sleeping when he heard Henri greet their unannounced visitor downstairs.

"Pascaline." He kissed her on both cheeks, the embrace formal rather than friendly.

"Ah, Sebastian. *Comment ça va?*"

"*Ça va bien, merci.*"

He gestured to the Chesterfield that sat facing the room's second set of French doors, which opened onto an internal courtyard. "Please, have a seat."

Pascaline perched on the edge, her posture rigid, hands clasped at her knee. "I'm sure you know the reason for my visit."

He took a seat on the velvet chaise opposite the Chesterfield, bracing his elbows on his knees as he leaned forward. "I haven't started it yet."

A disapproving lift of her brow. "And *the fall* remains unfinished?"

He gave a single nod, unwilling to share any more than he had to.

"Sebastian, even with the meds, the longer this continues, the greater the risk."

Henri came in and set down a silver tray with a china coffee service on the breakfast table by the inside entrance. Sebastian thanked him and poured the coffee, then dropped a cube of sugar into Pascaline's cup and stirred it with a silver spoon. He'd worked closely with Pascaline when he was a Primary, and he knew exactly how she liked her coffee.

"*Merci.*" She took the cup and saucer from him with a tight smile.

He sat back down without bothering to make himself one. "Can I speak frankly? Off the record?"

Two grooves appeared between her brows, worry lines he saw frequently during their battles with the hunters. "If you must."

"I don't know if she'll ever consent to turning, and I don't know if I could ever force her."

"Sebastian..."

"How much do the other leaders know?"

"They were notified of a new vampire-human bonding, and they have your names. That is enough."

"How long do we have?"

"I'm supposed to report back to confirm you've started the process."

He raked his hands through his hair, considering their limited options. "Can you buy me some time?"

Large, fearful eyes held his. "I can try, but it won't be long."

"She doesn't know about the consequences of declining an offer. I-I wanted her to choose freely, not under duress."

"There's too much at stake, Sebastian. You can't afford to be so idealistic."

"I have to try, Pascaline."

"And if the answer is the same a month, or a year from now, then what?"

He stood and paced over to the open doors, the urge to grab Emily and run making him tuck his fingers into fists.

Pascaline came to stand beside him, cup and saucer in hand. "Are the meds working?"

"To a degree—they take the edge off, nothing more."

She took a sip of coffee. "You should introduce her to Jean and Audrey. It might help her see things differently."

A bumblebee drifted from flower to flower in the courtyard, and he isolated the sound of its wings, took in the bright contrast of its stripes, the individual strands of black, yellow, and white that covered its tiny body, the fine pattern on its translucent wings— sounds and details that would seem flat and dull to human senses.

"You're right," he said. "I've focused on warning her about the dangers, so she really hasn't seen any of the positives."

Pascaline squeezed his shoulder. "I'll do what I can, but be careful with her, Sebastian, and don't waste time."

"Mom?" Emily sank into her pillow as the call connected.

"Emily! How are you? Are you having a good time?"

"Yes, it's been... I can't even describe how beautiful it is here."

"And Sebastian? He's been looking after you?" Her voice sounded distant and tinny.

"Yes." Emily stifled an unexpected sob.

"What's the matter?"

"Nothing. It's just that we've never been this far away from each other before."

"Oh, honey. You should be enjoying yourself."

"I am. But I miss you."

"Is your hotel nice?"

"Um, we're not staying in a hotel. It's a chateau."

"Oh my. Can your budget stretch to that? I know he paid for the flights, but even so, you must be burning through money."

"Well, it's his. It's his chateau." Silence. A crackle on the line. "Mom?"

"Just keep your feet on the ground, Emily. The lifestyle. Fast cars and fancy restaurants, champagne, and designer clothes. It's addictive."

"You know I don't care about those things."

"Then make sure you come home exactly as you are. Don't let him change you."

Her mother's words carried an unintended aptness that solidified her resolution to remain human, regardless of the danger. She couldn't become a vampire for Sebastian.

There was a soft knock on the door.

Sniffling and wiping her eyes with the back of her hand, Emily hopped off the bed. "I gotta go, Mom. I'll call you again in a few days."

"All right, sweetie. Take care of yourself."

She ended the call, tossed her cell onto the bed, and cleared her throat. "Come in."

Sebastian opened the door and leaned against the frame. "Hey."

"Hey."

"You sleep okay?"

She nodded.

"Homesick?"

"A little."

"You feel like a road trip?"

"Where to?" She tried to surreptitiously untangle her bed-rumpled hair but gave up when she noticed the amusement flickering in his eyes.

"Cannes."

"As in where they have the film festival?"

"Yes, but it's not at this time of year."

"What's there now?"

"Besides the beautiful Riviera coastline and fantastic restaurants?" He grinned. "One of the most exclusive nightclubs in the world and a yacht on loan from a friend."

She frowned. "I don't have anything to wear around yacht people."

"Then I guess we'll have to go shopping," he said with a laugh.

"Can't we just stay here?"

"Don't you want to see some of France? We can stop at places along the way, spend a couple of days seeing the countryside."

"There's countryside here."

"Come on." He pouted, his face all irresistible boyish charm. "I want you to meet my friends."

She slid off the bed and stretched. "Okay, okay."

"Wait." He pulled a velvet cube from his back pocket and held it up for her.

"What's this?" She took the box and pried it open.

The green diamond from the display cabinet sparkled within.

He lifted it from the box and threaded the long gold chain around her neck, fastening the clasp at the back so it came to rest between her breasts. "Never take it off."

"You reset it?"

"Yes. Because it should be worn."

"Sebastian..." She started to protest, but he silenced her with a kiss and then pressed his forehead against hers.

"That stone was all I could save of my family. Sometimes I still think about the flames, the smoke... I want you to have it. I want to see it out in the daylight again."

She looped her arms around his neck and pressed her lips to his.

They arrived in Cannes the following day as the neon-pink sun began its descent below the horizon. Warm air ruffled Emily's hair as she boarded the sleek white yacht anchored a stone's throw from the nightclub where Sebastian reserved a table.

He greeted the British captain and small crew warmly, then asked for drinks to be left on deck before dismissing them for the night. The crew did as he instructed with slick professionalism, dissipating into the French Riviera resort with quiet enthusiasm.

Emily leaned over the side of the boat to take in the view along La Croisette—the promenade that threaded its way between the expensive hotels and the beach. She smirked at a line of Ferraris, Lamborghinis, and Aston Martins parked below. Their own car looked conspicuously modest among the motorized show of wealth spread proudly along the street. A group of sweating men painstakingly rolled an orange Ferrari off the back of the yacht next to theirs with a cacophony of grunted instructions.

"Pretty vulgar, huh?" Sebastian ran a finger along the disdainful curl of her lip and threw a disapproving glance at the tangerine monstrosity. "There's money and then there's taste."

"I guess I'm lucky you have the latter. An orange car would've been a deal breaker."

The dancing reflection of the dying sun on the water threw wavering light over Sebastian's face, and a sudden nervousness seized her shoulders. Any minute now, a group of vampires whose collective age made her head spin would crowd the yacht. Would she be safe around so many of them?

"Are you okay?" Sebastian asked.

"This place..." She looked at the other boats and the expensively attired passersby strutting back to their hotels carrying bags from the same boutiques Sebastian cajoled her into visiting earlier. "It's a lot to take in."

"Even after the chateau?"

"The chateau was just you and me. It felt different. This is like Oak Ridge on steroids."

He laughed, but his gaze kept searching hers, like he knew she was deflecting. "Are you worried about meeting the others?"

She shrugged. "I feel like a lost lamb encountering a pack of wolves for the first time."

"They're my friends. They won't hurt you."

"But will they want to? I mean, they won't, but will they be thinking about it?"

"Stop worrying. There'll be plenty of other people on the menu for them to choose from."

She grimaced. "That's not making me feel any better."

"They won't hurt anyone."

She freed the breath she held. "Okay."

He squeezed her upper arm. "Stop worrying. You're with me. You'll be treated like a princess, I promise."

Putting his hands in her hair, he tugged her into a hug, the cotton of his olive-green shirt soft and warm against her collarbone. He rubbed the base of her neck in slow, sedate circles. Standing on tiptoe, she brushed her lips against his. He deepened the kiss, opening her mouth as their tongues touched in an absorbing caress.

"It's not even dark yet, you two!" said a boisterous voice from across the deck.

Sebastian beamed as he pulled away from her.

"Jean." He stood to meet the dark-haired vampire who sauntered onto the boat, casually carrying two bottles of champagne in one large hand.

Sebastian called in French to the immaculately dressed group following noisily in Jean's wake, his greeting met with French enthusiasm she couldn't begin to decipher.

An hour later, Emily went in search of the master cabin, leaving Sebastian to entertain his lively friends on deck. The spacious, plush room cocooned her from the noise above, its gold-framed mirrors and hidden lighting tracks illuminating the fear and uncertainty of her pinched lips and wide eyes.

Though Sebastian had kept her close to him, she couldn't quash the telltale tremor in her voice when he'd introduced her to each of his friends, not least because she recognized two of them from the vicious sparring display at the chateau.

Jean and his girlfriend, Audrey, came first. No, not girlfriend —*mate,* Emily corrected herself, remembering the possessive way the darkly handsome vampire with cobalt eyes as luminescent as Sebastian's fawned over the pretty blonde. All three of them had the same bright cat's-eyes. Eyes that seemed to glow and shimmer. Eyes that warned other vampires to stay away.

She wondered if Sebastian would be like Jean if they completed *the fall* together. No more maddening restraint, just unadulterated devotion.

Would she want that? She'd only observed the couple for a few minutes, but their closeness, the intensity of their interactions, was impossible to miss.

The twins, Jacques and Christophe, looked the youngest of the bunch with tousled platinum-blond hair and perfect tans. She reminded herself that though they appeared to be fresh from college, they could be decades, if not centuries, older than Sebastian, who'd joked about their "special status" as born vampires.

Naomi, a tall, graceful woman with curly black hair, chocolate eyes, and smooth molasses-brown skin brought them a gift: a solid silver photograph frame, as if she assumed they lived together.

An aloof, brooding vampire named Julien, whose jet-black hair and pale-gray eyes lent him an arresting, melancholy quality, arrived last and stood in silence, watching the water with dispassionate detachment while the others gossiped and laughed. She couldn't be certain, but she thought she recognized him from the fight at the chateau. She got goose bumps just thinking about the brutality of the violent exercise.

Though Sebastian translated for her here and there, Emily failed to keep up with the group's animated French exchanges. The quiet cabin offered a welcome retreat from her awkward, superfluous presence at Sebastian's side.

With a sigh, she pulled the horribly expensive black dress he'd bought her earlier that day from its bag, peeled away the tissue paper, and ran a hand along its unfinished silk. Her mother's warning against materialism rang in her ears. With a high neck and a short hemline, it wasn't the budget party-girl look she and Roxi frequently favored. Instead, it was darkly chic, its clean lines intimidating and striking.

She wriggled out of her shorts and top and into the black dress before she lost the nerve to wear it. In the bathroom, she dusted bronzer over her cheeks and worked a light smattering of silver eye shadow onto her lids, then reached for a geranium-red lipstick and boldly smeared it across her mouth. She usually preferred a nude lip, but she needed war paint tonight, camouflage so Sebastian's friends wouldn't see the floundering, small-town nobody she'd allowed herself to become.

She blotted her lips on a tissue, pressing them into a thin line at the realization she was wasting her life in Pine Lakes. She might not be motivated by money or traditional emblems of success, but she wanted to learn and explore and see the world. She couldn't do that if she continued to shadow her mother, yet the thought of leaving her behind, of accepting the terms of Sebastian's offer, crushed her heart.

Emily needed to find a compromise, to forge a path that could somehow unite all their needs and interests.

She fluffed and sprayed her hair, spritzed herself with a heavy, musky perfume, and stepped back to assess her work in the mirror. Satisfied with the sophisticated mask in front of her, she hurried into the bedroom, yanked on her new high-heeled, black, strappy sandals and a grabbed a crystal-embroidered clutch bag worth more than her car.

Taking a slow breath, she forced herself to go back on deck. Tall, lean, and poised, Sebastian stood talking to the twins, whose laughter ricocheted around the boat.

Max waved to her from across the deck, so she wound her way through the others to greet him. A willowy woman with waist-length, mousy-brown hair stood next to him, her arm linked with his.

"I owe you an apology," Emily said, reciprocating the kisses Max planted on each of her cheeks.

"Everything looks different now, eh?"

"It does. I'm sorry I was such a bitch to you."

"There's no need to apologize. Vampire bonds are complicated things."

"I'm Marie," said the willowy woman before she kissed Emily on both cheeks as Max had done. "Emily, it is nice to finally meet you," she said in the same beautifully accented English as Max, leaning into his body with comfortable familiarity.

"I'm guessing you two have been together longer than I've been alive." A silence that made Emily's spine tingle met her off-the-cuff remark. Cursing her carelessness, she realized they weren't mates, that Max's eyes were the muddy shade of oak leaves at the end of autumn and Marie's an ordinary hazel—they lacked the striking radiance of bonded vampires' irises.

"She's my wife," Max eventually said, his tone devoid of pride and satisfaction.

"Sometimes." Marie's lashes swept her high cheekbones, and her expression soured. "Sometimes I'm his wife."

He said something to her in French, and an angry flush colored her collarbone above the slinky white dress. Pulling away from him, now upright and rigid, he caught her hand and offered a placating murmur that Emily didn't need to translate to understand its purpose.

A reassuring hand at Emily's nape freed her from the awkward moment. She turned into Sebastian's hard body, welcoming the kiss he dropped onto the top of her head.

"Time to go." He gestured to Max and Marie, distracting them from their quarrel. "*Allez!*"

The party meandered off the boat in a chattering line, crossed the promenade, and stopped by a red velvet rope. A fashionably attired host greeted them with professional enthusiasm and ushered them past the long line of people waiting to go in, prompting an outbreak of lingering looks and openmouthed stares.

Emily held Sebastian back. "What's the deal with Max and his *wife*?" she whispered.

"They've been married on and off for eighty years."

"On and off?"

"They've separated at least a dozen times, divorced and remarried once. Relationships are difficult if you're unbonded—the knowledge either one of you might bond to someone else at any time is a heavy cross to bear."

They hurried after the others as the host led them up a flight of broad, red-carpeted, open-air stairs and across a rooftop garden furnished with boxy white leather chairs and solid wood cubes serving as tables. At the far end of the garden, he threw open a set of doors, unleashing a rush of cool, conditioned air into the humid night.

Emily followed Sebastian down a long, curved corridor lined with a plush cream carpet, happy to trail at the back of the pack with him.

Holding a fire door open for her, he leaned down and trapped her against it, pushing his body against hers and kissing her neck. "Later."

The single word sent a thrill through her body, but they were moving again before she could respond.

She felt the music before she heard it, the shuddering thump of the beat making the corridor walls vibrate as they made their way to the club's main room.

They had the best spot in the house, directly behind the DJ booth on one of several raised tiers that overlooked the dance floor. There was room to dance, and the horseshoe-shaped seating acted as a barrier to keep other patrons out of their way. She chose a seat between Naomi and Sebastian on the leather bench.

Advertisements for Bulgari, Veuve Clicquot, and Hennessy flashed across a bowed electronic board that wrapped around the upper portion of the room's wall, a taunting visual reminder of the clientele's wealth.

When she spotted a waiter making his way over, she reached for one of the white-and-gold menus on the low central table. Her eyebrows shot up at the prices. *Thirty thousand euros for a bottle of champagne?*

Naomi caught her expression before she could hide it and leaned closer. "It's extortion, isn't it? Can you believe it costs eighty thousand euros just to reserve a table in here?"

"Seriously?"

Naomi nodded, looking pointedly at the older, overweight man on the table next to theirs, who was surrounded by a bevy of attractive young women. She shook her head. "More money than sense."

Emily wanted to ask if Sebastian really liked this kind of thing, if blowing huge sums of money on extravagant nights was something he did often, but she knew he'd be able to hear her despite the pounding dance music and his conversation with the server.

Shortly after, a huge ice bucket with several bottles of champagne arrived.

"I heard you talking to Naomi," he said in her ear as the server filled champagne flutes with the liquid gold. "Don't worry about the cost."

"It's excessive, Sebastian."

"It's one night."

"Exactly. Don't you feel guilty about spending so much?"

He shrugged. "I wanted you to have fun tonight."

"A few beers on the beach would have been plenty of fun."

"You don't like it here?"

She crossed her legs at the ankle and folded her arms around herself. "It's too much."

"Relax. Pretend the champagne costs thirty euros."

"That's *still* expensive."

He laughed, his eyes dancing with amused approval.

An hour later, the club was full, and everyone was dancing. The champagne on the table had been replenished several times. Emily had no idea how much she'd had to drink. As soon as she took a sip, a server refilled her glass. But she was grateful to have the edge taken off her nerves, her inhibitions dampened.

Sebastian and his friends moved like professional dancers, with both precision and natural fluidity. She knew if it weren't for the champagne, she'd be sitting unhappily on the sidelines, feeling too awkward and clumsy to join them.

Naomi and the twins moved rhythmically together like stars in a music video while Audrey and Jean looked like they'd been dance partners for a lifetime—probably had, or perhaps longer—every move anticipated and met with its counterpart. Julien stood at the edges, cool and detached, watching and sipping his drink while Max and Marie sat locked in conversation.

Emily danced with Sebastian, her reservations forgotten, until he stiffened, and surprise widened his eyes. She twisted and followed his gaze. A pale woman with straight white-blond hair, sharp cheekbones, and a wide, cruel mouth stood behind her. Everyone stopped dancing, the tension in the group tangible.

Sebastian pulled Emily behind him, his stance protective, and began speaking to the woman. Emily's human ears couldn't distinguish a single word exchanged over the music. The woman shot her intermittent glares, her face animated and angry, the heat of her expression growing with each of Sebastian's calming gestures.

Turning to Emily, he squeezed her shoulder. "I have to go outside for a minute, okay?"

"Why?"

"I'll explain later. The others will take care of you."

"I don't need taking care of."

"Humor me. Stay close to them. Please?"

She froze, dumbfounded by the sight of Sebastian's retreating figure following the woman, his tall frame cutting a path through the crowd. She began to tremble, anger and disappointment flooding her.

Naomi sashayed over and held out a glass of champagne. Emily knew she'd already had too much, but she felt like she needed it. Had he really just ditched her?

She felt the eyes of the other vampires on her. Audrey leaned toward her, like she wanted to say something, but Jean pulled her back. The twins and Julien exchanged meaningful looks.

Emily turned to Naomi. "Who was that?"

Naomi brought her mouth close to Emily's ear. "That was Marguerite."

Emily searched her memory, certain she'd heard the name before. Recognition began to dawn with a sickening lurch of her stomach as Naomi said, "She's the psycho bitch who turned Sebastian."

15

Emily tried to mask her distress as her fears were confirmed. She forced herself to stop shaking and sipped the champagne before responding. "Sebastian said she was...good to him."

Naomi sat down and gestured for her to do the same. "From what I've heard, she manipulated him for decades. He was young and impressionable when she turned him, and she took full advantage. Sorry, I didn't mean for that to sound condescending. It's different with you. You're bonded."

Emily crossed her legs and gripped the edge of the seat, the sinking feeling refusing to go away. "How old is she?"

"Five hundred, give or take. She's been around a long time, that's why she's so bitter. Five hundred years and still unbonded. That would drive any vampire crazy."

Emily was about to ask what Marguerite wanted with Sebastian when Naomi pointed to her purse.

"Your phone's vibrating."

Emily fished it from her bag, holding her breath and hoping the message was from Sebastian.

Make sure you stay with the others. S

She showed the screen to Naomi, who pulled her to her feet

and guided her back to the group, talking to them all briefly. After a moment, they continued dancing, Jean pouring more drinks for everyone as the twins passed around the freshly filled champagne flutes. Emily didn't miss the way they closed in around her, shifting their positions to form an unbroken barrier.

She tapped Naomi's arm. "What's going on?"

Naomi just shook her head slightly, looking over Emily's shoulder. She followed the vampire's eyes to Sebastian, who approached with Marguerite.

Were they holding hands? She stared in disbelief and then turned away, white-hot anger burning through her.

Audrey caught her murderous scowl and leaned into her. "It's not what you think."

Emily tried to smile but knew it didn't reach her eyes. Sebastian and Marguerite loitered at the edge of the group, Marguerite whispering in his ear. Her hand lingered on his neck, the tips of her fingers stroking and patting his tawny hair like a pet.

Sucking in a breath, Emily rushed between the twins, ignoring their protests as she headed to the exit. Spilling through the roof garden doors on shaky legs, she braced herself against the railing that ran along the perimeter and lifted her face into the sea breeze to stave off tears.

She had to get away—she couldn't face the thought of watching him with Marguerite for another second. But where would she go? Not back to the yacht. For all she knew, Sebastian would invite Marguerite there too. She'd have to find a hotel, somewhere. She could figure out the rest in the morning when her anger stopped bubbling like lava. She shuddered and lurched down the carpeted staircase.

"Don't leave." Jean stood a few feet above her, his eyes luminous in the darkness.

She paused, halfway down the deserted steps, the sounds of revelers enjoying the lavish party wafting on the wind. "I'm not sticking around to watch that."

"You're bonded. No one else exists to him."

"That's not how it looks."

"He's marking her," Jean said.

"What does that mean?"

"He's protecting you by making sure she's not free to strike."

"Wouldn't he be better placed to protect me at *my* side instead of hers?"

"He can preempt any move she might make this way, and it's less likely she'll try anything while she thinks she has his attention. I know that's why he's over there with her because that's what *I* would do to protect Audrey."

"I appreciate you explaining what's going on, Jean, but I can't go back in there. I can't sit and watch them together."

"Tonight was important to him, Emily. He really wanted you to have fun and get to know all of us. He didn't know Marguerite would show up looking for trouble. Please stay for a few more drinks. You can hang out with Audrey, me, and the guys. Naomi will talk to Marguerite, distract her so she's not all over Sebastian in front of you, okay?"

Emily hesitated. She knew that Jean meant to help, that he knew Sebastian well *and* what it meant to be bonded.

"We're not..." She stopped herself, wondering if she was sharing something she ought not to divulge. But she needed Jean's insight, so she continued, "We're not fully bonded. We haven't"—she swallowed—"finished *the fall.* Does that make a difference? Is it possible he might still like her?"

"Absolutely not. You're his world now. Everyone knows that. Marguerite is just territorial, and this has come as a shock to her." A hint of disapproval lined his tone, the implication clear that Sebastian could've delivered the news more gently in the sigh that followed his words. "She's always thought of Sebastian as hers, even after he left her, left France. She never let go. Come back inside. Maybe it will help her accept reality if she sees you together."

He extended a hand, and after a moment, she ascended the steps and took it. He led her back inside, the crowd parting as it had done for Sebastian, everyone looking at Jean's strange cerulean eyes.

Sebastian sat next to Marguerite in the booth, his arm draped over her shoulders. His eyes pleaded with Emily as she assessed Marguerite's features beneath the colored beams of light sweeping over them in a relentless rainbow rhythm. Marguerite's smug expression did nothing to mask the cold glint in her eyes. Turning her back to them, Emily accepted another glass of champagne from Christophe. She tried not to look back, not wanting to give Marguerite the satisfaction, but she couldn't stop herself from glancing over her shoulder every few seconds.

Jean spoke to Naomi, and moments later, she joined Sebastian and Marguerite, engaging the cold-eyed vampire in continuous conversation. Sebastian slipped his arm away while she was distracted, picked up a glass of flame-colored liquid, and knocked it back in one swallow. A server quickly placed another in front of him, and he held the glass loosely between his parted legs, looking wretchedly down at the floor. It wasn't long before Marguerite began squeezing his upper thigh, nudging beneath his arm even as Naomi enthusiastically tried to point something out to her in the crowd. Sebastian's mask slipped back into place, and an artificial smile graced his lips. It might have been an act, and a necessary one at that, but it bruised her heart like a fist.

She didn't feel comfortable dancing—not with Marguerite's critical stare boring into the back of her head—so she sipped her champagne and gazed at the crowded dance floor below. A cute guy around her age smiled up and beckoned for her to come down. She smiled back automatically. Wasn't she supposed to be having fun? She didn't have to skulk helplessly while Sebastian appeased his ex.

Emily was about to go down when she felt Audrey's hand on her back. "She's leaving, thank God." She held Emily in place so she couldn't turn. "No, don't look. It's what she wants. Sebastian is walking her to her car to make sure she goes. Naomi is going with them. It will all be okay now, yes?"

Her heavy French accent leant her an endearing sincerity, and Emily wanted to tell her that everything would be fine, but she couldn't, so she managed only a half smile.

Audrey put her arm around her, hugging her. "It will get better. It can be difficult in the beginning. It was the same for us." She gestured to Jean, who was talking to Julien. "It's so intense, and there's no time to acclimate. But you will both get used to it eventually, and you'll be happy."

"I hope so." Emily couldn't say more, couldn't explain how she felt when the searing pain of what she'd witnessed still burned in her chest.

Audrey bobbed her head in assurance. "You will see. When you are turned, everything will be perfect. Better than perfect, and it will be that way always."

Not wanting to dampen Audrey's spirits or share her decision to remain human without telling Sebastian first, Emily smiled and focused on the crowded dance floor again.

Sebastian encircled her waist with his arms as his lips brushed her ear. "I'm sorry."

She didn't respond, didn't know where to begin.

"Emily?"

"When did you last see her?"

He shifted his weight behind her. "Last summer."

"Have you ever just been friends?"

He dropped his head down onto her shoulder. "We've not been together, not as a couple, since I left France, and that was a long, long time ago."

"But when you see her, things go back to the way they were?" She was guessing, but judging by the way his jaw clenched beside her ear, she wasn't far from the truth. "That's why she's so furious."

"I should have told her about you. We've both had other lovers, of course we have, but I should have told her I was bonded. I didn't think she knew I was in France."

She leaned against him for a moment, so he would know she wasn't mad, before pulling away. "I need a minute."

In the quiet empty bathroom, she noticed her head pounding, her tongue throbbing, thick and dry as the acidic after-bite of the champagne lingered in her mouth. She reapplied her lipstick with an unsteady hand and assessed her face in the mirror. She would never have the kind of terrible beauty Marguerite had. Despite her efforts, she looked unsophisticated and ordinary—pretty rather than striking.

Her hands felt clammy, the snug fit of the high-necked dress stifling. She didn't want to ruin her makeup by splashing water on her face, so she ran the cold tap and held her hands under it until the sobering chill began to sink into her skin.

"Did he take you to the river?"

Emily met Marguerite's glacial blue eyes in the mirror. Gripping the porcelain lip of the sink to keep her arms from shaking, she steeled herself for the coming attack.

Marguerite's lips thinned into a nasty little smile. "Why am I even asking? Of course he took you to the river."

She must have been in her thirties when she became a vampire —she looked older than Sebastian and his friends, her features more defined, a handful of lines beneath her lashes heightening the frosted azure of her eyes, scattered strands of silver among her white-blond hair.

Marguerite took a step closer and sneered. "Nice dress. He likes to make his conquests prettier, turn rag dolls into porcelain marionettes."

Anger incinerated Emily's fear, and she straightened, smiling at Marguerite's reflection. She shut off the tap, reached for a hand towel, and painstakingly dried her hands before turning to face the waiting vampire.

Raising her chin, she met Marguerite's intimidating stare. "Yes, he did take me to the river. We had a wonderful time, thank you for asking."

Marguerite narrowed her eyes. "You think you're special. You're not. You're just one in a long line of distractions. Soon he'll get bored, and he'll remember why there's only been one constant in his life."

"I guess we'll both have to wait for that day then." Alcohol fizzing in her bloodstream, she strode toward the door, pushing past Marguerite.

The vampire shot an arm out in front of her, holding the door shut. "I could end you right now, little rag doll."

The immediacy of the threat kicked Emily's brain out of its champagne haze. "Do you think Sebastian will come back to you if you do? Or do you think he'll turn his back on you permanently?"

Marguerite's nostrils flared. "I can smell exactly what you are." A giggle, girlish and insincere, fell from her mouth as eyes as sharp and cold as ice blades bore into her. "He hasn't even started turning you. I won't have to end you. You're on borrowed time."

"You're wrong." Emily swallowed, her throat slick with champagne bile. "He's on meds, so he won't hurt me."

Vicious incredulity brought out a dimple in Marguerite's cheek. "He hasn't told you." She applauded in affected delight.

"Told me what?"

"If the offer of vampirism is extended to you, you accept *or you die.*"

Emily knew she should bolt for the door now that Marguerite had moved her hand, but curiosity tightened her chest and shook a frightened question loose. "What are you talking about?"

A creeping smile. "Why don't you ask Sebastian?"

Emily could sense Marguerite's power now—the gust of rising predatory excitement. She yanked open the door.

"If you last long enough to hurt him, rag doll, I'll rip your fucking throat out."

Marguerite's threat rang in her ears, drowning out the euphoric rhythm of the club's sound system as she thrust her way through the crowd.

Sebastian was in front of her in a flash. "What happened?" He cupped her jaw in his hands, searching her face with fearful intensity.

She shoved him away and kept walking. Though she sensed him behind her, he didn't shout or try to stop her. She crossed the outdoor terrace, pelted down its broad, red-carpeted stairs, and stopped when she reached the low wall separating the beach from the walkway. She whirled round, tears pricking her eyes, and pushed at his hard chest.

"I'm sorry, Emily. I didn't think she'd come back. Did she hurt you?"

Enraged, she hit out, pounding her fists against his torso. He didn't move, didn't attempt to deflect the blows or restrain her.

"What did she say to you?"

"You trapped me." She backed away as her tears broke free. "When you told me what you were, when you offered to make me like you, you trapped me."

"No, I gave you a choice." Sebastian locked his jaw, cursing his stupidity. Max told him to speak to Marguerite, and he'd chosen not to. Now, she'd doused his woodpile of problems in gasoline and tossed on a lit match.

"Vampirism or a pine box six feet under? Not much of a choice." An accusing glare. "Will you be the one to kill me? Or will it be one of your fanged friends?"

"They had your back tonight, Emily."

"What for? I'm on borrowed time anyway, right?"

His gut twisted at the tears trailing charcoal rivulets down her cheeks. "*We're* on borrowed time, Emily. Both of us."

"You can't die!"

"No, but my mind can shatter into nothing."

"I didn't ask for this. I didn't ask for any of this. You've dragged me into a nightmare." Her voice broke into a sob on the last word, and a couple sitting farther along the wall turned and stared at them.

"We can't talk about this here." He offered her his hand. "Let's go back to the boat."

She ignored his outstretched hand and strode toward the yacht, her heels drumming a hard, angry beat against the paving stones.

The hushed lap of the water met them in the semidarkness of the upper deck. Sebastian slowed his pursuit and considered the least incendiary way to explain things to her. She dropped onto a leather sofa, the lights from other boats throwing a shadowy illumination across her strained features.

He riffled through a chilled drinks cabinet in the corner until he found a bottle of still water. "Do you accept that, sooner or later, I would've had to tell you what I am?"

He unscrewed the cap and held the bottle out to her.

She took it, her eyes no less thunderous. "You could've waited. You could've waited until I was sure of my feelings for you."

He lowered his gaze, not wanting her to read the hurt he knew his eyes would hold. "Are you saying you're not sure if you have feelings for me?" He kept his voice steady, but the question emerged with a telling sluggishness, a painful drag of words that tore at his chest.

"I was going to tell you when we got back to Pine Lakes."

His gaze snapped back up.

She dropped her face into her hands. "I don't want to be like you. I won't leave my mom behind. Not for you, not for anybody or anything."

"You'd still have years left with her—"

"That's not enough!"

"You're both human. That's the best you can hope for regardless. So you have to curtail your relationship by a decade or two? That's nothing!" His voice accelerated into a frustrated yell.

She lifted her head, stony-faced. "It's not what I want, and now because of *you*, I have to give up everything I care about."

He neutralized his expression, pushed the hurt and indignation beneath calm composure, and took a step closer. "No, you don't."

"Marguerite said—"

"It doesn't matter what she said." He thrust his hand through his hair, horrified by the promise he was about to make. "Turning a human without consent is forbidden by the Circle. Normally, the Circle gives a petitioning vampire seven days to expose our existence and convince the chosen human to join us. During that time, the human remains oblivious to the consequences of declining, and the vampire who made the offer is expected to stay close, enforce silence if necessary."

"Enforce silence?"

"If the human talks or refuses the offer, the vampire must kill them. If they won't do it, a Circle assassin is dispatched. If the human talks or changes their mind during the process of turning them, the consequences are the same. Our situation is different because I'm bonded to you. The Circle's edict is that I begin to turn you as soon as possible, with or *without* your consent. We can't force most humans to turn, can't risk creating an immortal who resents us, who might expose us to the world in retaliation. But if you become a vampire, Emily, you will bond to me as I have to you, and nothing else will matter. Everything that tied you to your humanity will seem insignificant. You'll be happy, loyal, devoted."

"That's not what I want," she said, her voice hoarse, face ashen.

"I said I gave you a choice. If you won't accept my offer, I'll do whatever it takes to guard your freedom." He dropped into a crouch that put him at her eye level and held her gaze from his position on the far side of the deck. "During my conscription, I was part of the Circle's elite fighting force—the Primaries. I was the most successful Primary they'd ever had, and by successful, I mean lethal. I led operations that took out thousands of hunters."

He spoke without pride; his perfect strategies and deadly combat techniques were well documented.

"At the end of my quarter century, they invited me to run all their military operations. I declined. Slaughtering misguided humans might be in our best interests, but it's unsettling, extinguishing life after life." He sighed, remembering the blood and shattered bones, head wounds and crushed organs. "I'll agree to take the role in exchange for your freedom."

"How long would you have to do it for?"

He squeezed his eyes shut for several seconds. "I'll be required to guarantee your silence, and I can't be certain they won't assign a team to shadow you anyway, to make sure you don't talk."

"How long." Hard flinty eyes demanded an answer from him.

"Accepting the position means becoming a Circle leader. That kind of power and influence comes with a lifetime obligation."

"You mean the equivalent of a human lifetime?"

"No, I mean eternity."

She paled. "Would I still see you?"

"That would depend on you. I'd have to travel, and my base would be at the headquarters in England."

"What about the bond? Could you manage that much distance?"

"With the meds, I think so."

"There are no other alternatives?"

"None that don't put your mother at risk." He paused while considering it. "We could run, take her with us, find somewhere off the Circle's radar where I could try to keep you both safe. But if they found us, they'd imprison me for my rebellion and execute both of you. And there would still be a chance the hunters could target me, not to mention the risk I could pose to you without the Circle meds if you choose to remain human."

"What if..." She trailed off and took a hopeless sip of water.

He weighed the options again then shook his head. "I don't think you appreciate the ruthlessness of the people you're dealing with, the lengths they'll go to protect and hide our existence. Asking that you remain human in exchange for my service is inconceivable as it is. The only reason they'll even consider it is because bonds are sacrosanct to vampires, and I'm the best weapon they have against the hunters."

"What if they say no?"

"They won't." Silence separated them, heavy and dark, and he hung his head. "I'm sorry I can't offer you a real way out of all this."

"Would you really make those sacrifices, if I asked you to?"

The weight of their bleak future pressed down on him. There was no solution that met both of their needs, but he'd rather suffer than force her into a compromise.

Hearing her get up, the soft sound of her shoes on the carpet, he stood, bracing for a slap, another furious outburst, or worse, silence.

Instead, there was a breath, her hands against his face as she lifted his head, her eyes searching his.

He cupped her face with both hands, traced her lips with his thumb. "There's nothing I wouldn't sacrifice for you. What do I need to do to make you understand? To prove the depth of this?"

Tension loaded with sensual demand wrapped its way around them as she held his gaze. Then her lips met his, and it exploded.

16

SEBASTIAN COULDN'T THINK. THERE WAS ONLY HER—THE PULSING aggression and need behind her kiss, the heady scent of her arousal perfuming the air. He lifted her into his arms, pleasure blinding him as she wound her legs around his waist and pushed herself against his erection. His groan broke their kiss, and she started to grind against him in a determined rhythm that made him shake with desire.

He met her lips again, their tongues tangling in a hot, wet dance, shoved her dress up past her hips, and squeezed her rear, her soft flesh overflowing his greedy fingers.

He dropped them down to the floor and stripped her dress off to reveal black lace underwear and honeydew skin. She leaned back and let him work her panties down her legs with a deliberate slide of his fingers along her skin. He tossed them aside and shed his own clothes in the blink of an eye. He paused, transfixed for a second by the glistening folds between her shamelessly parted legs. His fangs sharpened, and the bond urged him to seize his chance and claim his mate.

There would be time to explore and savor her later. Now they had to *fall*.

He flipped her onto her front, and his eyes became heavy lidded when she instinctively pushed up onto her knees and widened her legs. He kneeled behind her and reached round to shove the cups of her bra down, brushing her exposed nipples with one hand as he used his other to position his length against her moist core. Stifling a moan, he nudged his way inside her, giving her a few seconds to accommodate his width, before surging into her with a smooth, slick movement that took his breath away.

She cried out as she clenched around his full length, arching her back and meeting his thrust, setting a punishing pace that filled the air with the erotic scent of an almost fully formed bond. He pulled her upright against him, his arm encircling her waist as he remained buried deep inside her. With his free hand, he tugged her hair aside, his fangs aching at the sight of her exposed neck. She whimpered, and as he bit, she climaxed, her muscles tightening and releasing around him in an intimate caress. As the rich citrus-copper syrup of her blood hit his tongue, he joined her, his seed rushing into her in a mind-blowing torrent of sensation.

Spent but still hard, he withdrew and released her. She lay on the hard floor and propped herself up on her elbows, her swollen breasts straining and stiff-nippled above the bra cups he'd folded down. He leaned over her and grazed his fangs down her left breast in a deliberate trail. Then he sucked each nipple in turn while circling the other with his fingers. Impatient for more, he popped the clasp on her bra and pulled it away, rubbing his lips over her breasts. Sitting up, she gripped the back of his neck and guided him to suck and nuzzle where she wanted. She sighed when he reclaimed her mouth in a long, gratifying kiss, before he trailed his lips back down her body, between her breasts and along her stomach. He pushed her legs apart and dipped his head to her sex. She gasped, and he groaned with pleasure when he tasted the sweet residue of her orgasm mingled with his own.

This was how she should always taste, like she'd just been claimed by him.

He moved his mouth up to the sensitive little bud beneath her curls and sucked on it until she quivered with need. She pushed at his shoulders, and he let her shove him down onto his back and straddle him. He drank in the sight of her naked body, its delicate curves a siren song to his already overloaded senses.

She hovered over him for a moment, moisture from her wet core dripping out onto his hard, straining tip. Then, switching her position, she turned around and dipped her mouth to his shaft while lifting her sex to his face. Wild with need, he worked his tongue into her, panting as she took him in and out of her mouth with hard, frantic sucks. When she flipped back and lowered herself onto his shaft, pleasure scrubbed his mind until a powerful orgasm gripped them both.

Sebastian was not the choreographed, careful lover Emily had expected. This was unfiltered sex driven by brutal need and guileless instinct. There was no coy flirtation or playful seduction, only a fierce abandon that fused their bodies together in a frighteningly honest union.

Only now, in the aftermath, did he touch her with heart-stopping, reverent fingertips, his gaze one of tender appreciation as he slid in and out of her with a lazy sensuality that made her nerves somersault over and over again.

There were no words in the shadowy darkness, only the ripple of his muscles beneath her hands, the glow of his eyes, his claiming bite, and his sweet penetration of her senses.

Boneless and without coherent thought, she stilled as dawn's violet haze rose across the ocean. Eyes drooping, she let Sebastian drape a throw around her shoulders and carry her into the yacht's bedroom.

He kissed her forehead and laid her on the bed. "Sleep."

When she woke, he sat in an Eames chair opposite the bed,

dressed in dark-blue jeans and a white muscle shirt, his hair disheveled gold perfection that set the panther's eyes he had fixed on her alight with yellow-green flames that burned her soul.

She sat up, holding the throw tight to her chest. "What time is it?"

"A little after eleven." His clipped tone and knitted brows told her he regretted their recklessness as much as she did.

"Last night..." She waited, still clutching the throw, for the fallout.

"Yeah, last night."

"I guess we got caught up in the moment."

"I warned you."

"I know." Her throat tightened. "Sebastian, I know you can't get sick, but do I need to worry about pregnancy?"

"No."

When he didn't elaborate, she pressed him further. "You can't have children?"

He scowled at her. "Only bonded pairs are fertile. As long as you're human, I'm a bonded half."

"You're sure?"

"Pairs are only fertile once a century anyway." He ground out the words as if he would have preferred not to answer her.

"I'm sorry. I needed to check."

Silence.

"Are you mad at me?" she asked.

"Did you change your mind about becoming a vampire?"

She dug her nails into the sheets. "You're asking me to make a forever decision when I've only known you for a few weeks."

He straightened. "Do you think you might change your mind given time?"

"I don't know. I don't think so. You said you would find a way around it."

"And I would've if I wasn't fully bonded to you. Do you honestly think they'll strike a deal now? When all I can see, smell, hear, think about is *you*?"

"But the meds—"

"Don't appear to be strong enough to suppress a full bond."

"Will it settle? Audrey said that in the beginning it's intense, but that it gets better."

"I don't know. I can't think straight." He scrubbed a hand over his face. "I have to meet Pascaline in an hour."

"Will she be able to tell you're fully bonded?" Emily bunched the throw in her hands.

"I'll lie."

"Thank you."

He stalked out of the room without another word.

Pascaline sat at a table outside a seafront café, her usual gray pantsuit and the two little espresso cups in front of her incongruous among the relaxing tourists sipping soft drinks in their shorts and flip-flops.

She rose to greet him, her nostrils flaring as she leaned in to kiss him on first one cheek and then the other. "What have you done?" She recoiled. "You stink of sex. Please tell me she's a vampire and you haven't completed the bond without turning her."

"Don't worry. There's more than one way to satisfy a mate."

Pascaline curled her lip at his vulgar bravado, but she seemed to believe the bond remained incomplete, lifting a rose from the little glass vase on the table and holding it to her nose as she changed the subject. "I negotiated a year with the council leaders."

"Seriously? That's fucking incredible! I could kiss you."

She held out a manicured hand, continuing to twirl the rose in front of her nose with the other. "Please don't."

"Strings?"

"You don't complete the bond, you continue taking the meds, and you submit to weekly medicals."

"Done."

"If at the end of the year she still wishes to remain human, you will become a Circle leader, responsible for military strategy and execution. She will be covertly monitored for the duration of her life to make sure she doesn't talk. If she appears sick or injured, we will intervene. At some stage, we'll need to stop the aging process. We can't afford to have her die of old age. A dead mate will mean you're of no use."

"I understand."

"If she agrees to start the transformation before the year is up, then in deference to the bond, your service will be restricted to one century in your previous role with the Primaries." She laid the rose on the table with a sigh. "Do you think you'll be able to convince her to turn before the year is up?"

He flicked his eyes out to sea, focusing on a boat in the distance. "No, I don't."

"Then I'm sorry I couldn't get you a better deal. I know how you feel about leading the Primaries, why you shunned the Circle's offer the first time round."

"You got me the best deal you could. I'm grateful."

Her eyes scrunched in sympathy. "But you'll be trapped, Sebastian."

He blew out a breath as a bitter smile tugged at his lips. "That's what Emily said—that I'd trapped her."

"Does she have any idea what you're giving up for her?"

He shrugged. "She's young and uncompromising, but I..." His heart swelled with the emotion that invaded his mind and senses during *the fall,* and he couldn't get the words out, couldn't explain how he felt about her.

Pascaline squeezed his hand. "I know. I know."

When Sebastian got back to the yacht, he found Max prowling the sun deck like a caged lion. "What the fuck, Sebastian?"

"I don't need this now." Sebastian kept his head down as he walked past him.

Max's heavy footfalls pounded after him. "The entire boat reeks of bonding. How could you be so stupid?"

Sebastian spun round to glare at him. "Back off, Max."

"You need to start turning her. Right now."

"Pascaline negotiated a deal. I have a year."

"No, you can't risk it." Max's voice rose, panic and disbelief shrilling through his words.

"It's my decision, not yours."

"What did Pascaline say about it?"

"She doesn't know, so you need to keep your mouth shut around Marie. The Circle can't know I'm fully bonded or the deal's off."

"Are you fucking crazy?"

Sebastian ignored him, stalking down to the deck below.

"Sebastian? Are you listening to me?" Max followed him, his protests getting louder. "Fine. You know what? If you won't turn her, I will. Christ knows you'll both thank me in the end."

Sebastian slammed his fist into Max's nose before he had time to think. Max crashed into the drinks' cabinet, and the glass shattered in a glittering burst.

Sebastian was on him again before his friend could stand, beating him with a blind fury that Max couldn't match. Pumped with the protective rage of a newly formed bond, Sebastian struck with unstoppable force.

"Sebastian!" Small hands pulled at his shoulders. "Sebastian, stop!"

Her sugar-lemon scent threaded its way into his nostrils, calming him enough to step away and breathe.

Max stood, wiping blood from his nose with the back of his hand.

Sebastian nudged Emily behind him.

"What's going on?" She tugged on his arm.

Max edged toward him. "Sebastian? You have to listen to me—"

"This conversation is over. Get out."

"You're making a mistake." Max shot him a sad look over his shoulder, shook his head, and lumbered up the steps and out of view.

Sebastian remained tense, his body poised to strike, until Max disappeared.

"What was that about?"

"It doesn't matter."

Emily lifted a brow. "You just pummeled your best friend. It matters."

Sebastian sighed, and she pulled his mouth to hers in a kiss intended to reassure and soothe him.

He pulled away. "Pascaline got us a deal."

"She did? I don't have to become a vampire?"

"No, you don't."

Her eyes moistened with relieved tears. "Sebastian, thank you."

He glared down at her as he nodded in acknowledgement.

"I really am grateful."

"Will you do something for me in return?"

She hesitated, searching the hard olivine of his eyes for a clue to the kind of favor he might want. "What?"

"It's harder than I expected. The full bond, the way it's making me feel." He swallowed. "The Circle has given me a year's grace before my service begins. Will you move in with me? Just until I have to leave? I think it might make it easier to adjust to the bond."

"Okay." A dull ache started in her chest because she hadn't thought about their future beyond remaining human, hadn't grasped that eventually it would mean saying goodbye.

"I know you wanted to stay with your mom."

"I don't want to live with my mom forever, but I can't cut her out of my life completely."

He nodded, and she rested her head against his chest. He wrapped his arms around her, and she absorbed the comforting warmth of him with the kind of appreciation that only came with something finite.

17

EMILY PUSHED HER PLATE AWAY, UNABLE TO FINISH HER SECOND SLICE of chocolate cake. "I'm stuffed."

Heath licked his lips. "I'll finish it."

Something about the suggestion and the closeness it implied made her scrape her chair back from the kitchen table. "If you like."

He took the silver cake fork and offered her a mouthful of frosting. "One more bite?"

She shook her head.

He sucked the frosting from the fork, his eyes on her.

She giggled. "God, only you could make eating cake look dirty."

After working all week and catching up with her mom in the evenings, it felt good to finally have one of her friends over to Sebastian's home. Roxi's departure for college left Emily in a kind of social limbo. She lacked her old enthusiasm for the Pine Lakes party circuit. She simply lost interest without Roxi's cajoling influence, but she needed to have a life beyond Sebastian.

When Heath called, she answered after the first ring, relieved she wasn't adrift and friendless in a town where, sooner or later, people settled down and had families, or left to chase bright lights somewhere else.

Her mother's acceptance of her living with Sebastian caught Emily off guard. She even brought over a box of Emily's things, staying for a coffee so she could cross-examine Sebastian for the first time. He handled the exchange with the kind of smooth social ease to be expected of a 225-year-old vampire, which was a relief considering she'd been walking on eggshells with him ever since *the fall.*

He was volatile. His moods ranged from passionate to downright morose and passing through everything in between, and all the while he watched her, desire burning unchecked in his even, steady stare. The sex was intense, dizzying in its ferocity, crushing in its intimacy—his emotions overwhelming her each time the bond fused their bodies together.

"Are you sure you don't want another bite?"

"I'm watching my figure," she said in mock seriousness—they both knew she never counted calories.

"I don't blame you," he said, looking her up and down. "I like watching your figure too."

"Is this what you studied in college? How to flirt badly?"

"I'm not flirting," he said with an innocent shrug.

The door to the kitchen swung open with a thud, and Max leaned against the frame, his arms folded. "Emily, you need to sign for a delivery."

Max and Sebastian had navigated their way to a grudging reconciliation, the former spending a discomfiting amount of time in the house with them. She knew concern for Sebastian motivated Max, but she wished he'd give them the privacy they needed instead of third-wheeling at every opportunity.

She followed him to the hall. "I didn't hear the doorbell."

"That's because it didn't ring."

"Then why—"

Max jabbed his finger at her. "What do you think you're doing?"

She raised a brow. "Hanging out with my friend. Is that a problem?"

"It will be if Sebastian walks through the door."

"He asked me to move in with him, to make this my home. That means having my friends over."

"*That* is not a friendship. Sebastian is on a knife-edge at the moment. You know that. Hanging out with guys who want to fuck you will push him over."

"Firstly, it's guy—singular—and secondly, that's incredibly offensive."

"But not wrong."

She glared at him and then swept past. Flushed and shaking, she went into the kitchen, ignoring Heath's questioning look. "You want to get a drink somewhere?"

"Sure."

Max disappeared by the time they gathered jackets, cells, and wallets, which was just as well as Heath placed his palms against the hollows of her waist while she fumbled with the front door handle.

"Hands," she snapped.

"Quit being so uptight."

"Quit being so you."

"You used to like my hands on you."

She snorted. "I used to like cheese balls and peanut butter cups too. That doesn't mean they were any good for me."

He scowled, and they strolled across to his car, a new red BMW.

She arched a brow. "Did you rob a bank?"

"No. For your information, I've got a good job."

"Where?"

"At a big international research agency."

"In Pine Lakes?" She shot him a quizzical glance, knowing full well the only international company in the town was McDonalds.

"I work from home."

"Sounds too good to be true." She couldn't quite keep the

resentment out of her tone. Researcher sounded way more promising than waitress. "I hope you get the paycheck you're expecting."

"Jealous?"

She rolled her eyes and got in, pulling the door shut with a soft, expensive thud.

"Why don't we go to my place?"

Heath had never invited her to his home before, and the suggestion caught her off guard. "Are you living with family?"

In the years she'd known him, he never talked about his family, their conversations restricted to jokey flirtation and the shallowest of topics.

"No. I live alone now."

"I don't know if Sebastian would be okay with that."

"Do you need his permission?"

She bit her lip, realizing how hard she tried every day to keep Sebastian calm. It was as if *the fall* had triggered a seismic shift in his personality, bringing a dark, simmering anger to the surface where it shimmered like oil, waiting for a flame to ignite it. She avoided confrontations, diffused and soothed her way through the time they spent together because she couldn't challenge him, couldn't ask any more of him than he was already giving.

Or rather giving up—his freedom for hers, forever.

Yet she resented having to submit to a man—remembering her own mother having to placate and pander to her father—and felt a sickening malaise tighten her throat.

"Well?" Heath put the car in gear.

"Okay." Her croaked reply was a grasping reach for independence, an acceptance of the rebellious heart she always had. But she also knew that it was a betrayal, and as she sat back in her seat, unease began to pulse against her skin.

She expected Heath to have a dingy, small apartment, possibly with a standard-issue, lurking roommate for company, but the vast, bright space made her squint. Skylights set high in the pitched ceiling flooded the wooden floors below with light. The kitchen, dining area, and living room flowed seamlessly into one another, and several doors led off from the main space, presumably to bedrooms and bathrooms. There wasn't a roommate in sight.

"Surprised?" he asked with a touch of conceit.

"Yes."

She wandered into the middle of the room and turned in a slow circle. "Is it another perk of the new job, or do your parents pay for this?" She grinned, waiting for him to tease her about living with her mom for so long.

"They're dead."

Her face fell. "Shit, Heath. I'm sorry. You've never mentioned them before."

"It was a long time ago."

She remembered the first conversation she had with Sebastian about his family, struck by the similarity in Heath's choice of words, although Sebastian's "long time ago" would be many decades more than his.

"Who raised you?"

"I was adopted."

"Do you have siblings?"

"A half brother," he replied tersely.

"You don't get along?"

"We're on different sides."

"Different sides of what?"

He crossed the room to her, leaning in as he replied, "Life. Everything."

"Do you still speak?" She tilted her head back to look up at him.

"We've never really spoken." His eyes twinkled with amusement.

"You always do that."

"Do what?"

"Act like everything is a big joke only you know about."

"You're"—he faltered—"you're the first person I've spoken to about my family in a very long time."

His gaze lingered on her face, and when his eyes fell to her lips, she blushed.

"Are you going to make me a drink? Or did you bring me here under false pretenses?"

He gestured for her to take a seat on the leather sofa and sauntered over to a chrome machine on the kitchen countertop. "Coffee?"

"Perfect."

The smell of fresh coffee hit her, dispelling some of the tension.

"So do you want to talk about it?" Heath set a steaming cup on the low oak table in front of her.

"Talk about what?"

"Him." He dropped down onto the sofa next to her, his long leg brushing hers.

"There's nothing to talk about." Nothing she *could* talk about anyway. She suppressed a sigh, wishing she could discuss her predicament with somebody outside Sebastian's inner circle.

"Can't you see you're on a roller coaster with him?"

"It's complicated."

"Then uncomplicate it."

"I can't."

"Why not?"

She rolled her bottom lip between her teeth, debating how much she could tell him without breaking Sebastian's confidence and landing them both in hot water. "He...he wants to change me."

"Change you how?"

She hesitated before she answered. "To make me more like him."

"And that's not what you want?"

"No."

"Then find a way out."

She reached for the coffee, wrapping her fingers around the

glossy black mug and taking a sip while she processed the direction he pushed their conversation in, the destination he intended to reach.

He picked up his own mug and leaned closer to her. "What are you thinking?"

"You don't know him."

A tight smile coupled with a peculiar look. "I know *exactly* what he is."

She glanced away, hiding her reaction to the irony of that statement because Heath had no idea what Sebastian was. If he knew, he wouldn't be sidling closer to her, tilting her chin up so she'd meet his eyes.

"And I know you," he murmured. His gaze fell to her lips again.

"Don't." She deposited her mug on the table and stood.

He grabbed her hand. "Relax. I won't do anything you don't want me to."

She jerked her fingers free. "I'm not doing this with you. Will you just take me back?"

"What's the matter, Emily? Don't you trust yourself around me?"

Irritation glinted through his flirty provocation. Something had changed. This wasn't Heath being Heath. He wasn't looking to add another name to the long list of conquests he'd accrued during his short stint in Pine Lakes. She crossed her arms and went to the door.

He took in her stance, shook his head, and joined her. "Fine. I can wait. I'll be here when you need me."

"Right now all I need is for you to drive me home."

"Got it." He chucked her under the chin and opened the door, his expression enigmatic and closed.

Dr. Khan listened to Sebastian's heartbeat with a puckered brow, her head inclined, her vampiric hearing tuned into its rhythm. "I need to run some tests. Check the meds are doing what they're supposed to."

Sebastian leaned forward, the metal legs of the chair scraping the floor as his weight shifted. "I've been doubling the dose." He volunteered the information because he wanted her to focus on that, to look for elevated levels of the drug in his system instead of bonding hormones.

The lines between her brows deepened. "You should have spoken to me first."

He nodded, and she headed down the stairs of the three-story house the Circle set up as a makeshift clinic. The secluded property was less than half a mile away from his home and also the permanent base of a dozen Primaries, all prepped and ready to contain him should the need arise. The Circle couldn't risk another vampire-human bonding massacre. Dr. Khan was on call twenty-four hours a day, and this was the first of his scheduled weekly medicals.

He kicked his legs out in front of him and slouched back, trying to look relaxed when she returned with the syringe.

"I'm going to take some blood, have a look at what's going on with you."

He watched the needle go into his arm, the red fluid filling the plastic cylinder. "How long will the results take?"

"Not long. I have everything I need to run the tests here." She withdrew the needle and capped the sample.

He stood and lifted the black leather jacket he'd draped over the chair.

"Actually, would you mind waiting?" She glanced at the clock. "I'd like to go through the results with you, discuss your meds. I'll only be half an hour or so."

He shrugged and dropped back down into the chair. "Sure."

Ninety minutes later, he still sat there, his gaze doing relays between the clock and the door. His phone buzzed when he was halfway between the two for what felt like the thousandth time.

"Pascaline," he answered.

"You lied to me." Her voice chilled him even over the crackling phone line.

He scrubbed his hand over his face, defeat and frustration making it difficult to speak. "I'm sorry. I had to."

"Dr. Khan has reported it. The decision was made quickly, before I had a chance to try to speak on your behalf. Not that it would've done much good this time."

He gripped the phone. "What decision?"

Silence.

"Pascaline!"

"They've taken the deal off the table. Out of respect for the sanctity of bonds, they're giving you a week to convince her to accept your offer. But if at the end she continues to resist, she'll be captured and forced to turn and held in captivity for the duration of her transition."

"They expect me to stand by and watch while they—"

"No, Sebastian. Until her change is complete, you're going to take an unapproved new drug to counter the bond. It's politically sensitive—bond born campaigners are strongly opposed to its development because it should erase the bonding instinct altogether. There are significant risks associated with it, but the Circle needs a guinea pig, and you made yourself the perfect candidate. In addition, as penance for your deceit, at the end of the week, you begin your military service."

"I won't do it." He spat the words, his anger a fist hammering blow after blow against his chest.

"Yes, you will. If you care about her well-being, you'll accept the role as military leader and you'll make a good job of it. Don't try to run. They won't be so lenient if this turns into a manhunt. You know damn well the only reason they're even cutting you this much slack is because you're a valuable asset to them. The second they suspect you're incapable of complying, they'll make an example of you."

He stood and paced the room, trying to think of a way out.

"Don't make a bad situation worse, Sebastian." There was a muffled sound, as if she'd covered the receiver.

"Pascaline?"

"I have to go. I'm being called into an emergency tribunal to determine whether I deliberately misled them about the status of your bond."

His breath caught. "Shit, Pascaline."

"Yeah, shit." She sniffed. "Please, Sebastian. This doesn't just affect you and Emily anymore. My job and my freedom are on the line too."

She hung up without saying goodbye, and he turned at the sound of three sets of footsteps on the stairs.

Dr. Khan stood between two towering Primaries, both of whom had fought and thrived under his command little more than a year ago, and neither of whom would meet his eye now. They were dressed for combat in the force's discreet uniform of black fitted pants, black laced boots, and high-neck black leather jackets with epaulets featuring a single silver circle on one side. It was designed to be durable and to pass for human civilian clothing at the same time. Humans usually mistook battalions of uniformed Primaries for large, unusually clean-cut biker gangs.

"Take a seat, please." She gestured to the chair and shuffled behind her desk, leaving the Primaries to hover by the side.

"Obviously, your blood shows you're fully bonded." She paused, like a teacher prompting a disobedient pupil to confess to a misdemeanor. "How are your moods?"

"I'm managing them." He looked at the floor, determined not to glare at her.

"Sebastian, I need you to be honest with me." She tucked a lock of pixie-cropped black hair behind her ear and fiddled with her pen. "How are your moods?"

He huffed and glared at the ceiling instead of her. "How do you think?"

"I'm altering your medication." She scribbled something in a notebook. "Three tablets a day to be taken at evenly spaced intervals. They'll take a few days to kick in, but when they do, you should feel different—I want you to report any symptoms or changes to me. I'd also recommend frequent feeds. And I need you to wear this." She opened a desk drawer and pulled out a strip of black Lycra fitted with a small rectangular screen, not dissimilar to a watch face, in the middle.

"What's that?"

"A heart monitor. It will send a notification to the Primaries if your heart rate suggests a bond fracture."

"You've got to be kidding me. There are plenty of other reasons for an elevated heart rate."

"No, actually there aren't. Among our kind, emotional distress is the only thing that influences heart rate."

"Emotional distress doesn't mean a bond fracture."

"But it could. So you wear it, or you go into containment. Your choice."

"Fine."

She tapped her pen against the pad. "I understand the Circle leaders have given you a week before she has to turn."

This time he did glare at her. "Yeah, thanks for that, Dr. Khan."

She began rotating the lid on her pen. "I didn't have a choice. The risks to your mental health are too high."

"Can I go now?"

She stood, curling her fingers around the lip of her desk as she leaned on it. "Don't wait until the end of the week. Start turning her now, Sebastian, before this gets any messier."

Sebastian pulled up outside the house as Emily stepped out of a red BMW, the setting sun silhouetting her as she waved to the driver, who looped around the circular driveway and shot past him with a cocky smirk and a spray of gravel.

He got out and slammed his door. "Really?" He stalked toward Emily, who narrowed her eyes in readiness. "You've been with *that* guy?"

"He's my friend."

"A friend who didn't care enough to take you home from a party on the wrong side of town." He was less than a foot away, staring down at her, his chest heaving with unwelcome adrenaline.

"I'm not going to write him off because he screwed up one time." She was infuriatingly calm in the face of his storm, her breathing steady, her stance grounded and firm.

"How about when you were dying alone in a bathroom and he failed to even notice?"

"He didn't know I was in there."

"Because he didn't give a shit where you were."

She recoiled, anger flaring in her eyes. "This is ridiculous. I've known him longer than you. You can't expect me to drop him just because I have a boyfriend now."

"I'm not your boyfriend. I'm your *mate*. You'd do well to remember the difference."

"I don't remember agreeing to give up my friends."

"Well, I'm telling you to give up that one."

"You don't get to tell me what to do." She turned her back on him and began walking to the old Honda Accord parked at the side of the house.

He jumped in front of her. "Where are you going?"

"Get out of my way."

"Not until you tell me where you're going."

She squeezed her hands into white-knuckled fists. "Move."

"Tell me."

She sidestepped him, but he was faster, blocking her path with squared shoulders.

"What is the matter with you, Sebastian?" Her eyes glossed, and her lip quivered. "Can't you see how wrong this is? I want to leave."

He froze, chastened by her sharp words. He hung his head and stepped aside. He couldn't tell her the truth, couldn't shatter her heart with the Circle's edict, with his catastrophic failure to protect her freedom.

Emily stopped her car outside the little house and slumped in her seat. Her hands still shook, adrenaline and fear charging through her bloodstream. For a slow, drawn-out heartbeat, she thought Sebastian might not let her leave.

If he'd forced her to stay, it would've signaled a change. A change that meant she no longer had a say in the course of their relationship. A change that meant she no longer had a say in her own future either.

If he'd forced her to stay, would he have forced her to turn? She shivered and shoved away the memory of Sebastian's rage. She couldn't tolerate the force of his moods or the demands of his bond to her anymore.

She got out of the car, the cracked driveway and tired porch of her home welcoming her with warmth and familiarity.

Her mother answered the door in her uniform. "You don't have to knock, sweetie. This is still your home."

"I lost my key, remember?" Emily forced a smile and embraced her, grateful for the warmth and strength of her arms.

Her mother looked at her, sharp-eyed and inquisitive. "Is everything okay?"

"Do you have time to talk before you leave for work?"

After a quick glance at her watch, her mother pulled the door back in answer.

Curled up on the faded pink sofa that had been the spot for so many conversations with her mother over the years, Emily forced herself to begin. "I had a fight with Sebastian."

"About?"

She sipped the sweet tea her mother had made them both. "He doesn't want me to see Heath."

To her surprise, her mother laughed. "I can't say I blame him."

Emily gawped, stung by her mother's endorsement of Sebastian's behavior.

"Come on, sweetie, you were in love with the guy for years."

"I was not in love with him," she interrupted.

"All right, all right. Had a crush on, whatever you want to call it." A dismissive wave of her hand preceded a sip of tea. "Then all of a sudden you get together with Sebastian and Heath's interested in you."

On cue, her cell started ringing, the screen alight with Heath's name. Wincing, she sent the call to voice mail. "I didn't realize you'd been paying such close attention to the situation."

Her mother's gaze fell to the silenced cell, a knowing half smile shaping her lips. "Mothers don't miss much. Anyway, my point is, can you really blame Sebastian if he feels insecure about you spending time with Heath?"

Insecure. Emily hadn't thought about it like that. She picked at the sofa's piped edge. "I thought... I feel like he's trying to control me, like Dad did with you before he left."

"This isn't the same as that. Your father was trying to make me into someone who met his parents' criteria for a suitable wife. It didn't matter what I did. It was never good enough, and that frustrated him—it frustrated both of us. Sebastian feeling uncomfortable with you seeing Heath... Well, that's because he cares about you."

"I don't want a man telling me what to do." She looked down and picked at the piping some more, realizing with each scrape of her nail that her discomfort had more to do with her relationship with her father than Sebastian.

"Relationships are about compromise," her mother said. "One day you'll need him to give up something important for you. Today he needs you to make a sacrifice for him."

Emily's breath hitched, tea slopping over the sides of her mug as she slammed it down on the coffee table. "I need to go." She gave her mother a quick hug. "Thank you for making me see how stupid I'm being."

"Not stupid. Cautious."

"Love you," she mumbled into her mother's shoulder as she pushed off the sofa and headed for the door.

"Love you too." Her mother's words reached her as she pulled the front door shut behind her and stepped out onto the porch.

"Feel better?"

Her head snapped up at the masculine voice. Warm cinnamon eyes met hers from beside the red BMW parked on the street. "What are you doing here, Heath?"

He crossed the cracked driveway and joined her on the small porch. "Your pet vampire looked pissed when I left, and I was worried about you, so I circled back. When you weren't there and didn't answer your cell, I came here."

A tremor danced up her spine. "What did you call him?"

"*Vampire.*" He watched her with narrowed eyes. "I know, Emily. I've always known."

Speechless, she backed up against the door.

"Don't be scared. I'm here to protect you."

"From what?"

"From him. From vampires in general." He extended a hand toward her. "Will you come with me? There are things I need to show you, things I need to explain."

When she didn't move, he inclined his head, his gaze one of pleading sincerity. "Please, Em. You can trust me."

18

SEBASTIAN SLAMMED THE REFRIGERATOR DOOR SHUT AND TORE INTO another blood bag, hoping to dull the spiking aggression that would no doubt push his heart rate to Dr. Khan–alert levels.

He sucked in his cheeks and swallowed, crumpling the empty bag, indecision paralyzing his ability to do anything other than drink. He wanted to convince Emily to turn. At this point, it wasn't the worst option. But he also clung to the hope that somehow, he could guard her free will and prevent the intervention the Circle had threatened.

Raking a hand through his hair, he strode across the dark kitchen and hallway, reaching the front door as crunching footsteps came to a stop on the doorstep. Pulling open the door, he was faced with two uniformed Primaries.

He waved a dismissive hand. "I know, I know. My heart rate was high, but it's fine now. I'm okay."

"That's not why we're here." The taller of the two held out a photograph. "We were instructed to carry out investigations into all Miss Heart's male associates, to assess whether they posed a threat to your bond."

Sebastian surged forward, and the Primary who spoke took a step back. "You've been spying on her?"

"With respect, that's not the issue." He held up the photograph, forcing Sebastian to look at it.

Heath sat in a dated diner drinking coffee opposite Harry Clark, one of the hunters' most senior members in the US. Harry, who— thanks to the wonder of harvested vampire blood—looked to be in his late twenties when he was in fact in his late two hundreds, grinned at Heath with telling pride.

"They got to Heath? Harry's been mentoring him?"

"Perhaps."

His gaze flicked from the photograph back to the Primary. "You have a different theory?"

"It's possible he's a long-term affiliate."

"But Emily's known him for years. What evidence do you have?"

"Nothing before his arrival in Pine Lakes."

"Meaning?"

"It could just be a routine new identity, that he replaced one he'd outgrown and started again, coincidentally in the same town as your future mate."

"Or they planted him here," said Max, who stood behind Sebastian now. "But how could they possibly predict a bond?"

The Primary passed the photograph to Max. "We really need to speak to Miss Heart."

"She's not here. I'll track her." Sebastian pushed past the Primaries, ready to break into a sprint.

"No." Max gripped his shoulder. "I'll drive. If you track and chase now, the predator will take over. If she's with him, how do you think she'll react to you tearing her friend limb from limb in front of her?"

"It doesn't matter. I need to get to her. It'll be quicker if I run." He shrugged off Max's hand.

"It does matter. He hasn't hurt her so far. There's no reason to think she's in any danger—he doesn't know that we're onto him."

Sebastian ground his teeth and stalked over to Max's car. "Fine. You drive, and I'll direct you along the scent trail."

"We'll follow on foot with the rest of the team," the Primary said as Max got behind the wheel. "Send us the location when you have it."

They pulled out at speed. Sebastian opened the window and leaned out. "Head south."

Max turned a sharp right off the private road, the car's tires spinning in complaint.

"Keep going toward town." Sebastian sat back, confident he had the scent, but heavy with anxiety. "You got anything to drink in here? I need blood, or I'll rip his head off when I get in there."

Max kept his eyes on the road. "There's a flask in the glove compartment."

Sebastian popped it open, pulled out the smooth silver flask, and froze. Piled beneath it lay a logbook, a pair of sunglasses, and a set of keys. A keyring with a plastic-encased photograph held the dull metal keys together. The little girl in the photograph, who beamed up at her mother, couldn't have been more than six or seven, but her smile was unmistakable.

"Can I use your cell?" he asked Max, as the car careened through a stoplight. "I left mine at the house."

Max passed it to him, keeping his eyes on the road. "You think she'll pick up?"

"Maybe." Sebastian hid his fury and fear, scrolling through the call list, then the messages in search of proof.

And there it was—a text message to a nameless contact sent three minutes previously—the two little words wrapped their fingers around his throat and squeezed.

He knows.

Sebastian locked his jaw and buried his emotions, letting the cold strategist in him, the mastermind behind so many bloody victories, come to the fore. "Pull over."

Emily followed Heath up the stairs to his apartment, taking the steps two at a time.

"We don't have a lot of time," he said, shimmying his key in the lock with impatience.

"Why not?"

He flung the door open and ushered her through. "Because they know about me, and your bond means Sebastian can isolate your scent across long distances. He'll track you here."

"So?" She followed him into a bedroom. He collected a laptop, tablet, and a couple of folders off the floor, tossing them all into a gym bag from beneath the bed.

"So I'm a hunter. And they know it."

He pulled open a bedside drawer and grabbed a gun and a set of silver-handled blades from inside.

Emily gaped at him.

"To slow them down," he said, tucking the gun into the back of his jeans' waistband and sliding knives into the sides of his boots and every available pocket. "Come on."

He dashed out into the main living space, pausing by the open front door.

She hovered by the bedroom. "I'm not running. I don't have any reason to fear Sebastian, and as of right now, I have absolutely no reason to trust you."

"We don't have time for this, Emily!" Heath bounced on his toes, then groaned, and reached inside the bag, retrieving a folder. "Fine. I wanted to do this somewhere safe, but if you insist." He strode to the coffee table and laid out image after image with rapid sweeps of his hands. Next came well-thumbed stacks of stapled paper, striped with lines of neon highlighter. "*This* is a reason to fear him."

With several reluctant steps, she joined him, gasping as she looked down at the carefully documented massacre on the table-top. "What is this?"

Heath didn't answer. He didn't need to—the brutal images and highlighted snippets of horror did the talking for him. There were piles of mutilated bodies—rows and rows of men and women with their throats ripped out, limbs and heads torn off, bloodied corpses with broken bones jutting through yellowing skin, entrails glistening like tangled strings of garnets.

She clapped a hand over her mouth, nausea burning in her chest. "Sebastian did this?"

"He orchestrated it. He's smart, detached, ruthless—an excellent soldier and general, I'll give him that." He began gathering up the pictures. "Still want to wait for him to get here?"

She remained where she was, unable to look away from the bloody battlefield Heath methodically arranged on the glass table. "Why?"

"Why what?" He swept the photographs together and stuffed them into his bag with the papers.

"Why did he do it?"

"Does it matter?"

"Yes." She felt her nails bite into her palms and realized she was clenching her fists.

"Fine. I'll talk you through it. But not here." He hefted the bag over his shoulder, clutching the two straps with one hand.

"How long have you been a hunter?"

He glanced at the front door. "Emily, we have to go."

"How. Long."

"They took me in when I was a child. Both of my parents were dead, so they raised me."

"When was that?" Her voice sounded hoarse, her throat tightening with each breath she took.

He dropped the bag and strode over to her, squeezing her nape with gentle fingers. "I promise I'll explain everything, but I can't do it here." He took her hand and tugged.

"No, I'm not going anywhere with you." She jerked her hand free and backed away. "You're not who you said you were. You're a stranger. And a liar."

"Emily, it's still me. Name, age, occupation, none of those things matter. I'm still the same person."

Her mind spun, flashing memories of all her interactions with Heath, searching for inconsistencies. "Why did you come here?"

Before he could answer, a vicious blur sped through the open door and pinned Heath to the far wall. Emily's eyes focused as the movement slowed.

Sebastian's right hand coiled round Heath's neck. His upper lip pulled back in a silent snarl that revealed his fangs like a cobra about to strike. Heath met his stare without flinching, his mouth set in a thin angry line as Sebastian lifted him off the floor, his grip tightening.

She vaulted over the coffee table and pulled at Sebastian's arm. "Stop!"

"He's a hunter." He spat the words without looking away from Heath to meet her pleading stare.

"I know, Sebastian. But you have to stop."

Blinking, he turned his murderous gaze to her with the slow swivel of an apex predator in full control. "Are you working with him?"

"No! Of course not."

He continued to stare in terrifying silence, his clenched jaw hardening and sharpening his features.

"Please, Sebastian. There are things we need to ask him, things we need to know. Things *I* need to know."

He tightened his fingers around Heath's neck.

"Sebastian!" Desperate to get through to him, she cupped his face, knowing she was putting herself between a tiger and its kill, but also knowing she couldn't stand by and watch him squeeze the life out of someone.

She released the breath she held when he loosened his grip and allowed Heath to slide down far enough to plant his feet on the floor.

"Wait." She stilled Sebastian's arm when he moved to release Heath with the wary reluctance of a guard dog. "He has a gun and knives."

Heath shot her a glance laced with incredulity and frustration while Sebastian patted him down with his free hand, pocketing the gun and handing Emily the knives. Unsure what to do with them, she crossed to the coffee table and deposited them on top, the metal clattering against the polished glass.

Sebastian turned to look at her for a long drawn-out moment before stepping back, leaving Heath to crumple to the floor where he spluttered and coughed.

Obligation dragged her to Heath's side to check if he had any injuries, though Sebastian's hurt stare followed her. Satisfied, she returned to the other side of the coffee table and perched on the edge of the sofa, keeping the knives in grabbing distance.

Fifteen feet to her right, Heath struggled to stand and sagged against the wall. Sebastian stood ten feet to the left of him, angled so that both Emily and Heath were in his line of sight.

She grasped the edge of the sofa, the dark-brown leather squeaking beneath her sweaty fingertips. "Heath told me he was raised by hunters."

Sebastian's lip curled. "Did he tell you what he's doing here?"

"No, we were just getting to that. Heath?"

He shook his head and gave a bitter laugh between rasping breaths. "He knows why I'm here."

"To take me down. I've been on the hunters' capture list for twenty years. But that doesn't explain your relationship with her. You were here before me."

Heath's face contorted with undisguised scorn. "And they say you're perceptive."

"Heath." Emily shook her head in warning, unsure of her

ability to restrain Sebastian's impulse to attack a second time. "I'd like to know why you came here too. Why you befriended me."

"It will sound bad. You have to understand, Emily, what he's done, who he is. He has to suffer—he has to pay." He spoke with a quiet bitterness that took Emily's breath away.

Sebastian glowered at him, understanding pinching the corners of his eyes. "You used her. You've found a way to predict bonds and knew that if I bonded I'd be vulnerable."

Heath shot him a snide half smile, his dry, heaving breaths beginning to ease. "Getting warmer, genius."

Emily raised a hand as Sebastian took a step closer to Heath. "Explain."

He straightened, his eyes locking on Sebastian. "You vampires are so ignorant. You think your bonds are a great mystery. We didn't *predict* anything. We studied bonded pairs, found patterns in the DNA of each half of a bonded couple, and searched for a human whose DNA would fit Sebastian's pattern."

"Because vampire-human bonds are more volatile." Emily's breath caught.

Sebastian shook his head, pieces of a decades-old puzzle falling into place. "That's why mates in particular have been hunted." He exhaled. "Not just because they're easier to predict and manipulate, but because you were studying them, figuring out how the bond works. By hunting bonded pairs, you got to do your research and continue to grow your supply line. And the spike in vampire-human bondings over the last twenty years, the atrocities that followed—were you triggering those bonds? Testing your research?"

Emily reached for the knife on the table, closing her fingers around its cool metal handle. "Were you going to hurt me to make him crazy? To make him easier to capture?"

Heath's eyes widened. "No. You were never in any danger. I came here to get to know you, to make sure you were the right choice, that you had the strength of character to cope with a bonded vampire. We didn't set anything in motion until you were old enough to handle it. That's why I went away and came back. We protect human life—we don't destroy it. That's why I'm here now, to make sure *he* doesn't hurt you."

"Some protection." Sebastian eyed Heath with all the contempt of an eagle for a crow.

"Careful, vampire. I've been a hunter for two centuries. I'm good at finding weak spots."

Emily hissed and stood at the revelation of Heath's true age, and Sebastian moved closer, putting himself between her and Heath.

"How do you have my DNA?" He growled the words, and Emily sensed him fighting to stay in control.

Heath sighed. "Because you and I shared just enough DNA for us to figure out the required sequence in your potential mates."

"What are you talking about?" She hadn't seen him move, but Sebastian stood in front of her now, his back touching her left shoulder as he used his body to shield her without blocking her view.

Heath stared at Sebastian, his gaze cold and unwavering. "I was born in a village in the shadow of a great chateau. The hunters took me away when I was a little over a year old, but they made sure I knew who I was, who my parents were, and what had happened to them. What happened to my mother and me."

Emily saw the muscles in Sebastian's back ripple with tension beneath his shirt as Heath continued.

"My mother named me Francois, after my father."

Sebastian stiffened.

"Sebastian, did you know him before?" She studied his profile, registered the disdain lifting his upper lip.

"I think he's saying he's one of my father's bastards."

"Sebastian!" Appalled at his archaic prejudice, she edged away from him, distancing herself from the white-hot rage radiating between the two men. "He's your brother?"

"A *half* brother, perhaps."

"You said all your family died in the fire."

"They did."

"But if he's your brother..."

"He's not anything to me. I can't recall ever seeing him before I met you."

"Let me tell you a story, Emily." Heath's words sounded clipped and tight.

"Save your breath." Sebastian seized Emily's hand. "We're leaving. If I see you again, I'll kill you where you stand."

He'd pulled her to the door by the time she found her voice. "Stop! I want to hear what he has to say."

"No, you don't."

"Have you finally put the pieces together, Sebastian?" Heath's tone chilled her from across the room.

Sebastian's face darkened, his grip on her hand tightening. "Emily, this isn't just about hunters versus vampires. This is personal for him, and that makes him dangerous. I need to get you out of here."

She jerked her hand free. "If you want to leave, then go, but I'm staying." He gave her a withering look, and she forced herself not to shrink beneath the heat of it.

He gritted his teeth. "I'm not leaving you alone with him."

"Then you'll have to hear him out too." She raised her chin defiantly and moved to the sofa with false calm.

Sebastian forced himself not to wrench Emily off the sofa, tightening his fists as he glared across the room at Heath.

The rangy blond began to speak again, his story spilling out of his mouth in a caustic froth that shook his reedy voice.

"I can't remember my mother, but I'm told she was cursed with great beauty. Cursed because nobody working in the Baux-Blosset chateau wanted to catch the Marquis's roving eye. She had the misfortune of becoming one of his favorites, of bearing a son. *Me.*

"She named me after him even though she hated him. She thought the gesture might win his favor, and I suppose, in a way, it did. We were allowed to stay in the servants' quarters at the chateau, which is why we were both there the day it went up in flames."

Sebastian closed his eyes for a second. He knew where the story was going now—the horrible ending it rushed toward.

Heath paced in front of Emily, his head lowered, as if the floor offered a window to the past. "My mother and I were trapped with three other servants by a burning beam that fell from the ceiling. The only other survivor told me what Sebastian did—or rather, what he *didn't* do—as soon as I was old enough to understand."

He jabbed an accusing finger at Sebastian. "Tell her! Tell her how you turned your back on a young mother and a child barely old enough to walk. Tell her how you left us to burn to death so you could run to your own mother's rooms to recover as much jewelry as you could carry. The flames licked the skin from our bodies as the smoke filled our lungs, but you didn't hesitate. All you cared about was salvaging some of your family's wealth before it was too late."

When Heath's story reached its crescendo, Emily put the back of her hand to her mouth. Her shoulders heaved beneath her thin denim jacket, and Sebastian couldn't tell whether she was crying or hyperventilating.

He took an unsteady breath. "That's not why I ran to my mother's rooms." He made himself look Heath in the eye. "You're right. I should have helped you. You were right in front of me, cowering from the flames between us. Flames I could easily have walked through. But I chose to help my mother instead. I went to save her first. I thought I could come back for you."

"But you didn't come back for us, and you didn't save your

mother, did you? Though you did save plenty of her priceless baubles."

Emily's disapproval crawled across his skin like the aftermath of a slap as Heath's words continued to fall around them like bombshells. He could only watch as she paled, her fingers wandering to the green diamond pendant that hung out of sight beneath her dress.

"She wasn't there." His voice sounded small and distant, the echo of roaring flames and screams drowning out his words. "I saw her brooch on a dresser, and I took it. I knew she'd be devastated if she lost it. I grabbed the rest because if any of my family survived, I thought they could trade the jewelry for refuge, shelter, anything."

Keeping Heath in his sights, he went to Emily and reached for her hand. "Please, you have to believe me. I made a terrible choice. I could have helped them, and I chose not to, but I didn't leave them to burn so I could loot for valuables. I left them because I wanted to save my mother and my sisters."

Heath spoke from behind him. "The hunters saved me. They'd come to help the injured and were told there was a child trapped inside. Despite what Sebastian and his kind say about them, they're good people. The organization was established to protect, help, and heal those in need. Before modern medicine, vampire blood was the best cure, the only cure for most injuries and illnesses, so they became vampire hunters, salvaging what they needed to aid their own. They dragged me from the fire, healing my burns and smoke-damaged lungs with a single vial of vampire blood."

Heath's features tightened, and he thrust a finger toward Sebastian again. "The hunters were so busy treating the injured that they let him leave. They said he didn't look back. He left us to die in there even though he could have helped, even though being a vampire made him invulnerable to the flames, even though he knew his blood could heal others."

"It's forbidden." His voice was a whisper, weak and shallow in the wake of Heath's diatribe. "We can't heal humans unless they've accepted an offer to turn."

"Yet you healed her when she was sick."

"She's my mate. I couldn't let her die."

"But you could let a child and countless others die right in front of you."

Emily slipped her hand from his and pushed her palms against her face. He stroked her shoulders, trying to calm her, to remind her that he was more than the two-dimensional monster from Heath's past. He wondered if Heath would take the opportunity to attack him, but he stayed where he was, his blond hair in disarray, brown eyes full of hate.

At last she lifted her head, her shoulders stiffening beneath his fingers. He pulled back and moved to stand a few feet away from her. He braced himself for her rejection, knowing it would seal both their fates and shatter him into a thousand dangerous pieces. Heath's tale played to all her prejudices and moral bias, leaving her swelling with sympathy for him and bristling at the behavior of the cruel aristocrats.

She leveled her eyes at Heath. "Did you spike my drink?"

Heath blinked, opening and closing his mouth before he answered. "It was the only way to move the bonding along. I wouldn't have let you come to any harm."

"She was dying. She almost didn't make it." Sebastian surged forward, his body fighting his brain's fragile restraint.

"I was managing the situation. The dose was measured, just enough to force you to heal her, just enough to make it convincing."

"And if I hadn't?"

"I had the means to help her if necessary." Heath turned pleading eyes toward Emily. "I'm sorry. I did what I had to."

"But he avoided me after that," Emily said.

"It didn't matter. Healing you created a blood bond, and it did what it was supposed to—it amplified your already strong connection. It was only a matter of time before you went looking for each other."

She turned to Sebastian. "Why did you come to Pine Lakes? How did they get you here?"

He swallowed, bile coating his tongue. "Max."

"Max?" Bewildered eyes met his. "Max betrayed you?"

He answered with a single curt nod, unwilling to reveal his corrosive fury in front of the hunter who had been plotting against them from the beginning. "Your keys, the slashed tires... The two of them have been working to force us together from the start."

Heath took a step toward Emily, his palms upturned. "Emily, I truly am sorry for pulling you into this. At first you were just a pawn, a way for us to stop future massacres on the scale you saw in those photographs."

"And a convenient way for you to avenge something that happened two hundred years ago." She stood, a tremor running through her legs.

Heath ignored the reprimand and continued. "But you've come to mean a lot to me, Emily. My feelings for you are genuine, and I only wish we'd met under different circumstances."

Sebastian shot forward. "Your feelings for her?"

A snarl escaped his lips, followed by a low, threatening growl. It didn't matter if Heath, or Francois as he used to call himself, was pumped full of vampire blood and in command of all the artificial strength and virility it bestowed. Sebastian could still break every bone in his body.

Emily placed a warning hand on his arm, easing his tension back to a humming, pulsing menace.

Heath addressed Emily with big, pleading eyes that made Sebastian sick to his stomach. "Emily, I'm admitting all of this because I want you to know that I realize my mistakes. And I'm sorry for everything. But it's different now. In watching over you, I got to really know you. I think it hit me as soon as I saw you again in Pine Lakes, but I was so bent on revenge that I ignored it. You grew up while I was away, and you became...breathtaking. I fell in love with you."

Sebastian tightened his fists, his fangs sharpening as he fought the urge to shut Heath up by mauling his throat.

Emily didn't acknowledge Heath's declaration of love. Instead, she curled her fingers around Sebastian's wrist, anchoring him to her and stopping him from acting on the violent impulses surging within him. "What if he had turned me?"

Heath's wary gaze flicked in Sebastian's direction and then back to Emily. "One of the reasons we chose you was because of your connection with your mother. You were never going to sacrifice that relationship for immortality."

"But if I had, would you have caged me like an animal too?" Fear and betrayal splintered her stuttered words.

"Emily, I'm telling you I want you to be with me."

Sebastian palmed one of the knives. "He was your friend, so I won't hurt him if you don't want me to, but I really think it would be in your best interests to let me finish this now."

Emily shook her head, sending cold shivers through his heart.

"Can't you see what he is?" Heath extended a desperate hand to her. "He's a murderer. You think you can't trust me because I'm a vampire hunter. But I've never taken a life. We capture—we don't kill. And we do it to help others. How many innocent people has he slaughtered? He proved his reckless disregard for life when he left me to burn to death as a child, but do you have any idea how many people he's drunk to death? An aristocrat whose *raison d'être* was excess. You can imagine what his blood lust was like in the beginning." He rounded on Sebastian. "Tell her how many people you drained for the fun of it."

He ground his teeth. "I found control difficult at first. There was no bagged blood in those days—you had to learn restraint while drinking from the source. It was harder for me than most." He turned to Emily. "I've never denied killing."

Heath scoffed. "No, you're actually proud of your Circle victories. Yet *I'm* the bad guy in all of this."

She raised her chin. "You need to leave, Heath, while you still can."

"Emily." Sebastian began to growl a protest, but she silenced him with a tighter grip on his wrist, her fingers biting into his tendons.

Heath moved to within striking distance, bold arrogance lifting his chin as his gaze tilted to Emily. "Come with me."

"That's not happening." Sebastian vibrated with anger at his nerve.

Heath backed toward the door. "Emily."

"*Go.*" Her voice shook, and Heath finally heeded the warning, disappearing through the front door, his footsteps echoing beyond in a rushed thud that faded into nothing.

"You shouldn't have let him go." Sebastian didn't look at her. He feared the revulsion and loathing he'd see in her face, but he needed her to understand how dangerous the hunters were. "There are Primaries on the way, but there's no guarantee they'll catch him."

Emily continued to watch the door. "I don't want them to catch him, Sebastian."

19

"YOU'RE MAKING A MISTAKE." SEBASTIAN STRODE TOWARD THE DOOR, his eyes like wildfire.

He pulled out his cell and tossed calm, cold orders to the Primary on the other end.

For the first time, Emily saw the general Heath warned her about. The ruthless strategist who wiped out human lives. For all the flaws Sebastian owned up to having, he never revealed the true extent of his violent past. The cold detachment that allowed him to suppress his feelings and humanity, to massacre thousands, to walk away from a mother and child surrounded by flames—not to mention the unrestrained blood lust he admitted to indulging as a new vampire.

"We need to leave." He extended a commanding hand to her.

She shook her head, disappointment crushing her windpipe and making each breath hurt. "I'm not coming."

"Emily." He took a step toward her but stopped when she retreated farther into the room.

"You're not—" The heat of his gaze incinerated her thoughts, and she faltered. Bowing her head, she stared down at the floor, unshed tears making a kaleidoscope of her vision. "You're not who I thought you were."

"It wasn't the way he said it was. Wouldn't you choose to save your mother in the same situation?"

She met his incandescent stare. "I'm not just talking about the fire."

"It was a different time. I was a different person. That's not who I am now." Closing his eyes, he took an unsteady breath.

"Isn't it?"

He glared at her. "This is exactly what he wants. You're behaving exactly the way he wants. Can't you see that?"

"Even if I could get past all the things you've done and the fact that you kept the true extent of it from me... There's still the bond. What you feel for me? It was *engineered*. Planned." She wiped the first tear to break ranks with the back of her hand. "It—it's not real. It's forced."

His flawless golden skin became taut, the chiseled cheekbones beneath jutting out in sharp relief. "If you knew how I felt, Emily, there'd be no question of it not being real. There's only one way for you to truly know how it feels, but you won't even consider it."

"It's not what I want."

"You don't want love? Consuming, burning, elevating love?"

She shook her head. "I don't want something that's not freely given."

His sharp, narrowed gaze drove a stake through her heart, holding her in place. "Is *he* what you want?"

She tried to process everything—Sebastian's past, Heath's deception, the complexities of the bond. Silence fell between them, heavy, thick and as cold as a snow drift. Was Heath what she wanted? He had been once. But he'd lied to her, used her as bait, and what she felt for him years ago paled in comparison to her love for Sebastian. She *loved* Sebastian. She knew it in that moment, recognized it with more certainty than she'd ever felt about anything in her life before, and it hurt. Because the hunters had manufactured it all.

She squeezed her eyes shut for a second, trying and failing to stem the flow of tears that rushed free as she opened them again. "I don't want Heath. But I don't want this either."

He flinched, his composure wavering as a muscle in his jaw pulsed. Bracing his arms against the kitchen counter, he gritted his teeth as he began to shake.

"Sebastian?"

"You need to go." A single tear fell onto his cheek, and inky-black swirls spread from his pupils like an oil spill. "Quickly."

Sebastian's body reacted to his heart's anguish, and a terrible change ripped through him. His vampire nature surged, and he couldn't fight it. He felt himself disintegrate.

He began convulsing, the granite countertop cracking beneath his hands.

"Run!" He bit the word out, knowing it would be the last thing he said.

"Run!" He bellowed it this time with all the fury and fear of a wounded animal. He heaved his eyes upward, so she would see the bond fracturing.

"Sebastian?"

He saw the horror in her eyes as she realized his warnings about the dangers of vampire-human bonds had not been exaggerated. The blind terror as she stumbled and fled. He clung to what was left of the crumbling countertop, fighting the awful need to pursue her.

But it was too much. He couldn't fight it.

He would end this for them both.

Emily took the steps three at a time, flying down the stairwell without pause for thought or breath. She threw herself against the exit doors and staggered out into the dark parking lot, whirling round at the sound of screaming tires to her left.

Heath's passenger door swung wide. "Get in!"

She blinked, hesitating though she knew it cost valuable seconds.

"Get in. You're not safe. He'll kill you!"

Still in the grip of paralyzing inertia, she didn't move or speak. Maybe she should go back and talk to him. Maybe it would be safer for everyone if they found a way to live with the bond and Sebastian's dark past.

"Emily!"

Heath's shout jolted her, animating her limbs into numb but rapid motion. She clambered into the car, slammed the door, and fumbled with the seat belt as he floored the gas and shot out onto the road.

Twisting in her seat, she stared at the towering brick building, waiting for Sebastian to burst out in a blur of speed that'd outstrip the car in seconds. But he didn't.

Heath's anxious brown eyes met hers. "It'll be okay. I can keep you safe."

"My mom—"

"I have people watching her. She'll be fine. You're the one he'll come for." He lifted a hand from the wheel. "I need your cell."

"Hang on." She pulled it out of her jacket pocket and fired off a quick text to her mother and Roxi, claiming Sebastian was taking her on vacation again so she'd be out of contact for a while. The lie stiffened her fingers, but she hit send, knowing Heath's open window meant he'd toss the phone as soon as she gave it to him. She watched its trajectory with a stab of disquiet as her only means of communication broke into useless pieces of metal and glass at the side of the road.

They drove through the night without stopping. Heath tried to talk to her, but she couldn't manage more than a few brief, noncommittal responses. He wanted to know what she said to Sebastian, but she wasn't ready to talk about it, and even if she had been, she didn't want to give him the satisfaction of a blow-by-blow account of the heartbreak.

Sebastian was right about one thing—Heath had exactly what he wanted now.

But she couldn't resent him for that. She couldn't blame him for his vendetta. He'd lost his mother because of Sebastian. The people who'd raised him had honed his hatred and anger into a powerful weapon. She couldn't even blame him for dragging her into it. It wasn't personal, even if his lies did feel like razor blades pressing into her skin.

After a while, she drifted off into an exhausted sleep, the monotony of the engine and gentle vibration of the road beneath blocking out her whirling confusion. She woke to a pretty seaside town full of wind-shaped cypress trees and picturesque shops and boutiques. The sun broke free of the horizon and washed away the last of the shadows, but her dark mood remained.

They pulled up outside a white one-story building nestled on a cliff top.

Heath opened her door, but she didn't move. "Is this far enough?"

"No, but being this close to the sea will make it harder for him to track your scent. We should be okay here for a few days."

"And then what?"

"We keep moving."

"When can I see my mom again? And Roxi?"

"I have a team ready to bring Sebastian in. Once he's secure, I'll try to arrange for them to visit you. You'll need a cover story though. The less they know, the safer they'll be."

"From the Circle?"

A curt nod. "They're ruthless, Emily. With everything you know, finding you will be a priority for them."

She sighed, realizing how much Heath compromised her life when he threw her into Sebastian's path. "Are you going to hurt him?"

He shot her a quizzical look. "Are you *worried* about him?"

"I don't want him to get hurt."

Heath folded his arms across his broad chest and watched her with narrowed eyes. "He'll heal, Emily."

"What will your people do with him?"

"We have a facility where we can contain him."

Heath leaned into the car, reaching across her to release her seat belt. He offered his hand, and she took it, stepping out of the car and straightening in the face of the gusting breeze. Waves crashed against the rocks below in hushed explosions of white spray. She smoothed the creased peach dress over her thighs and pulled her denim jacket closed, the hard swell of the green diamond pendant cold against her heart.

Heath waited for her on a little stone path bordered by beach grasses leading to a weathered front door. The similarities between Heath and Sebastian were obvious now. They had the same masculine, sultry mouth, the same shape of eye, though Heath's were warm amber brown rather than the preternatural shade of green Sebastian's had become after he met her. She winced at the memory of his startled expression in the coffee shop when she'd asked him about his eye color, unable to suppress the feeling that she'd crushed something precious.

She swallowed the lump in her throat and crossed the threshold into a lounge with a whitewashed wooden floor. Voile curtains billowed in and out of open windows in the light wind, and laughter spilled out from somewhere farther inside.

"Other hunters." Heath squeezed her shoulder. "Relax. *They're* not the bad guys."

He led her to a dining room where two women and three men in their early to mid twenties ate breakfast. Loaded forkfuls of pancakes and bacon punctuated their animated chatter.

"You're back!" One of the women jumped up and threw her arms around Heath's waist. She was all legs, her heart-shaped face framed by light-brown waves stripped back a few shades on top by the coastal sun.

Heath returned her hug and stepped aside so everyone could see Emily. "I brought someone with me."

Ten pairs of eyes strip-searched Emily. "Hi," she said.

The woman stiffened at her greeting while the others exchanged puzzled looks, but nobody said anything until a stocky strawberry blond with a smattering of stubble cleared his throat. "So things went well?"

Heath glowered at him. "The situation is being monitored. Emily has decided to stay with us until the dust settles."

She bristled. She hadn't decided anything—she'd acted on impulse, taking the only safe route without giving any thought to what she would do next.

Heath ushered her farther into the room and pulled out a chair for her. Did he expect her to make polite conversation with strangers who wanted to capture and imprison the man who, tainted past or not, she loved? Even this artificial, concocted love fueled a protectiveness she failed to reason away.

"You should eat something." Heath lifted a loaded platter from the center of the table, piled pancakes onto a plate, and passed it to her.

She looked at the greasy stack with trepidation but took a seat. "I'm not really hungry."

"Anna is a fantastic cook." He sat down next to her and pushed a knife and fork toward her.

She prodded at the food, her stomach tight with nerves and emotion, while the others conducted a stilted conversation about a storm that was due to hit the following day.

A whispered exchange began between Anna and a short-haired blonde in khakis at the far end of the table.

With a pointed look at them, Heath cleared his throat. "You can speak freely in front of Emily. She's with us now."

He squeezed her knee beneath the table, the contact startling her as much as the suggestion that she was somehow "with" the hunters.

With a lift of her brow, Anna stopped talking.

"Please, go ahead, we'd all like to hear what you have to say."

Pursing her lips, Anna complied. "If she's here, where's Blake?"

"The field unit are in pursuit."

"And when they have him?" Elbows on the table, she steepled her fingers. "He'll need to go down to Level Six, and it's at capacity. We weren't expecting you to bring him in yet. You said she needed more time."

Emily scraped her chair back so she could look at Heath. "More time for what?"

He glared at Anna, who responded with a provocative shrug. "You said we could speak freely."

"You can." He turned to Emily, his cheeks flushed. "More time to see who he really is—that's all."

"What do you want us to do? Relocate some of the others?" Anna asked.

"No, the other levels are overcrowded as it is." He paused, pulling a chunky silver pen from his pocket and tapping it on the table. "The trials are complete. We may as well start phasing."

A smile spread across Anna's suntanned face, two rows of bone-white teeth appearing as she sat back in her chair. "Awesome!"

An icy finger of doubt traced a cold path up Emily's spine, warning her not to question the group though she wanted to know exactly what Heath meant by "phasing."

Excited but meaningless comments, like "time to even the score," and "can't wait to teach the bastards a lesson," frothed around her before settling back down into the stagnant foam of small talk.

Drained and unable to continue with the social niceties, she pushed her chair back with a conversation-stopping screech and stood. "I'm kind of tired. Is there somewhere I can rest for a while?"

"Of course." Heath stood with her and gestured to the door.

He led her to a small bedroom that overlooked the craggy descent down to the rocks below. There was a single bed, a bedside table, and a lamp, and nothing else. The walls were painted the same stark white as the rest of the house, but the sparse furnishings made it feel more like a cell than a guest bedroom.

"The bathroom's down the hall," he said. "I'll check on you in a little while."

In the clean but damp bathroom, she splashed her face with cold water and assessed her pinched, pallid complexion in the mirror above the sink. *Fuck.* What had she done? She'd still been processing everything she'd learned when she turned on Sebastian. She reacted without giving him a chance to explain, spoke her mind without stopping to think first, carelessly triggering the awful mental implosion he'd warned her about. Would the meds counter the bond's choke hold, or would he end up like Astrid? An immortal basket case with no hope of recovery.

She hurried back to her room, blocking further thought by holding her breath and counting, inhaling, and then holding her breath and counting again. A soft tap on the door interrupted her mind-numbing rhythm. She didn't respond.

A moment later, Heath maneuvered his brawny upper body around the door. He came in wordlessly and sat next to her on the edge of the bed, looking at her with resolute warmth.

He reached out and tucked her hair behind her ear, trailing his fingers down her cheek. "You did the right thing."

She didn't have the heart to tell him that it had effectively been Sebastian who ended it and not her. She might have lashed him with her damning words, but she'd been waiting for him to talk her down, to explain away his past, to dismiss her doubts about the legitimacy of the fabricated feelings the hunters set up for them.

Except he hadn't. He shattered right in front of her, like the most fragile glass, and now only the sharp, broken pieces remained.

Hot tears scalded her face, but before she could wipe them away, Heath stopped their descent with three swift kisses to her wet cheeks, and then he pressed his mouth to hers. His lips felt like Sebastian's.

Maddening despair at what she'd thrown away drove her to shove him off her. "What are you doing?"

"This is how it's supposed to be, Emily."

"We're not 'supposed to be' anything."

"You need time. I get it."

"That's not it." She wound a finger through her chain, feeling that it somehow connected her to Sebastian.

Heath seized her hand with a scowl and then tugged the pendant over the top of her dress, his brow crumpling.

"He gave you this."

"You recognize it?"

He ran a finger across the stone's smooth facets. "This is the stone that cost my mother's life."

"I didn't have time to give it back to him."

His mouth set into a hard line. He yanked the chain, breaking the clasp, and pulling it from her neck. He dropped it onto the nightstand. "Well, you can return it when we have him caged."

The thought of hurting Sebastian even more jarred, and with a violent shudder, sharp-edged suspicion broke free.

"What were you waiting for, Heath? The bond was completed in France. Max must have told you that. Sebastian's been vulnerable ever since. Why didn't you tell me the truth as soon as we got back? You could've captured him weeks ago."

Hostile eyes met hers, and with a jolt, she realized he hadn't been waiting at all. He'd begun the final stage of his plan before they'd even completed the bond.

She jumped off the bed with a disbelieving exhale. "The flirting, the touching, all the time you suddenly wanted to spend with me. You wanted me to fall for you. You wanted him to be like Astrid—to lie down and give up so you'd have an easy capture."

He stood with unsettling calm, his movement fluid yet poised, like a stalking leopard. "No, I don't want him to lie down and give up. I want him to *suffer*. It's what he deserves. I grew up without a mother because of him. I've dedicated my life to protecting humans and fighting vampires. I've lost friends, lovers, and family because of his military campaigns. I've suffered enough. I deserve to be happy."

"What are you saying?"

"I chose you, Emily. I chose you for *me*, not him."

"I don't understand."

He seized her hands in his. "We're in love, and that means I get to be happy while he suffers. I don't have to feel guilty about swapping vengeance for happiness because my happiness, *our* happiness, is my vengeance. Every single day of his unending life, I will make sure he knows we're together. That will torment him more than the most excruciating torture ever could."

She extricated her hands from his, wrapping her arms around herself. "But we're not together, Heath. We're not in love. I love Sebastian."

He scoffed. "No, you don't. You think you love him because of the bond, but it's not real. I should know—I created it. Before the bond, you wanted me. That's what was real."

20

Sebastian's eyes began to focus, and inch by inch, he became aware of the beige wall in front of him. He tried to turn his head, to speak, but it was as if he were submerged in resin, conscious but unable to act. He tried harder, straining with all he had, but it was futile.

"Sebastian, you're okay. Try not to struggle. You're here with me in the clinic we set up for you. You've been asleep for a while, so you need to wake up slowly. Take your time."

Dr. Kahn's voice, slow and steady, pulled him farther from the beige wall.

"Vampires don't sleep." He swallowed, his tongue swollen and dry for the first time in two centuries.

"That's right, Sebastian. Vampires don't sleep. That's why we've created new sedatives to help vampires who need to rest."

He blinked, and the beige wall disappeared. Dr. Kahn loomed in front of him. Drawing breath with a rasp, he tried to stand. "Emily..."

"Increase VamSure dose, please." Dr. Kahn continued to stare at him while a man dressed in white scrubs filled a syringe.

"What is that?" He tried to move his arm without success, the limb pinioned to the bed he lay on, the force holding him there invisible and intangible.

"It's just something to help keep you calm, Sebastian."

"Why am I here?"

"What do you remember?"

He closed his eyes and thought for a second. "Heath claiming to be my father's bastard, spewing his own fucked-up version of my past. Emily taking the bait, choosing him over me."

His words sounded oddly monotone, as if someone else said them. He recalled all of it now, recalled how he felt, how he imploded into a violent, unthinking force, snapping bones and tearing limbs off anyone who tried to slow him down. Yet it didn't bother him now. It didn't bother him at all that Emily was out there somewhere playing house with the hunter.

Sure, he wanted to eviscerate the sly bastard when the time was right, but he felt nothing for Emily other than a run-of-the-mill base attraction that was easy to ignore.

"How does that make you feel?"

He shrugged. "Like she's a prize idiot and they deserve each other."

"You don't sound angry."

"I'm not."

"What about the bond? Do you still feel its pull?"

He concentrated. "It's there, but it's not like before. It's irritating but not overwhelming."

"Good, that's good." She checked a monitor in the corner of the room. "Everything looks good. You'll be able to move again soon— we just need to adjust your meds gradually. You'll be here for a couple more days so we can monitor you, but you should be good to go fairly quickly."

"Back into service?"

"That's for Pascaline to discuss with you."

His gaze fell on the austere black uniform hanging on the back of the door. "They don't waste time."

"The hunters have been making alarming progress. They've learned things about our kind even we didn't know."

"You've spoken to Max?"

"He helped bring you in, shared everything he'd learned about the hunters with the Circle. It's the only reason they haven't locked him up."

"Did he share his reasons for betraying me too?"

"I don't know anything about that. You should ask the Assembly."

Twenty-four hours later, he waited with Pascaline, who'd survived her disciplinary hearing, as the Assembly of the Circle began its emergency session. The familiar ageless faces looked at him with him unguarded interest from the velvet cushioned chairs arranged around the board room table. They'd flown in from the Circle's global headquarters in central England, prioritizing this briefing at one of the organization's US offices above all other business.

Alexandra Townsend, a bony British brunette with sharp judgment and a sharper wit, cleared her throat. "Let's get started, shall we?" Nods of consent bobbed up and down around the table. "Firstly, Sebastian, I would like to apologize for the circumstances which have brought you to our ranks. We had hoped you would join us freely—please, believe me when I say obligating you as punishment for your transgression was a last resort for us. We've lost significant ground since you left, and we need your strategic vision if we're to regain it. Your reluctance to accept a position within the Assembly left us with no choice, and frankly, forcing you into the role as penance reminded our subjects that we will enforce our laws. But I apologize, nonetheless, for the severity of our decree —we all apologize."

She looked around the room, where more head bobbing revealed just how desperate they were for his help.

"Actually, on reflection and in light of recent events, I'm more than happy to count myself among your number." He leaned back in his chair. "It's an honor to be offered a place on The Assembly, and any reservations I had about continuing to use force against the hunters have been dismantled by their personal, ruthless targeting of me."

Alexandra nodded. "Their campaign against you would have been uncovered much earlier if we'd had stronger military and intelligence leadership."

"And if Max hadn't been working with them." He shot Alexandra a pointed look, waiting for her to assure him of future sanctions against Max.

"His reasons for helping them were complicated, Sebastian."

"Meaning?"

"They promised him an engineered bond to Marie, and he thought if he could convince you to turn Emily before you completed the bond, you could dodge what your half brother had in mind."

A sigh pushed past his lips at the memory of Max's persistent attempts to persuade him to start turning Emily. "I see."

"He thought you could both win."

"Did they keep their promise?"

She grimaced. "Marie bonded to another vampire a few days ago."

"Shit." He wanted to hold on to his anger at his best friend, but he couldn't help but sympathize with Max's frustration. He'd loved Marie for centuries, and his motives for deceiving Sebastian were understandable, laudable even.

"It's unclear whether they could have manipulated a bond that way. In your case, they found, rather than created, a match. But, Sebastian, according to Max, the hunters have uncovered things about us, our biology and bonding, that we ourselves had no idea about." She placed the palms of her hands on the table. "We can't allow them to continue. You need to finish what you started."

Emily curled her fingers around the mug of sweet tea, trying to banish the chill that had clung to her skin since she'd arrived at the hunters' base a week ago. She slouched in borrowed sweats and a shirt and crept into the living space on silent feet, determined to catch a glimpse of the recording that played on the large TV. The gathered hunters whooped and cheered at the footage for the third time that morning.

She angled her head to take advantage of a gap in the bodies grouped around the back of the sofa and focused on a sliver of screen. A handsome male vampire's fangs extended, his pupils darkened, and then he started to shudder. Rivulets of blood snaked from his eyes, nose, and ears, but he gritted his teeth, his nostrils flaring until he fell to the floor with a choking cry. He convulsed for several awful seconds before he stilled.

"Boom!" Anna exclaimed and rose from the sofa. "One down, two thousand and seventy-one to go."

"Impressive," said the strawberry blond called Noah. "You did that one?"

"Nah. Heath sent a demo so we'd know what to expect."

He rubbed his hands together. "When do we start?"

"Just waiting on the order."

Retching inside at the cruelty of what had to be Heath's "phasing," Emily made herself speak up, tremors shaking her hands. "I'd like to help."

Half a dozen bodies and heads swiveled in surprise.

Emily cleared her throat. "I've seen what they're capable of, experienced it firsthand. I want to be part of this."

Anna arched a brow, her lips curving with grudging approval. "The more hands, the better. Come with me."

Emily left her mug on the window ledge and followed Anna down the hall and through a door that'd always been closed, behind which was an elevator. Anna swiped a lanyard from her pocket over an entry panel, and they squeezed into the tight space.

Emily's heart kicked with each floor they passed. *What was she doing?* She felt compelled to help the trapped vampires, but she didn't have a plan or tough girl smarts—she didn't even fully understand why she wanted, no *needed*, to help them. Her skin crawled around the hunters—she suspected they weren't the benign force they claimed to be. The pleasure they took from their conflict with the vampires was apparent in everything they said and did. They didn't treat the war as a necessary evil the way Sebastian did. They were gleeful in their hatred of vampires, and they relished the prospect of battle and bloodshed.

The elevator doors slid apart to reveal a well-lit subterranean corridor tunneling through the dark rock of the cliffs. The right-hand side was lined with cells.

"It takes a shit load of metal and concrete to contain these bastards." Anna strolled along the corridor and gestured to the evenly sized cells as "Here—take a look." She pulled open a peephole.

Emily placed her eye to the circle of reinforced glass, the scene beyond distorted but no less disturbing. A female vampire in a ragged, bloodstained dress banged her head against the far wall of her cell, a bloody wound appearing and healing in seconds before she repeated the action.

"How long has she been here?"

Anna shrugged. "A century, I guess."

"And you couldn't provide a change of clothes?"

"It's not a fashion show. You go in there, and she'll rip your throat out in a second."

As Emily watched, a metal pole emerged from the wall, its end fashioned into a sharp blade. The vampire didn't flinch as the blade slit her throat, blood gushing out and trickling down into a drain at her feet.

"This is how you harvest the blood?"

"Every hour."

"Why doesn't she fight it?"

"She watched us brutalize her mate. She doesn't care what happens to her as long as she's trapped, but you let her out, and she won't stop until she gets to him."

"Where is he?"

"In a different block. They're part of an experiment looking at the long-term effects of mate separation."

Emily swallowed. "I see."

"There's an even better one over here." She skipped to a cell a few feet away, beckoning for Emily to put her eye to the peephole.

Inside was a dark-haired male vampire with alabaster skin. He bit into his wrist, sucking greedily until he blanched and began to vomit with violent heaves that shook his body, the blood puddling at his feet before slowly sliding down the drain.

Anna laughed. "Killer, isn't it?"

"Is he part of your separation experiment?"

"Oh no. His mate was human. One of our guys coaxed her into bed to see what it would do to him, and *voilà*—this sick little puppy emerged."

Emily wanted to throw up as violently as the vampire had.

"Come on." Anna wandered back to the elevator. "I'll show you the nursery."

The "nursery" was a million miles away from the pastels and teddy bears, cribs and nursing chairs the word alluded to. The cold, cavernous space, every inch as bleak as the prison cells, housed rows of steel troughs set up to contain infants.

"They look helpless, but they're strong. They kept pulling their regular cribs apart, so we had to design these." Anna kicked one of the troughs, rousing an angry cry from its tiny occupant.

Fighting the urge to comfort the wailing baby, Emily followed Anna farther into the space. "There are so many of them. I thought vampires struggled to conceive."

"Focusing our efforts on bonded pairs has proved revelatory for two reasons. First, as you know, it helped us to better understand their weaknesses, and second, in studying the biology of bonded pairs, we discovered a unique quirk in their reproductive systems that makes conception next to impossible in human terms. Their fertile window only appears once every hundred years or so. We fixed it so they're fertile all the time, and they've been breeding like rabbits ever since."

"Why don't they just abstain? I mean, if they know you're going to take their children, why would they carry on reproducing?"

Anna sniggered. "Bonded pairs can't keep their hands off each other. It's disgusting. But you ought to know that." She turned her back on Emily's glare. "Those who try to abstain are forced to watch us terrorize the children we've already taken off them."

"But what's the point in creating more vampires? I thought your whole purpose was to annihilate them."

"This is why." Anna held up the arm of a whimpering infant, revealing a plastic tube full of blood secured to its arm with what looked like several layers of tape. "Harvesting from their spawn is much more efficient than the slash and drain method you saw earlier."

Feeling violent for the first time in her life, Emily fought her desire to knock Anna's teeth out, keeping her fists by her side.

At the far end of the cavern, a man held a wriggling infant, a bottle of blood in his free hand.

"Don't they need milk?" Emily watched as he forced the nipple past its lips.

Anna shook her head and smirked, as if Emily were particularly stupid. "Normally the mother would use her fangs to open her own vein, but they take bottled human blood well enough eventually."

Anna spun in a slow circle in the middle of the cavern, her palms upturned. "This is the future. This is why we can start phasing. With just a couple of breeding pairs, we have a solid, reliable bloodline. An easy-to-harvest, limitless supply. We'll cyclically phase out older, stronger infants and replace them with newborns."

Emily choked back her nausea and pushed shaking hands into the pockets of her sweats. "What do you do with all the blood?"

"We drink it, of course. The more our numbers grow, the more blood we need to keep us fit, healthy, and young."

"I thought you used it to help people?"

"We do. Each of us has brought close friends and family into the fold. We're a community, and we look out for one another. We make a couple of discreet sales each year too—that's what funds all this."

Emily bit down on her tongue as she followed Anna back into the elevator.

"Last stop." Anna waltzed out of the elevator, her ponytail swishing from side to side. "Go ahead, look around. Everyone's locked up tight, so you have nothing to worry about."

Emily took a few reluctant steps forward, loath to observe any more of the hunters' inhumane practices. The screeching grind of metal on rock made her whirl round, her sneakers scraping the uneven floor.

Anna waved from the other side of a heavy-duty barred gate that Emily hadn't noticed as she left the elevator. "Do I look stupid to you? I'm two hundred years old, bitch. I wasn't born yesterday."

"You're making a mistake, Anna," Emily yelled as the other woman strutted away, flipping her the finger as she went.

"Fuck." Emily hissed as the elevator doors slid shut.

Heath would let her out as soon as he found out, but what if Anna hid the truth from him? What if she said Emily left? He could be out there for days, weeks, looking for her while she wasted away down here. Who knew how often they checked on their prisoners? And if he did let her out, how would she hide her disgust for what he'd been doing? How would she conceal her determination to get the vampires out?

A cough sounded from the nearest cell. Emily steeled herself and crept to the cell door and then put her eye to the peephole.

"Is someone there?" A female voice, rich and husky.

"Don't talk to them, Leah. You know it only makes things worse." A male this time, his words clipped with ennui and defeat.

"This one smells different."

"So it's another new recruit."

"No, this one smells...bonded."

"It smells human to me."

Emily took a breath. "I-I am bonded."

"A human bonded to a vampire?" Leah's voice was tinged with urgency this time.

"Yes."

"What's she doing down here?" A male voice from a cell on the opposite row chimed into the conversation. "Shouldn't she be fucking around while her mate goes crazy like all the other human vermin?"

"Is that what they've been doing?" Emily asked, her voice strangled with emotion.

"Lately it is." Leah sighed.

The human Anna mentioned on the other level hadn't been a one-off—Heath had been rehearsing his revenge, practicing his plan and testing its efficacy before setting it into motion with Emily and Sebastian.

"Where's your mate?"

"I don't know." Her voice faltered as her breath caught.

"She betrayed him like all the rest."

The hostile male's judgment tightened her chest. She pulled away from the peephole, crouching on the cold floor as she hung her head and tried not to throw up. "No, it's not that simple."

A scornful laugh before the same voice said, "It never is."

"I need to get to him, but I'm trapped here. I was trapped even before Anna locked that gate."

"Maybe. Maybe not," said Leah's mate, the rich timbre of his voice commanding. "What if we could help each other?"

Emily swallowed. "How?"

"There's a key hanging on the wall behind you."

Emily stood and turned, her gaze locking on the electronic swipe card that hung from a lanyard on a silver hook fixed to the wall.

"The cell keys don't leave the wards," he continued. "You could let us out."

Anna wasn't stupid, though apparently she thought Emily was. The key hung there, like a tempting apple on a tree, because Anna suspected she sympathized with the imprisoned vampires. Anna *wanted* Emily to let them out, to give them the opportunity to be the monsters she despised. When the vampires mauled and murdered Emily, it would eliminate her competition for Heath's attention. Heath wouldn't blame Anna for her death if Emily chose to set the monsters free.

"If I let you out, you'll attack me." She murmured the words but knew they heard.

The two males were silent, but after a few seconds, Leah answered. "I just want my babies back. If you can help me, I'll make sure no harm comes to you."

"*Leah.*" Her mate snarled the rough warning.

"Shut up, Marco. This is our only chance of getting out of here. If you kill her, you'll be playing into Anna's hands."

He growled, a base noise that vibrated with danger.

"We haven't had blood for a long time. He's not usually this aggressive. But I can control him, I promise."

Emily glanced from their cell door to the steel bars in front of her. "Even if I let you out, there's still the gate."

"I think the three of us could move it."

Leah's unspoken request punched fear deep into Emily's gut. She looked at the second cell door and then cast her gaze along the two rows of cells that stretched to the far wall. There must have been at least a hundred on each side. "What about all the others?"

"You'd free us all?" It was the hostile male's voice, only now he sounded surprised.

"What they're doing... It isn't right. I want to free you all. But I don't want to die."

"We'll protect you." His offer rang with sincerity.

Emily closed her eyes and mouthed a silent prayer before striding over to the key. Lifting it off its hook, she approached Leah and Marco's cell on shaking legs and swiped the little plastic square through a black slot. A green light appeared, and she held her breath as she depressed the handle and pulled the door open.

One second, Marco and Leah were in the cell—her slender, pale hand clutching his deep-mocha arm—the next they were behind her, Leah's gaze taking in the space with frantic sweeps from floor to ceiling.

"It's okay." Leah held one hand up in a calming gesture while keeping the other wrapped around Marco's bicep. "We just wanted to get out of there before you changed your mind."

"I wasn't going to change my mind. What they're doing has to stop, and if it c-c-costs..." She took a breath to steady the fearful stammer that shook her words. "If it costs my life, then so be it."

Marco's face softened, his silver eyes warming with determination. "You don't need to fear us. Leah gave you her word. I give you mine as well. We'll keep you safe."

With a nod, Emily headed to the hostile male's cell and swiped the card. The vampire inside was tall with brown hair that curled around his face. His hard blue eyes told her he was unbonded.

Like Leah and Marco, he rushed from the cell in a near-invisible blur of movement. "Thank you."

"You heard our agreement, Simon." Marco gave him a pointed stare.

"I won't bite the hand that fed me." Simon disappeared and then reappeared by the barred gate. "Shall we get this done?"

"What about the others?" Emily ran her fingers over the lanyard while the three vampires pushed at the bars, strain etched on their faces.

Simon shot a skeptical look over his shoulder. "You and Leah get the infants. We'll handle everyone else."

"We'll need help," Emily said. "There are a lot of babies down there."

Leah turned, her expression pained. "How many guards?"

"Just one when I was there."

"Okay. Marco, Simon—free the bonded pairs first. Have them meet us down there. Make sure they understand Emily is under our protection."

With a final heave, the vampires separated the gate from its base, lifting it to rest against the far wall in near silence.

Leah took Emily's hand and led her not to the elevator, but to a narrow stone staircase to its right. "We probably won't have long. They perform checks every thirty minutes."

They hurried down the steps, which had been cut into the rock and were slippery with damp, Leah pulling Emily behind her. When they approached the door on the nursery level, Emily tugged Leah back.

"The guard in there, don't kill him, okay?"

Leah's look burned Emily.

"I know they're monsters, but you don't have to be. I don't want their blood on my hands."

Leah hissed. "I can't stop the others."

Emily nodded in grim acceptance, and Leah reached for the door, vanishing as she crossed the threshold. A millisecond later, the guard was unconscious at Leah's feet, and she turned, taking in the rows of steel troughs before disappearing and reappearing in front of one to Emily's right. Lifting the small infant to her heart, she cradled him, a tear racing toward his upturned face.

Emily leaned over the nearest crib and began removing the tape that held the plastic tube to the infant's arm. "How many babies did they take from you?"

"Three," Leah said. She sniffed the air and dashed to another crib, still cradling the first child as she lifted out a second naked infant. "Our children don't age at the same rate as human babies. Liza is three and Hector is four."

The mewling babies in Leah's arms looked no more than a few months old. "How could they keep them like this? They don't even have blankets."

Emily eased a tube from the arm of the sleeping baby in the crib and then left him and moved onto the next one. "There are so many."

"The others will be here soon. We'll—" Leah fell silent as the lights flickered and then died, plunging them into pitch darkness.

21

EMILY WORKED FASTER TO PLY THE TUBE FROM THE BABY'S ARM. "Does this mean they know what we're doing?"

"I don't think so." Leah's voice tightened with tension. "The dark doesn't hinder our vision, so it'd put them at a disadvantage. We should hurry anyway though. Can you see well enough to carry on?"

Emily felt her way over to the next trough, her fingers brushing the hair of the crying baby inside. "I can manage."

She pulled the tube free and made her way to another trough. When the stairway door rattled, she crouched beside the crib. She couldn't see the vampires who spilled into the room, but she felt them, the air around her stirring as they sped to their babies. Cries of anguished relief rent the air as they were reunited with their tiny offspring. A lullaby of hushed comforting noises and whispered names followed, softening the shadows and brightening the dark.

Emily detached another length of tubing and felt someone lift the unfettered baby.

"Is that all of them?" She projected her voice into the darkness.

"Yes. Time to go." Anxiety clipped Leah's words.

"What about the other vampires?"

"Marco and Simon will have freed everyone on our level by now. They'll tackle the hunters while we get the children out."

"But what about the lower levels?"

"It's too dangerous," said an unfamiliar female voice. "The old ones and the ones whose bonds have been damaged—they're too volatile to let loose."

Emily thought about the male vampire who bit into his own wrist with such heart-piercing melancholy and tensed with the stab of knife-sharp anxiety that carved out the memory of Sebastian's tormented features when she left. "So we just leave them there?"

"The Circle will come for them," said Leah. "We need to go."

Emily felt the other vampires rushing from the room, quiet as moths in the night.

"Emily? Are you coming?"

"Yes."

"Here." Leah pushed a bony, kicking baby into her arms. "Can you carry Hector for me? I have two more to hold, and I don't want them to wriggle free."

Emily held the squirming baby in the crook of her arm, surprised by the strength of his movements. "Which way?"

"Hold on to the back of my shirt."

They made their way up the stairs at a pace that must have been painfully slow for Leah, but she didn't leave Emily behind. When they pushed open the door to the main house, the sudden flare of light made Emily squint. Blood spattered the walls, and thuds and shouts reverberated from all corners of the building.

Leah stayed close as they ran for the front door, racing out into the fresh air beyond. To their right, a group of four male hunters brawled with a lone vampire near to the cliff edge. With a lopsided grin, the vampire dived into the waves below, his shirt flapping in the wind like a victory flag. The hunters turned away in defeat and shifted their focus to Emily and Leah, their mouths set with grim intent.

With an apologetic look, Leah pulled Hector from Emily's arms, squeezing him between the two crying babies she already held. "Run."

The word lingered though Leah had vanished, and Emily broke into a sprint, an angry shout bursting behind her. She bolted to the far side of a parked pickup and squatted for cover. She tried the door handle, cursed when she found it locked, and then peeped around the back of the pickup. The hunters approached the truck. She tensed, ready to sprint to a white van parked farther down the driveway, but something swept her from the ground. The force overwhelmed her so quickly and effortlessly it could only mean one thing—vampire.

The vampire threw her over a shoulder, and she struggled uselessly, the landscape around her blurring with the speed of her attacker's supernatural pace. She focused on the only thing unobscured by the speed of movement and shivered at the sight of her attacker's distinctive white-blond hair.

Marguerite stopped at the back of the van and tossed Emily inside. She landed against a warm body lying face down on the floor. Heath's blood-streaked yellow hair and broad masculine shoulders shook with each rasping breath he took.

"Hello, little rag doll." Marguerite's taunting smile flashed before she slammed the doors shut with a laugh so cold it stung.

Sebastian pulled up outside a tired warehouse on an abandoned industrial complex about an hour's drive from the fallen hunters' base. Marguerite called him a week ago to say she had Emily, but he'd been too busy supervising the US branch of Primaries in their pursuit of the fleeing hunters to respond.

Now that the Primaries had captured or killed the majority of hunters in the area and only the elusive head of the snake remained, he decided to pay Marguerite a visit.

Squinting at the rust-stained cladding that covered the enormous shed, he watched as Marguerite emerged from a little door cut into the side of the building.

"What took you so long?" She strode toward him, irritation pinching her delicate features.

Leaning down, he kissed her on both cheeks. "What did you expect, Marguerite? That I would drop everything? My new meds counteract the bond. I don't need her. I don't even know why you did this."

He neglected to mention the piercing headaches or the black spots that had disrupted his vision since he began the new meds, or the just-manageable nausea that made him want to throw up every time he fed.

"What if I can offer you something better than meds?"

"Such as?"

"Such as no bond to medicate."

He lifted a skeptical brow. "How?"

A satisfied smile curved her lips. "Follow me."

She led him into a lofty space with one narrow, dusty shaft of sunlight falling through a lone window set high in the far wall. In the shadows beneath the window, Emily and Heath sat against a cinder block wall, their arms bound in front of them, Heath's head sagging against his chest.

Emily peered through the half-light at them. "Sebastian!"

She laced his name with relief and joy before casting her eyes down, guilt apparently dampening the surging hope of her exclamation.

He trained his gaze on Marguerite. He didn't care to see the heartbreak and fear on the expressive little face he had loved so deeply. "You should have told me you had him too. I'd have come sooner."

He tilted his head in Heath's direction. "What happened to him?"

Marguerite grinned and licked her lips. "He tastes like you. Cinnamon and whiskey."

"Heal him. I want to hear his explanation."

Marguerite obliged, biting into her wrist and yanking Heath's head back as she held it to his open mouth.

Heath's eyes flew open, and he threw his weight against Marguerite, who chuckled and put him in a choke hold. "Tell him what you told me last time we were alone, sugar-blood."

Marguerite released him from her grip, and he coughed. His gaze slid to Emily. "If I do this, you'll release her?"

Surprise sparked in Emily's eyes, but she said nothing.

Rolling her eyes, Marguerite tossed her silver-white hair over her shoulder. "If it all works out like you say it will."

Lurching to his feet, he squared his shoulders and eyed Sebastian with unreserved hostility. "Like it or not, we're brothers, which means we share enough DNA to bond to the same person." He looked at Emily with a naked longing that made Sebastian's nerves ignite despite the meds. "If I turn, I'll bond to her, and my newer, stronger bond will usurp your established one. It's nature's way of preventing two vampires sharing a bond with the same mate."

Though he knew a handful of born vampire siblings, like the twins Jacques and Christophe, Sebastian could only recall one pair of made vampire siblings, created by a maddened ancient vampire who defied the Circle's restrictions to recreate the long dead family she once cherished. Her two sons were in their twenties when she accepted an offer of vampirism to ward off a debilitating malaise she feared would kill her. After five centuries of pining for them, she stalked two brothers of similar age, each with the same flame-red hair as her sons. After she turned them, the Circle locked her up before the madness drove her to do anything worse. The Assembly gave the brothers a chance to accept their new state, and both proved themselves to be loyal and discreet until they disappeared. Heath had been thorough and ruthless in his revenge research; the siblings must have provided him with all the biological data he needed to find a way to identify a suitable mate for Sebastian based on his own DNA.

An angry flush spread across Emily's face. She glared at all of them as she got to her feet. "I don't want him to bond to me."

"What's the matter, rag doll?" Marguerite pouted. "Isn't he the catch you were hoping for?"

Ignoring them both and focusing on Sebastian, Heath continued, "The amount of time it takes to transition depends on the blood type of the vampire doing the turning." He pointed at Marguerite. "She says every vampire she's ever turned has transitioned in twenty-four hours."

Sebastian confirmed the assertion with a curt nod.

Emily lifted her chin. "Sebastian, I need to speak to you. Alone."

Giggling, Marguerite grabbed her by the neck and backed her against the wall. "Rag doll, didn't anybody explain that you're not calling the shots anymore? He won't jump on your command."

Sebastian watched Marguerite's enjoyment with a weariness that came from decades of witnessing her humiliate and intimidate his girlfriends. With a sigh, he cleared his throat. "Marguerite?"

"I'm having fun, Bastian. Don't be a stick-in-the-mud."

As she began to tighten her fingers, Heath's face darkened. "Let her go, or I won't do it."

Sighing, Marguerite released her and sashayed over to Sebastian.

Voice hoarse, Emily took a defiant step forward. "I said I wanted to speak to you."

Gritting his teeth, he stepped away from Marguerite. "Fine."

"You've got to be joking, Sebastian—" Marguerite's protest died as he fired her a withering look.

He crossed to Emily and loosened the rope binding her wrists so she could shake it off herself. He didn't look at her, but he felt the heat of her eyes on him.

"What are you doing?" Marguerite clutched Emily's wrist.

"Seriously, Marguerite? Are you worried either of them could outrun us?"

"No, but I don't see why we should make them comfortable."

Ignoring her, Sebastian gestured for Emily to follow him outside, unsure why he was giving her this opportunity to explain herself. There was nothing she could say to change his mind. He wanted to be free of the bond once and for all.

Sebastian's detached demeanor sickened Emily. He led her outside without so much as a backward glance, his gait free from tension as he pulled the groaning metal door closed behind her. Squinting in the bright sunlight after days confined to the warehouse, she had to cast her eyes down to the sunbaked orange ground for a few seconds before she could make out her surroundings. She only left the main room in the warehouse to use the grimy bathroom lit by the depressing glow of a single fluorescent ceiling tube.

When she looked up again, Sebastian stood beneath a lone tree in an abandoned lot, its only occupants Marguerite's van and the R8.

She strode across to him, stopping a few feet away, the shade of the canopy casting wind-animated shadows across them both. "I made a mistake, Sebastian. The way I reacted. Everything happened so quickly, and I needed time to work through it all. I didn't intend... I left with Heath because I was afraid."

He watched her without so much as a flicker of emotion, his body still and relaxed, his hands casually suspended by his sides.

"I know leaving with him was unforgiveable, and maybe you hate me now, but I missed you the whole time. If I'd known it was safe to come back, I would have run to you, I swear."

Still he remained where he was, his features impassive.

Confused, she moved closer and reached up to cup the side of his face. "Sebastian?"

He brushed her hand away as if it were a fly. "Is this what you wanted to talk to me about?"

She blinked, startled by his dismissive boredom. Then she noticed his dead eyes, the glowing green now flat and void of feeling. "What's wrong with you?"

"How do you think it is that I'm so calm, Emily? That I'm able to stand here without wanting to separate your head from your neck?"

She balked. "More meds."

"When you left, the bond fractured, and that made me a danger to everyone, especially you. The drugs make it so that I don't care whether you take your next breath or not."

"Tell me how to make things right."

"I want it undone."

"We can fix this. Don't let him bond to me, please. The things he's done..."

He shook his head with an amused smile as he passed her, moving toward the warehouse. "Still so judgmental."

"Wait! Did the others tell you about the weapon?"

He paused, his back to her.

"The hunters have a weapon that can kill vampires. If the others didn't tell you, it's because they didn't know, but I've seen it. I've seen what it can do."

He turned, crossing his arms like an irritated teacher. "If you think lies and fairy tales are going to get you out of this, you're mistaken."

"I'm not lying. They're planning a cull."

He laughed, the rich, chilling notes freezing her heart. "Vampires can't be killed. Try to sprinkle the bullshit with a little truth next time if you want it to sound plausible."

He pulled the squealing warehouse door open for her and waited.

Frustrated at being treated like nothing more than chattel to be passed along and traded at will, she spun on her heel and broke into a run. Dry, orange dirt scraped beneath her feet for less than a second before he took her down, her knees hitting the cracked earth shortly before he pressed her face into the dust. Despite everything, the nearness of him, the heat and weight of his body sent a thrill through her nerves, and she squirmed beneath him, fighting to turn and look at him.

He stood with a disgusted grunt and tugged her wrist. "Get up."

"You need to listen to me." She tried to shake his hand from her arm, but it was useless, and he pulled her inside with rough force, shoving her toward Heath, who lay crumpled on the floor, a thick chain now looped around his neck, tethering him to the wall behind.

Marguerite sauntered out from the shadows to their left, casually wiping blood from her mouth with the back of her hand. "Forgive me, you were taking such a long time I thought I may as well make a start."

"It's done? You've exchanged blood with him?" Sebastian's half smile squeezed Emily's heart, forcing quick shallow breaths from her.

"All that's left to do is wait for him to wake up and bond to her, and then we can finally kill the bitch and drive him mad in the process."

"You promised him you'd release me."

"Is she always so literal?" Marguerite asked Sebastian with a smirk.

"We're not killing her. If this doesn't work, or it wears off or whatever, I don't want to be a bonded vampire with a dead mate."

"She knows too much. You have to kill her."

"Not happening." He gestured to Heath. "Even if this works, the Circle will want him coherent, not mentally broken because his mate's dead."

"But they have drugs now. They could make it so neither of you care if she's dead."

"Again, we don't know what we're doing. We don't know if the meds would be half as effective in the case of a dead mate. All of this is unchartered territory. I'm not tearing up my insurance policy."

Marguerite scowled, ignoring the phone that started ringing in her pocket. "You used to be fun."

With a sigh, she retrieved the phone and flounced toward the door. "Keep an eye on them. The signal is crappy in here."

Emily sank back into her spot against the wall and watched Sebastian take a foil packet from his jacket pocket, drop a pill into his mouth, and swallow.

"What's the matter? Aren't the meds keeping you as numb and dumb as you'd like?"

He met the bitter sharp words with an even stare. "They're keeping you alive."

"It's not too late Sebastian." She got back to her feet, unwilling to plead on her knees. "If you get me out of here before he wakes up, he won't bond to me, and we can find a way to work this out. *Please.*"

"You made your choice."

"No, I said some stupid things, and you lost control. I hadn't *chosen* anything."

"I warned you what would happen."

"*Please,* Sebastian. Haven't I redeemed myself? I freed all those vampires. Doesn't that tell you that I hadn't picked a side? That I hadn't chosen him over you? Sebastian? Sebastian!"

He walked out of the room without bothering to reply or look at her again, leaving her in the shadows with Heath.

22

THE FOLLOWING MORNING, HEATH BEGAN TO STIR. SEBASTIAN TENSED, anticipation sharpening his senses to the hunter's quickening pulse.

Emily sat against the wall with her knees to her chest, her wrists bound again and her head tucked into her legs to hide her face in a futile attempt to avoid eye contact with Heath, to delay the bonding he claimed would happen on his transition.

Heath pushed himself up into a silent crouch, lifted his eyes to Sebastian, and tugged on the chain fastened around his neck. His gaze slid across to Emily, whose body heaved with quick little breaths like those of a trapped rabbit.

"Well?" Marguerite asked, placing a hand on her hip. "Are you going to get on with it?"

Heath's nostrils flared, and the tips of two piercing fangs appeared beneath his upper lip, eliciting a smirk from Marguerite. He ignored her and kneeled beside Emily.

"Ems?" His voice, hushed, soft, and coaxing, slithered toward Emily. "You need to turn around now."

She didn't move.

"Ems, please. I'm not going to make you stay with me. If we do this, you'll be free to go. No more Sebastian, no more me, no more vampires."

"Why would you help me?" Her knees muffled the murmured words.

"Because I understand why you did what you did. You don't have a reason to hate vampires the way I do, so our methods must've seemed barbaric. You have a good heart. That's why I chose you. You didn't deserve any of this, so let me make things right. The Circle will leave you alone after the way you helped those vampires. You'll be free. I'm sure of it."

Marguerite scoffed but said nothing. In truth, Heath was probably right. The Circle would likely repay Emily's act with her freedom, conditional of course on her silence. Sebastian didn't care either way. He just wanted the bond gone so he could feel like himself again. He couldn't understand why she hesitated, why she clung to their broken bond when it had brought them nothing but problems.

"Emily?" Heath placed a tentative hand on her shoulder, and she turned, her eyes downcast, her cheeks glistening with tears.

She looked up and met his brother's gaze.

Sebastian sucked in a breath.

Marguerite seized his hand.

But the relief he hoped for didn't come.

He felt no flood of release, no emotional shift or physical change, only a surprising sadness, a sense of absence and loss.

"Did it work?" Marguerite stepped in front of Sebastian and studied his eyes.

"You tell me."

Her mouth twisted in fury. "His eyes are the same!" She whirled round, pointing at Heath. "You lied."

Heath turned away from Emily, proving Marguerite wrong with his intimidating green-eyed stare.

"Perfect. Now you're both bonded to her."

"Do you feel like you're still bonded?" Heath asked Sebastian, those new fangs still jutting over his lower lip in warning.

"No."

"Then it's done. I kept up my end of the bargain. Untie her."

Reluctant to take Heath at his word, Sebastian crossed his arms. "We can't do that. I have no guarantee that this has worked, or what effects it may have in the long term. She stays here. You both do."

Emily swore at him as she got to her feet, and Heath roared beside her, the untamed emotions of a new vampire evident in his primal behavior. He lunged, and with the lightning speed and strength his transition afforded him, he broke the chain.

Emily somehow anticipated Heath's movement and sprang in front of him, falling into his arms before collapsing on the hard concrete floor with a smack.

Heath dropped to her side, pulling at his hair. "Fuck! No, no, no. Fuck! Do something!"

Sebastian moved closer and saw a little silver pen lying on the floor for the first time. Kneeling beside Emily, he plucked a dart made from the same dull silver from her chest and realized with a stabbing pain in his heart that she hadn't lied about the weapon.

"What is this?" he asked Heath with a growl. "What's in it?"

"I don't know. Toxins, enough to kill a vampire in seconds."

"Is it lethal to humans too?"

"I don't know! It took our scientists years to come up with a concoction that worked. Fuck knows what they put together to do it." He tore at his hair again.

"Can you contact them?"

"They'll be off grid after everything that's happened."

Sebastian bit into his wrist, then reached for his cell with his other hand, and dialed for a Circle medical team.

"What are you doing?" Marguerite pulled at his arm. "You don't need her. It's better this way."

He shook her off, pressing his wrist to Emily's mouth. "She just took a bullet for me."

The call connected, but Heath rushed him, knocking him onto his back as he barked a request for a Circle medical team. He shoved Heath away with a curse, and the cell flew from his hand.

"Don't do that!" Heath shouted.

Marguerite circled, looking for a way to restrain him.

Heath put himself between Sebastian and Emily. "Don't give her your blood. The toxin is deadly to vampires. Your blood in her system could make things worse."

Heath wiped at the blood on Emily's lips with his sleeve.

Marguerite pounced, landing a flying kick to his head. Heath roared again, fury darkening his pupils before he charged. His body hit Marguerite's with pounding force, and she arced into the air and landed with a crack.

Sebastian darted back to Emily's side and began checking her vitals.

Marguerite flipped up and spat blood. "Why are you trying to help her, Sebastian?"

She threw Heath against the wall with a scream.

"Because it's the right thing to do." The lie stung as it left his lips.

He didn't have a newly acquired conscience.

The bond *had* gone, dissolved into nothing as if it'd never been there at all, and without it, without the confusing pull and whispering torment that the meds only partially suppressed, he could finally think and feel without prejudice.

And what he felt as he looked down at Emily, ashen and fighting for breath, was love.

Not the obsessive, bruising love of the bond, but the nurturing, tender love that crept in behind it, unnoticed and unaffected by everything that had happened.

"I think she's waking up."

Sebastian's somber words drifted through the fog around Emily, focusing her on a direction instead of the swirling nothingness she couldn't seem to see past.

She tried to say his name, to ask him to speak again, but only succeeded in pushing a croak past her dry lips. She heard a female voice and felt slender but strong arms support her as she tried to push herself up, the nylon of what she realized must be a hospital gown rubbing against her skin. She dragged her eyelids open and took in a beige-walled hospital room, unremarkable apart from the metal chains that hung from the ceiling above a table laden with a variety of other restraints.

"It's okay," the female voice said. "Those aren't for you. You're in a Circle medical center. We rarely treat physical conditions. The restraints are for vampires suffering from fractured or stressed mate bonds. We have to chain them until we can stabilize them."

"Is Sebastian here?" The dry rasp of her throat forced her to cough, and the woman came to stand in front of her, holding out a glass of water. Emily took it with shaking hands and drank it down in one large swallow.

The woman took the glass and refilled it at a sink in the corner. "I'm sorry. We're not used to human patients. I should have considered dehydration." She handed Emily the glass with a smile. "In answer to your question, Sebastian was here. He hasn't left your side until now."

Emily gripped the glass with stiff fingers, hardly daring to believe what Heath and Marguerite set in motion could have failed. If Sebastian was here, did it mean the bond survived? Did it mean he'd forgiven her?

"The bond is still intact?"

The woman tilted her head, her short black hair glinting white beneath the overhead lights. "I'm Dr. Kahn. I've been monitoring Sebastian since he bonded to you, supplying the meds he needed." She sighed. "I can't say with a hundred percent certainty whether the bond you shared has been dissolved or not, but there are physical and mental signs that it's no longer in play."

Emily tried to ignore the rush of disappointment. "If I share a bond with Heath now, does that mean I'm going to feel about him the way I feel—" Her cheeks heated at the slip. "I mean, felt about Sebastian?"

"Sebastian asked me a similar question," Dr. Khan said with a knowing smile. "I think you've both been overestimating the influence of the bond on humans. From what I can gather, even the hunters thought bonds shaped human feelings and behavior to an extent. Our latest research shows its impact on human emotions is negligible. In short, what you felt for Sebastian is, well, what you felt for Sebastian."

"Oh." Emily tried to process Dr. Khan's statement. All this time, she thought her love for Sebastian was a by-product of the hunters' scheme, a kind of biological manipulation that produced simulated emotions. Even before Heath's revelation, deep down, she always suspected the bond drove her unrelenting attraction to Sebastian. He'd said as much, and why else would she have abandoned her rules and her dignity so readily?

While they were apart, despite believing the bond controlled her feelings, she concluded she wanted Sebastian anyway. Now that she knew she felt real love, everything looked different to her. Every conversation, every touch, every conflict. She'd truly loved Sebastian all along.

"How do you feel physically?" Dr. Khan asked.

"Tired." Emily's stomach growled. "And hungry, I guess."

Dr. Khan flushed. "Please accept my apologies, again. I'll have some food brought to you."

"Dr. Khan, can I ask you a question? If I become a vampire one day, will that mean I bond to Heath?"

"Only if you're right in front of him, close enough to look into his eyes, and I don't see any reason for that to happen, do you?"

Emily shook her head, ignoring the twist of pity she felt for Heath.

"Is turning an option for you? It would certainly make things more straightforward for the Circle. The pardon they've given you for declining Sebastian's offer is unprecedented and unpopular among some factions."

Emily tensed at the thought of the Circle's reaction if she hadn't saved all those vampires at the base. "I don't think so, but maybe one day."

Dr. Khan nodded.

"When can I leave?"

"You should be fine in a day or two. You've been incredibly lucky. Beyond the injury to your sternum, the dart doesn't appear to have harmed you. Looking at what it contains, if it hit Sebastian, or any other vampire, I have no doubt it would prove fatal."

Emily squeezed her eyes shut for a moment, recalling the convulsing vampire in the hunters' video footage of the drug at work.

"Can I go home?" She pictured her house, her mom sitting on the faded sofa sipping tea, and a fearful nostalgia rippled along her nerves. She longed to see her mother. She even missed Pine Lakes, though she couldn't imagine slotting back into her old life—her job, the parties, the small town—without feeling the crushing absence of Sebastian.

"I think there are some security issues you need to resolve with the Circle first."

"Oh." She fisted the bedsheets in a thick twist of fabric.

"Don't worry. After what you did, they're not going to lock you up and throw away the key." Sebastian leaned against the doorframe in an austere black jacket with military epaulets and a high collar.

His full lips didn't curve into the smile she loved, but a new playfulness lit his eyes. His brown eyes.

Dr. Kahn approached him, and he stepped aside to let her pass. "I'll be down the hall if you need me."

Emily pulled the starched sheet higher, awkwardness tautening her body when Sebastian sat on a plastic chair beside her bed. "How long have I been here?"

He leaned toward her, his forearms resting on his knees. "Less than twenty-four hours. I didn't know where else to take you."

He stared at her, his warm caramel eyes hardening. "You shouldn't have saved me. It was fucking stupid, and I didn't deserve your help."

She flinched at the reprimand. "You could just say thank you."

To her surprise, he reached out and took her hand in both of his. "Thank you."

She held his gaze, and heat began to curl its way up her spine. "Your eyes changed back."

"Yeah." He released her hand, his fingertips brushing hers as he moved. "I owe you an apology, a thousand apologies, for the way I behaved. I couldn't think straight. The bond clouded everything, and the meds might have kept my impulses in check, but they made me numb. I didn't care about anything or anyone. I'm sorry, Emily, for all of it."

"It was my fault you ended up like that."

"No, it wasn't. You didn't ask for any of this. You got stuck in the middle of a war, used as a weapon in a centuries-old vendetta. None of this was your fault."

"But if I'd listened to you—"

"You'd have been stuck in a relationship that wasn't right for you. That wasn't right for either of us."

She tried to swallow the pain that tightened her throat. The bond was gone, and with it, any feelings Sebastian had for her. Pursing her lips, she attempted to push out the truth—that he was perfect for her. From the beginning, she'd let her relationships with other men cloud her judgment, first equating Sebastian's wealth with her father's cruelty and then allowing Heath to poison her perception of him. But she couldn't speak, couldn't risk baring her soul only to be rejected, couldn't chance the humiliation and the pain.

He steepled his fingers, resting his elbows on his knees. "I'm not just here to apologize. The Circle's council have asked me to put an offer to you."

"I thought I was free to go."

"You are. But they'd like your help, if you're willing to give it."

"My help?" Her voice rose on a note of incredulity. How could she help a collective of centuries-old vampires?

"They'd like you to work with them, as a consultant."

"I don't follow."

"The hunters operate globally, Emily. The US arm has taken a hit, but there are networks all over the world. We're focusing on Europe next, and we want you to help us. It would mean moving to England initially, and there would be a lot of travel..."

"Would I be working with you?" Hope sparked in her chest, kicking her breathing up a notch.

"No. I'll be on the front line with the Primaries. Our paths may cross occasionally, but we won't be working together."

The little spark of hope turned into an ashen ember that lodged in her throat. "I don't need a pity job offer, Sebastian."

"The Circle doesn't do pity, Emily. Trust me. You'll be well remunerated for your assistance."

"Did you put them up to this? Because you feel guilty?"

"No." He paused, his brown eyes scrutinizing her. "They want your insight. You were inside a base, listening to their conversations, watching their movements. You probably saw and heard things you didn't even realize were significant. The Circle wants that information, and they want your take on intel they have on other operations around the world."

"What happened to Heath?" The question popped out before she could stop it.

Sebastian dropped his hands and straightened. "The Circle

wants Heath alive, for now anyway. We're already close to replicating the hunters' toxins, but Heath has too much information for us to consider executing him yet."

"I wouldn't wish him dead."

Dark-gold lashes descended, shuttering his eyes as he stared at the floor between his legs. "I understand. You have feelings for him."

Afraid to explain that the man she had feelings for was sitting right beside her, she shrugged. She didn't wish Heath harm because despite everything, she knew he loved her, and she appreciated the sacrifice he'd made in exchange for the promise of her freedom. She didn't feel the kind of aching need she felt for Sebastian, a desire and love so intense it paralyzed her. But she'd already pleaded with him for another chance at the warehouse. Her pride wouldn't allow her to do it again, and for him, there could be no point in a relationship without a bond. He wouldn't want to end up like Max.

"I need to go back home. I haven't seen or spoken to my mom in weeks. She must be frantic."

His mouth twisted in irritation before resettling into an impassive line. "You can explain you have a job offer over the phone. If you go back there, we both know you won't leave."

"Pine Lakes is my home."

He stood, towering over her for a second. "Will you at least think about it?"

"All right."

To her surprise, he bent and dropped a swift kiss on her forehead before heading for the door.

"Get some rest, Emily," he said without looking back.

The shady roads on the outskirts of Pine Lakes sent Sebastian's heart skittering into memories of him and Emily. She shuffled next to him in the peach sundress she'd been wearing when she left, the small bag he'd retrieved with it from the hunters' base resting in her lap. Her gaze tracked the blur of trees beyond the car window, and he had to stop himself from reaching for her hand.

He shifted up a gear, trying to shake off the echo of attraction. The bond had gone, so why did he feel so...*drawn*?

He couldn't stick around to find out. He respected her choice. Home and family had always been more important to her than anything else, and he couldn't stay in Pine Lakes. Even if he shirked his Circle obligations, the hunters knew about his connection to the town. The only way for them to be together would be for Emily to leave everything behind, and she would never do that, so why bother even trying to explain his feelings to her? It wouldn't change anything.

"Are you okay?" She looked pointedly at him drumming his fingers against the wheel.

"It's just this place."

"Brings back bad memories."

"Highs and lows."

"For me too."

"Then why are you so attached to it?"

She nibbled her lip and turned back to the window without answering. Anger licked at his heart like a flame. She'd clung to her past from the beginning, letting childhood hurts and prejudices act as obstacles to their future. If she'd agreed to turn, would they be happily bonded now? Traveling? Living at the chateau? Enjoying life together? She'd rather stay here, in this backwater, to protect a mother who didn't need her and to agitate a father who wanted her gone, than pursue her own dreams and desires.

He glared at the road ahead as the trees began to thin and the town started to sprawl in an unappealing swirl of concrete and steel. After another minute of agonizing silence, he turned onto Emily's street. The car slid to a stop by her tired front yard. He left the engine idling and turned to her.

"Don't speak to anybody about what you know. Don't mention vampires, hunters, or the Circle. If anyone asks about me, you tell them it didn't work out and I moved away to pursue business interests in Europe. I'm sure I don't need to explain the consequences of any slips—the Circle would be swift and ruthless in their response."

"Sebastian..."

"If you change your mind about the job, call this number."

She took the stiff white card from him. "Is that your number?"

"No. Tell the operator your name, and he'll connect you to the right person."

Sighing, she slipped the card into her pocket and unfastened her seat belt.

He moved faster than her, exiting the car and opening her door before she could do it herself.

A half smile curved her lips as she accepted his extended hand. "Always such perfect manners."

He ignored the compliment, bowing his head formally as he released her hand. "Goodbye, Emily."

"Goodbye, Sebastian."

She threw her arms around his neck in a tight hug that crushed what was left of his heart to dust.

She waited on the little porch while he got back in the car and then raised her hand in a final wave before he pulled away.

He watched her retreating figure in the rearview mirror, ignoring the stinging in his eyes and the sickening ache in his gut. They were both finally free from the bond's stranglehold, free to make the choices that were right for them. Emily had made hers without regret or hesitation, and he had to accept that.

Emily lingered on the doorstep. Sebastian's courtesy, his cool, polite façade as he'd said goodbye, hurt. She preferred the medicated cruelty he'd shown her at the warehouse to the unaffected amber eyes that'd just studied her with nothing more than reserved interest. The door clattered open behind her, preventing her from dwelling on the pain of his departure.

"Emily?" Her mother's arms closed around her in a familiar welcome. "I didn't know you were coming back. How was your trip?"

"Eventful." She couldn't help but smile at her mother, who bounced on her heels in delight.

"It's over, Mom. Sebastian and I... It didn't work out."

"Ems, I'm so sorry. You should've called."

"I lost my phone."

"Come inside. I'll make you some tea before I go to work."

"Thanks, Mom." Emily leaned into her mother's side, grateful for the warmth and acceptance.

"Roxi, look who just showed up."

"Roxi's here?" Emily crossed the threshold, her gaze landing on the faded pink sofa occupied by a semirecumbent brunette leafing through a glossy magazine.

"Ems!" Roxi bounded up to her, squeezing her in a hug that she reciprocated with equal vigor.

"Would you like another soda, Roxi?" Emily's mother called from the kitchen.

"Yes, please, Mrs. Heart."

Emily dropped onto the misshapen old sofa. "What are you doing here? Shouldn't you be in college?"

"Grad school was kind of boring." Roxi flopped down next to her. "I decided I'd rather be back here with you. Imagine my disappointment when your mom said you'd run off with your new boyfriend."

"Firstly, he's no longer my boyfriend, and secondly, I didn't exactly 'run off.' That aside, why would you drop out? Have you even got a job here?"

"I'll find something. I'm not in a hurry."

"Rox, good jobs aren't exactly easy to come by in Pine Lakes."

"Would you stop being such a downer? I'm back, you're back, so we should make plans for tonight."

Emily's mother bustled in with a cup of tea and a can of soda.

"Thanks, Mom."

"I'll see you after my shift?"

"I'll be here."

"Good. I've missed you."

"Me too," said Roxi, already scouring her socials. "So there's a party over on the other side of town later…"

23

EMILY RUMMAGED IN THE TOP DRAWER OF HER DRESSER, LOOKING FOR a black bag to go with her gold minidress. This would be the last party she went to in Pine Lakes, and she wanted to wear something special to say goodbye.

The last month had been uncomfortable, like trying to squeeze into clothes from her adolescence. Bob let her have her old shifts, and she and Roxi fell back into their familiar pattern. But with every shift and every party, the feeling she was wasting her time, wasting her life, grew stronger and stronger. She glanced from the black plastic wall clock ticking loudly above her bed, to the little white card on her nightstand, making sure she still had enough time to place the call before she left.

She told her mom about the job offer, describing it as a research role in an international intelligence agency and explaining security restrictions meant she couldn't say much about it, other than it being a great opportunity that would allow her to travel and develop professionally. Her mother's backing had been enthusiastic, relieved even, and Emily realized she had no desire to see her only child chained to her side for the rest of her life. She wanted her to live and experience the world. Any obligation to stay in Pine Lakes had been of Emily's own construction.

She didn't know what the Circle would say or if the offer would even be on the table anymore. It had been two months since Sebastian had made it, and she'd had no contact with the organization since. But she knew now that even if the job didn't work out, pursuing it offered a route out of Pine Lakes, a stepping-stone to her future.

Roxi made no real attempts to find a job suited to her interests and qualifications, content to stay on the party carousel, and with Emily by her side, she would be in no rush to move on with her life. Perhaps the same was true of her mother, who went on a date for the first time since her father left while Emily was away. Emily thought she was supporting the people she cared about by staying in Pine Lakes, but maybe she'd been holding them back.

The idea of indirectly complying with her father's wishes by moving to Europe still rankled, but she couldn't let her bitterness steer her anymore. Staying in Pine Lakes would damage her more than it did him.

She closed her fingers over the smooth leather folds of the purse she wanted, wedged at the back of the drawer beneath a disorganized pile of sunglasses, scarves, and bracelets. With a tug, she yanked it free, dislodging memories of it lying on the floor of her room in the hunters' base, and Sebastian returning it to her with her dress and shoes in the Circle clinic.

She grabbed a lipstick from the dresser top to stuff inside with her keys, unzipped the bag, and blinked.

The green diamond Sebastian gave her sparkled against the dark lining in a silent plea. The last time she saw it, after Heath tore it from her neck, it lay shimmering on the nightstand where he dumped it.

Evidently it found its way back to Sebastian, but why put it in her bag? Why would he want her to have it now? She rolled the stone between her fingers, its smooth facets calming her even as her mind raced with the possibility that Sebastian still cared. She reached for a simple chain hanging with a clutch of other necklaces from a nail in the wall above the dresser. She threaded it through the pendant's loop to replace the chain Heath broke, unlatched it, and swept her hair aside so she could fasten it. Her reflection stared back at her from the small oval mirror on the wall, willing her to make the call.

Perching on the edge of her bed, she picked up the card and began tapping the numbers into her cell. She slipped on her high heels as ringing echoed down the line, her breath quickening with each drawn-out second that passed. The ringing stopped with an abrupt click followed by silence.

"Hello?" Emily pressed the phone closer to her ear.

"Name, please." The man's voice had the stiffened enunciation of a British accent.

"Emily Heart." She stood as she spoke and began to twist a lock of hair around her index finger.

A pause, followed by the sound of computer keys being depressed in rapid succession. "You're calling about the contract offer."

"Yes."

"Consultant based in Birmingham, England. Starting salary $100,000 plus annual bonus, accommodation, car, and private healthcare. Start date immediate."

Emily swallowed as the man continued, reeling at the prospect of earning $100,000 in a year.

"Do you intend to accept the offer?"

"Yes," she croaked.

"The contract is to be signed in person. We will arrange transportation for you."

"When?"

Another pause. "The end of the week. You'll fly privately. We will call with details of the airstrip and time."

"Okay."

"Goodbye."

"Wait!"

"Yes?"

"Do you know how I can contact Sebastian? I have an old number for him." She'd tried to call him when she decided to accept the job offer, but an automated out of service message played.

More key tapping sounded. "I have alerted Mr. Blake of your wish to speak to him."

"Oh, okay. Thanks."

The call ended with the same tinny click it had begun with, and Emily fell back onto her bed, pushing her hair away from her face with shaking hands. She'd done it. No turning back now.

Yellow seeped out into the blue dawn beyond the window as Emily looked around her bedroom for the last time. Pale rectangles haunted the walls where she'd removed tacked photographs, stowing the sun-faded prints in the netted pocket beneath the lid of her case. She donated her small collection of party dresses to Roxi, apart from a couple good enough to pass for cocktail dresses should a suitable occasion arise in her new line of work.

She brushed a speck of dust off her fitted black jeans and stood, turning in a circle before she shrugged a light cardigan on over her white cotton shirt and collected her case.

She'd said her goodbyes to her mother last night because her work shift clashed with the five a.m. departure. They hugged and cried and sobbed encouragement to one another until it was time to part. It hurt, but it would be okay.

Emily dragged her case down the hall and out onto the porch, turning to ease the door shut. When she turned back to the road, a black Mercedes with darkened windows waited by the cracked driveway. Sebastian leaned against its door, the predatory grace of his imposing frame and seductive smile hitting her full force.

She couldn't help but return the smile. "What are you doing here?"

In three smooth strides, he stood in front of her, his eyes burning with intensity and longing. Without a word, he cupped her nape and pulled her lips to his in a devouring kiss that she reciprocated with startled fervor.

He pulled away, his hands still tangled in her hair as his gaze fell to the sparkling pendant resting on her collarbone. "I heard you wanted to speak to me."

She narrowed her eyes in question. "I did. I do."

He took her hand and held her at arm's length, watching as he waited for her to speak.

"I know the bond is gone and that changes things for you, but I...I still..." She took a breath. "I'm in love with you."

He closed the gap between them again, responding to her confession with a lingering, flutter-soft kiss. "I've always been in love with you, Emily Heart."

She frowned at his brandy-brown eyes. "But I thought the bond was gone."

"This is me, Emily. This is how I feel without the bond, without the threat of implosion, the mood swings, and instability. This is who I really am. And I still want you."

Her breath caught with elation and fear. "What if you bond to someone else?"

"It took me over two centuries to find you, so I'd say that's unlikely."

"But not impossible."

"We have the hunters' research. I can find out where the other known matches are, and I'll avoid them. That will reduce the odds of it happening."

"And if you change your mind? If you want to be bonded again?"

"I'm in this, Emily, with you and you alone for as long as you want me." He laced his fingers through hers before casting his burnt-gold lashes down. "But I understand if your feelings for Heath mean you can't be with me."

"When I saw you last, you said you thought I had feelings for Heath and I didn't contradict you. I didn't want you to know the truth because I was afraid of how you'd react. There used to be something there, Sebastian. But greater than that is my absolute revulsion for the things he's done, for what he's condoned and encouraged and been a part of without regret or conscience. And greater than *that* is my love for you. I love you, Sebastian."

He folded her in his arms, exhaling into her hair. "Say that again."

"I love you."

Taking her hand again, he grabbed her case and led her to the car. "Are you ready for this?"

He gave her a hypnotic smile full of promise.

She let him open the door, and she slid into the dark interior in answer.

He studied her with naked fascination and then started the engine.

Smiling, she looked out at the road ahead of them. "Drive."

Thank you for reading! Did you enjoy? Please add your review because nothing helps an author more and encourages readers to take a chance on a book than a review.

And don't miss more of the *The Bonded Vampire Chronicles* with book two, BOND CRUSHED, available now. Turn the page for a sneak peek!

You can also sign up for the City Owl Press newsletter to receive notice of all book releases!

SNEAK PEEK OF BOND CRUSHED

Marguerite examined the beetle on her fingertip. Ladybird. Black, four red spots. Harlequin. Invasive. She grunted and flicked it into a bowl of water to drown. Annoyed, she repeated the process for its cluster of companions on the wooden window ledge. Black, two orange spots. Orange, sixteen black spots. Orange, twenty black spots. Black two red spots.

She tucked stray strands of silver blond hair behind her ear and carried the bowl of dead insects down the lopsided stairs, through the open front door and out into the overgrown cottage garden where she tipped them onto the grass for the birds to eat. Cataloguing the colorful invaders eased her conscience. She disliked killing them, but she couldn't leave them to feast on the larvae of her beloved moths whose numbers continued to dwindle.

The ebony and crimson Cinnabars were her favorites, the beauty in their shamelessly contrasting colors far superior to the lauded butterflies that flitted about the fields, fluttering and posing like ladies at court. Cinnabars didn't restrict themselves to the night shadows like other moths; they thrust their way into the daylight, surpassing the quivering wings of the peacocks, admirals and gate-keepers with their steady style and grace.

A lone harlequin ladybird survived the cull and made its way back over the cobblestone path towards the tired timber-framed cottage. Marguerite ground it beneath the heel of her boot, wiped her feet on the doormat and went inside to wait for the female pheasant who would come to eat the ladybird's perished fellows.

She settled on an armchair by the small leaded window that overlooked the patchy turf and shoved away the memory of Sebastian's manicured green lawns and all the times they'd run across them, chasing each other into the wide-open spaces with laughter and lust in their hearts. *Sebastian.* Two centuries of trysts proved impossible to forget, no matter how hard she tried. She squeezed her eyes shut, the raw burn of the sight of him with his mate, Emily, returning for the hundredth time that day. *Ex-mate*, she reminded herself, at least she'd found a way to extinguish their fledgling, forever bond. Although he still wanted the bold young human, even without the damn bond.

She stared out at the wild garden and the empty meadows beyond. Time passed and the slow sun swam to its Westerly slumber. When the last splashes of light started to fade, the scrawny female pheasant picked her way through the grass, her dull brown feathers blending with the dying autumn foliage. She came alone as always, no majestic male by her side.

Marguerite waited for the pheasant to peck the last scattered seeds and insects from the ground, then she piled logs and kindling in the grate and struck a match. The fire caught and she focused on the flames as she did every evening. The burning wood crackled with echoes of a never forgotten childhood, of fires lit by her family, of warmth and comfort and happiness. The time before...

She lifted the poker from its hook in the recess of the sandstone fireplace and prodded the logs, trying not to think about what came after. Pale flesh and fevered brows flashed through her consciousness anyway. Vomit and blood and lifelessness. Filthy city streets and hunger. A man, tall and frightening and strange.

She shuddered, put the poker back and reached for the box of tiny wood carvings she kept beneath her chair. She took them out one at a time and placed them on her lap. She rotated each one, pressing the edges and points with ritualistic care...Owl, hare, fox, moth...Adder, raven, rabbit, stag...

The ghosts began to whisper.

"...*Pat-a-cake, pat-a-cake, baker's man,*
  Bake me a cake as fast as you can..."

"...*Margaret! Margaret! You must take your sister and go. It's too late for me.*"
  "*I don't want to, mother. I don't want to.*"
  "*It's too late Margaret. Your father is gone. I will follow soon. You must leave.*"
  "*We need to bury him and...*"
  "*No! Stay away. Stay away. You must go before it touches you too. Take your sister. Go...*"

"...*Pat it and prick it,*
  And mark it with E..."

"...*I can help you. If you want. Come.*"
  "*Where?*"
  "*Somewhere warm.*"
  "*Mother said never to go anywhere with men.*"
  "*Your mother isn't here now, and you will starve if you don't freeze first. Come. I can help you...*"

"...*And put it in the oven for Margaret.*
  And me..."

"...*Margaret, no. You mustn't leave.*"
  "*I'll come back, Edith. I'll bring food.*"
  "*Margaret, no, no...*"

"*This won't hurt. I'll only take a little, and afterwards you will forget it. I give you my word.*"

Time passed. She didn't know how much. The sun blazed outside but damp chilled the air in the cottage. The cold fireplace held only ash and soot. She trudged into the tiny kitchen and found her lifeless phone on the counter. She plugged it into its charger with a reluctant push, then rummaged in the chest freezer that occupied the wall by the backdoor and removed three bags of blood pilfered from the nearest hospital. She thawed them in the microwave and drank them one after another, straight from the bags.

Thirst quenched, she went outside and assessed the landscape.

Daffodils, crocuses, and grape hyacinths had erupted in erratic bursts of color around the garden, fighting the grass and weeds that threatened to destroy their moment in the sun. Spring had sprung while she sat dormant in the chair, the months ignoring her internal struggle as they rushed past winter in their relentless race with the seasons.

Panic tightened her chest. She hadn't lost this much time before. It was getting worse.

She yanked several nettles encroaching on the doorstep from their earthy bed, ignoring the stinging rash they left behind, which healed seconds later. Crouching, she began rooting out dandelions, ground elder and chickweed. Heaps of unwelcome foliage formed around her in minutes as she cleared the beds and borders before tackling the bindweed and ivy that invaded the hedgerows. She carried the weeds to the bottom of the field at the rear of the cottage and dropped them into a ditch with satisfaction.

The time lapses left her exposed and vulnerable, but she couldn't deny their restorative effective. She'd bought the cottage in a forgotten expanse of English countryside when she could no longer ignore the symptoms of her mental decline. Buried in hundreds of acres of useless, boggy woodland and meadows, it offered her isolation and absolute privacy. A place to run to when she couldn't hide her failing sanity. A place to release the ghosts that haunted the corridors of her deteriorating mind. It reminded her of her childhood home in a village not too far away, of her long dead family and friends, and the simple life she might have lived.

A mint moth landed on her sweater, crawled towards her shoulder, then settled, content to rest on the warm cotton. She smiled and took it inside where she opened the stiff windows. The house released a breath, blowing out the trapped, fetid air and inhaling the April breeze. At least, it smelled like April, like nests and cowslips, cherry blossoms and lambs. But with climate change she couldn't be sure. She lifted her phone from the counter and turned it on. The white bar moved across the screen, and she waited with trepidation for the time and date to appear.

12.03. Friday 29 April.

It vibrated with a reminder. *Find a mate. Find a mate. Find a mate.*

She had no recollection of writing it but the warning from her unconscious couldn't be clearer. She pocketed the phone and set off for the steep hill at the edge of her land—the only place with enough of a signal to make a call. At the top, she looked down at the patchwork of fields, the sheep grazing on a neighboring farm in the far distance, the lane that wound its way through the countryside and the powerlines that punctuated the greenery—the sole evidence that centuries had passed since she last lived in a place like this.

She clutched the phone and listened to the monotone ringing with dread. Was she really going to do this? She had no choice. The line clicked and an impersonal voicemail prompt sounded.

"I need your help," she said and hung up.

Sebastian would recognize her voice. She sat on the wet grass and waited for him to call her back. They always helped each other. She hoped he would help her now, that his newfound love wouldn't erase his loyalty to her. Because if she didn't find a mate soon, her mind would fail completely and irretrievably.

Don't stop now. Keep reading with your copy of <u>BOND CRUSHED</u> available now.

And don't miss more from Christie Clayton at www.christieclayton.com

Read more of the *The Bonded Vampire Chronicles* with book two, BOND CRUSHED, available now.

And discover more from Christie Clayton at www.christieclayton.com

When a vampire bonds to a human, the consequences can be catastrophic.

Five-hundred-year-old vampire Marguerite Fontaine is teetering on the brink of mental ruin. The affliction, which plagues older vampires, only has one cure—a mate bond. But when Marguerite finds her mate, human musician Mikey Madeley, he falls short of her exacting social standards. She decides to take an experimental new drug to suppress the feelings triggered by her bond, freeing her from a lifetime of misery with an unsuitable mate.

Devastated and confused by her disappearance, Mikey agrees to help a group of ruthless vampire hunters capture Marguerite. He finds himself torn between wrath and desire for her, his misguided pact with the hunters hanging over him like an axe. When they are reunited, he is no longer able to bury his overwhelming need for her, their bond drawing them to one another despite his fury and her disdain.

Will Marguerite continue to deny her love for Mikey? And can Mikey forgive her for abandoning him before it's too late to stop the hunters?

Please sign up for the City Owl Press newsletter for chances to win special subscriber-only contests and giveaways as well as receiving information on upcoming releases and special excerpts.

All reviews are **welcome** and **appreciated**. Please consider leaving one on your favorite social media and book buying sites.

Escape Your World. Get Lost in Ours! City Owl Press at www.cityowlpress.com.

ACKNOWLEDGMENTS

When I finished my draft of *Bond Bitten*, a former Harper Collins editor looked at my first chapter and synopsis. Her declaration that bonds were not romantic was crushing and inspiring in equal measure. I loved the mate bond trope, I still do, but I was willing to try something different and the idea that vampires might create medication to suppress bonds and take control of their romantic destinies took shape. So, thank you, Emily R, for your honesty and directness.

I was lucky enough to work on *Bond Bitten* with one of my favorite paranormal romance authors. Lindsay selflessly shared her time and thoughts with me, though she had her own unforgiving workload and deadlines. I could not have wished for a better mentor.

I'm hugely grateful to my acquiring editor Melinda for championing Bond Bitten and saving it from the confines of my desktop, and to Lisa, Heather and the Mystic Owl and City Owl team for their editorial guidance and assistance.

With heartfelt thanks also to Abbey, the first person to read and thoughtfully critique a very unpolished draft of Sebastian and Emily's story, and to Sam for her carefully considered suggestions.

Finally, thanks to MiblArt, for producing this incredible cover under extremely difficult circumstances.

ABOUT THE AUTHOR

CHRISTIE CLAYTON is a fresh new romance author from England. She loves to write haunting paranormal and contemporary love stories with strong protagonists and gripping plots. When she isn't writing at home in her quirky old cottage, she enjoys walking, reading, gardening and daydreaming. Christie likes to travel and she uses places she has visited as settings in her books. She's a diehard fan of

Buffy the Vampire Slayer, *The Vampire Diaries* and anything with fangs. *Bond Bitten*, the first book in *The Bonded Vampire Chronicles*, is Christie's debut novel.

www.christieclayton.com

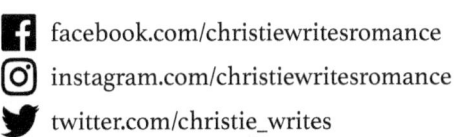

facebook.com/christiewritesromance

instagram.com/christiewritesromance

twitter.com/christie_writes

ABOUT THE PUBLISHER

City Owl Press is a cutting edge indie publishing company, bringing the world of romance and speculative fiction to discerning readers.

Escape Your World. Get Lost in Ours!

www.cityowlpress.com

facebook.com/YourCityOwlPress

twitter.com/cityowlpress

instagram.com/cityowlbooks

pinterest.com/cityowlpress